Taking Stock

Scott Bartlett

Mirth Publishing
St. John's

TAKING STOCK

Library and Archives Canada Cataloguing in Publication

Bartlett, Scott

Taking Stock / Scott Bartlett ; illustrations by Susan Jarvis.

ISBN 978-0-9812867-2-3

To anyone who has suffered from mental illness

Chapter One

Sam first met me in the middle of committing suicide.

I'd been standing on the stool for a while, to tell the truth. In the shed. It was wobbly—the stool. Poorly-made.

Before I came in here, I thought I'd made up my mind. I felt ready. I felt killing myself was the logical thing to do.

But I stood, stool wobbling, rope hung from a ceiling beam and draped around my neck, for a long time. A crow started cawing, and wouldn't stop.

Crows have a remark for every occasion.

A few minutes before Sam came in the stool almost fell over. I grabbed the rope above me and managed to keep my balance. My heart hammering against my chest, the rope scratching against my neck.

I decided to decide whether to kill myself soon. On account of the scratchiness.

The arguments in favour of suicide seemed numerous. I'd spent the last of my inheritance. I had no résumé—I'd never had a job, and didn't feel like looking. Two years before, I stopped talking to my only remaining friends because they fell in love with each other. Ever since, I'd been a complete recluse.

And I really wanted that crow to shut up.

I started to consider whether the lawn mower was too close. I envisioned my dumb, flailing body trying to use it to survive. Its foot finding just enough purchase on the mower's handle to prolong asphyxiation. Its fingernails clawing dumbly at the noose.

That's when the door opened wide, and the bright light made me squint. A silhouette stood framed in the doorway. "What are you doing?" it asked.

"Nothing."

"It looks like you're committing suicide."

"Really?"

"Well, no, not really. That rope is too long, for one."

"Oh. Geez."

The silhouette took out a silhouette of a cell phone and dialled three numbers. "Hi, I need an ambulance at 37 Foresail Road. I just found the young man who lives downstairs attempting to commit suicide in our shared shed. No, he's not hurt. I'll keep an eye on him till you get here. No. I don't think the police will be necessary. Okay. Thanks." He put the phone back in his pocket. "I don't believe we've ever been formally introduced. I'm Sam."

I removed the noose from around my neck and stepped down from the stool. My thigh cramped. I ignored it, and offered my hand. "Sheldon."

"Why did you pick the shed to kill yourself in, Sheldon? Didn't you figure I'd be the one to find your body? Awful first impression."

My cheeks heated up. "The ceilings are too low in my apartment. Anyway, I was going to make up for it. I left you everything I own in a note. Including my bike, in the corner there."

"I don't know how to ride one."

"Oh. Well, I left you a lot of books, too."

"I like books. Anything else?"

"A cat."

"I'm allergic."

"Oh."

Silence. For a moment I couldn't think of anything to say, which was somehow worse than him walking in on my suicide attempt.

Then I thought of something: "So, what were you coming in here for?"

"Lawn mower."

"You're the one who mows the lawn?"

"Yeah. Did you think it mowed itself?"

"I thought the landlord did it."

"You don't look out the window much, do you?"

The ambulance arrived. The sirens weren't on, and it didn't pull up in any kind of rush. The driver got out and gave us both a friendly hello. He showed no special interest in either of us—just opened the back door. I climbed in, and so did Sam.

"You're coming too?"

He shrugged. "Nothing better to do."

"What about the lawn?"

"I tend to procrastinate."

*

Spending three weeks in hospital on suicide watch is not very enjoyable. After that, it feels good to come home and fall into your own bed.

For me, though, that sentiment doesn't survive the night.

I wake up drenched in piss. It's on my neck and chest. It's in my hair and mouth. The sheets are soaked. My throat is raw, and the air is thick with the pungent odour of ammonia. The cat looks at me from the computer desk, tail twitching.

"You little bastard," I say in a hoarse whisper.

My Mom used to say that belongings should embody social relationships. That's why they're called 'belongings'. A keyboard helps you email your friends, a book can be borrowed, a painting elicits discussion, a glass holds a guest's drink. She used to periodically purge all her possessions that didn't facilitate her interaction with others, and she taught me to do the same. During these purges, if she came across an unwanted item she thought I might like, she'd toss it on my bed. We called them culture bombs.

The day she died, my belongings died, too. Objects that used to represent parts of my relationship with her—inside jokes, favourite games—were dead things, now. Inert.

Except the cat. The pudgy calico. The little bastard, who used to rub against the legs of guests, who suffered even me, and adored Mom. The cat who, since she died, stalks around the apartment, fur bristling, hissing. Who shreds my books and scratches my ankles. Who pisses on me, apparently.

Mom named him Brute. I call him Marcus Brutus.

*

Sam and I weren't sitting in the emergency waiting room long before I started wishing I'd brought a book. I'm very tolerant when I have a book. Otherwise I'm forced to look at reality, which in my experience is glacial and dull. A nurse took my blood pressure, and after that we were told to wait. Which we did. For hours. I guess the suicidal aren't a priority unless they're really feeling motivated.

Around suppertime I asked Sam, "Why are you still here?"

"Told you. Nothing better to do."

"I heard your phone ring like six times."

"No one important."

"I'm not, either."

"You kidding? Trying to kill yourself makes you VIP."

"Not really. You just don't want to sound like an asshole when you tell people you found the kid who lives downstairs trying to kill himself. You want to be able to say you stayed until he was safely committed, and you did all you could."

Sam scratched his nose. "Did you know most people who are hanged urinate and defecate as they die?"

"So?"

"Is that really how you wanted to be found?"

"How I appear after I die is irrelevant to me. Dead people don't care how they look, or about anything else."

"Are you sure about that?"

"Yes. Trust me. I'm sure."

A nurse finally called my name, and led us down a series of corridors to a room with a bed and a couple chairs. It turned out this was just a waiting room in disguise, since another hour passed before I saw anyone. When I did, it was another nurse, and she asked Sam to leave the room while she spoke with me.

She asked what my relation to him was, and why I thought I was there. She asked if I'd been hearing any disembodied voices or strange noises. She asked if I was sleeping well. She asked if I'd been having trouble concentrating. She asked about my appetite. She asked if I was irritable.

Then it was on to yet another room, for another two-hour wait. Sam asked me if I was currently attending school, and I said, "Ever notice how every conversation you've ever had gradually became more and more pointless, until it finally spirals headfirst into redundancy?"

Sam tilted his head a little to one side.

Until I met Dr. Cervenka the chairs were made of plastic or wood, but once he became available I was shown to a room with soft, leather seating. Cervenka took a couch. I took an overstuffed armchair and watched him study a clipboard.

"Sorry about the wait. How are you feeling?"

"I guess 'ennui' would be the word."

"That's a good word. Why don't you explain to me what brought you here?"

"I was about to off myself when my neighbour intervened and called an ambulance."

"Succinct. Why did you want to commit suicide?"

"Nothing about living interests me."

"Have you had thoughts like that before —that life isn't worth living?"

"Yeah."

"Have you tried to act on them before today?"

"No."

"Why now?"

"I ran out of money. Living is expensive."

"You could get a job."

"I don't want to."

"Well, are you still inclined that way? Do you feel like you're a danger to yourself?"

"Suicide still appeals, if that's what you mean."

The doctor nodded. "Looks like you'll be staying with us a while."

*

Unlike mine, Sam's apartment has a porch. It leads into the living room, which features a couch, an armchair, a flat screen TV, and a hodgepodge of cabinets, dressers, and chests. There are also more video game systems than I can name. Not many guys pushing 40 have that many video games.

"Sorry about the PJs," Sam says. "Though, you're lucky I'm wearing more than underwear. When you live alone, fashion sense is the first thing to go."

"I didn't have any to begin with."

"You want a beer?"

"What?"

"Beer—it's an alcoholic beverage brewed from fermented sugars."

"Oh. I'll have a beer."

He goes into the next room—the kitchen, I assume. There are swinging saloon doors, which flap back and forth at his passage. I sit on the couch.

"Careful, though," he says, passing me a sweating bottle. "I was reading about your meds—apparently they increase the effects of alcohol. How does it feel to have your freedom back?"

"Good. I guess." I twist, and the beer hisses.

Sam sets his beer on the coffee table and sits beside me. My leg twitches.

"You guess?" he says.

Let's play What Does Sam Want to Hear.

"I need a job. I want to get a job."

Sam smiles. "Good. Work gives life meaning. You know, they did a study where they put a rat in a cage, with a metal bar hooked up to a food pellet dispenser. Once the rat figured out how to operate the dispenser, the scientists put a tin cup filled with pellets in one corner of the cage, and the rat was given a choice between free food and food it had to work for. They did this with 200 rats, and only one of them chose not to press the bar."

"Maybe I'm that rat."

Sam shakes his head. "I don't think so." He sips his beer, peering at me. "You're still taking your meds, right?"

Two knocks on the door—the second harder than the first. Sam looks at me, then looks up at the ceiling. "Excuse me." He gets up and walks to the porch.

"Hey, Sam," a low voice says.

"Hi, Gord. Come in. I have a visitor."

Gord enters ahead of Sam, and he stops in the doorway, blocking Sam's path. "I don't know him."

"Yeah, Gord, this is Sheldon. Sheldon, Gord."

"There aren't supposed to be strangers here."

"It's okay, Gord, he—"

"He a cop?"

"No, he—"

"What does he do, then? Where do you work, kid?"

"Nowhere, at the moment."

"You don't work anywhere? He's a cop, isn't he? I'm not buying from you, Sam. I'm telling everyone about this. You're done."

He turns around. Sam looks at him, expressionless. "Sit down, Gord."

"You can't keep me here. That's illegal. I know my rights."

"Sit down, Gord."

"Sam, I'm serious, if—"

"Sit down."

Gord stands there, hands balled. Sam raises his eyebrows. Gord sits in the armchair and stares at me.

"Sheldon's a friend," Sam says. "He lives downstairs. Has for years."

"How come I haven't met him, then?"

"I recently met him myself."

"What do you do, kid, seriously? Do you live with your mommy?"

"No."

"What do you want to be, then? When you grow up, like?"

"I used to want to be a writer."

"A writer, hey? I could give you some pointers. I'm a writer myself."

"Really?"

"Wrote my will last week."

I fake-chuckle. "It's good to be prepared."

Gord grins. "This kid's not a cop. Got any weed, Sammy?"

"Plenty."

"Break it out. Let's see how it tastes."

We go out onto Sam's deck, which overlooks our backyard, as well as a great stretch of suburbia beyond it. There's a dresser out here, in the deck's far corner, and from the top drawer Sam takes a bag of marijuana, a pack of cigarette papers, and a long, thin book. When he lays the latter on his lap, I see it's the illustrated version of *A Brief History of Time*. He produces a playing card from within its pages, and uses it to sweep some weed into a line. He starts rolling it. When he's finished, he takes a lighter from his pocket, lights the joint, and inhales once. He passes it to Gord.

Gord takes a long drag. "Delicious." He inhales twice more and holds it out to me.

"I don't smoke."

"Suit yourself. Hey, Sam, you still having that dinner tomorrow?"

"Yep. At 6:00."

"Great. You're a good cook, Sammy." Gord gives him the joint and stands up. "I better get going. I want an ounce."

"Come inside. I'll be back in a few, Sheldon."

My beer is gone, and honestly, I'm feeling it. Buzzed as I am, though, I still can't relax. There's a tension in my chest that never really goes away—like a spot oxygen can't reach, no matter how deeply I breathe. Mom used to say I got that from her.

"Sorry about that," Sam says when he comes out.

"So you're a drug dealer?"

"Yeah."

"How'd that happen?"

Sam shrugs. "I have a cousin who's been growing it since junior high. I turned 26, and I lost my taste for working hard to meet other people's goals. Quit my job, borrowed some money, and bought a pound of pot from my cousin."

"I see."

"Would you like to join us for dinner tomorrow night?"

I try to think of an excuse. "Um."

"The rest of the guests won't be like him. Promise."

I hear a car start, and the crunch of gravel as it pulls out of the driveway.

"Is that him?"

"I guess, yeah."

"He's driving stoned? You're okay with that?"

"It's not my place to enforce anything."

"Well, I can't come to your dinner."

"Sorry to hear that. Can I ask why?"

"I've had my fill of social interaction. I get tired of people pretty fast. Try to avoid them, normally."

"That hasn't been going too well for you."

"People disappoint."

"Maybe it's not them."

"Goodbye."

"See ya."

*

I wrote my first story in grade three. It was about a superhero with the power to turn anything into food, just by touching it. Like King Midas, but not really. Mom was ecstatic I'd found my passion. She bought me lots of writing books. She registered me in programs for young writers. She made me practise writing every day. For years, every story I wrote was homework for some course.

She enrolled me in other stuff, too. Piano lessons. Soccer. Figure skating. Rock climbing. Gymnastics. Hockey. I don't think she had any concept of gender roles. She registered me for little league, but I never played a game. Before the first one started, the coach hit some pop flys for us to catch. Except, one wasn't a pop fly. One was a line drive that smashed into my face and raised a bump between my eyes the size of an egg. When it hit me, I spun around like a ballerina and landed on all fours. Blood dripped onto the sand. On the way to the hospital, I considered that I would probably die.

Eventually, I quit everything—even writing, though that happened later. Kung Fu, I stayed in for a while. Earned a couple belts. Pushed up, sat up, jumped jacks, ran laps. Once, the instructor called me a mental giant. I wasn't sure whether he was praising my cerebral fortitude, or calling me tall and retarded.

I wonder what my instructor would have said if he'd seen me sitting around a psych ward, wearing a pair of Velcro Reeboks.

They took away my sneakers around the same time they took my freedom. They didn't explain it, but I knew why. Laces are problematic.

I had no money, so Sam bought me these Velcro shoes. He also bought me *Crow*, a book of poems by Ted Hughes, after I mentioned it's something I've been meaning to read.

To be honest, I was a little surprised when Sam brought me the sneakers. I hadn't expected to see him anymore.

*

When I was a kid, I discovered I could play catch with myself by throwing a tennis ball at the sloped roof of our shed. I'd play for hours, never able to anticipate where the ball would go once it bounced off the shingles. The empty lot across the street was always filled with kids throwing balls, but the pressure to catch one thrown by another person was too much. In the backyard there was just me, and my determination to get better. We only stayed in that apartment one summer, and in later years I missed the shed.

That sounds like a sad story, but telling it to Sam, I can only laugh.

Sam scratches his chin. "Within this anecdote may lie the true reason you're not attending my dinner party tonight. Tell me. Did you throw with your right hand, or your left?"

"My right. I'm right-handed."

"Oh. Never mind, then."

"Why? What does that have to do with anything?"

"I'm thinking of a study I was reading about the other day. They found that left-handed people are more likely to experience feelings of apprehension and self-doubt when faced with new situations. For lefties, the right hemisphere of the brain is dominant, and apparently that's the half responsible for most negative emotions."

"Well, I was born left-handed, but Mom kept switching stuff to my right hand when I was a baby. She didn't want me to be a leftie in a world built for right-handed people."

Sam whistles. "Goodness."

"I have a right-handed body and a left-handed brain."

"You're screwed up."

"I don't even know which side of my brain I'm supposed to be using!"

"I guess that's your answer, then. That's what's wrong with you. I understand now why you declined my dinner invitation. You have things you need to sort out."

"No. I defy my biology. I'll come."

Sam grins.

"But don't tell anyone I was in a psych ward, okay?"

His grin fades a little. "It's nothing to be ashamed of."

"It shouldn't be. But it is."

In attendance at the dinner are Sam, a bunch of other middle-aged people, and me. A few of them glance at me askance, but nobody reacts like Gord did. As for Gord, he's sitting near the wine, alone.

I don't have much experience making small talk with men and women twice my age. For that matter, I don't have much experience making small talk. I'm not sure where to start, or whether I want to. My chest feels particularly tight. I hang out near a basket of flatbread.

Sam walks over, sipping from a glass of wine. "Hey, Sheldon. Glad you came." He turns to a guy standing nearby. "Ted, have you met Sheldon?"

Ted shakes his head, and comes over. "Hey."

"Hi."

"This is the first day of Sheldon's new social life," Sam says.

Ted's eyebrows raise. "Oh? Congratulations."

I force a chuckle.

Sam says, "Are you enjoying the appetizer, Sheldon? I made it especially for you."

"It's good bread."

"Not just any bread. It's unleavened bread. And see that bottle over there? That's wine."

"Yep."

"Do you know what they ate at the Last Supper?"

"Wine and bread?"

"Bingo."

I glance around. "Where's Jesus?"

He pokes me in the chest. "Right here. And your crucifixion is tomorrow morning. The actual hour is flexible—you can show up at your convenience. But you'll be nailed to the cross of customer service." He sips some wine. "I got you a job."

"Really? Where?"

"The grocery store down the road."

"Spend Easy?"

"Yep. I know someone there who's putting in a good word for you. Do you have much you can put on a résumé?"

"Not really."

"Well, write one, and include whatever you can think of. Bring it in and ask for the manager. Don't tell them I sent you."

"Why not?"

"Just don't."

Something starts beeping in the kitchen. "That's supper," Sam says, and goes to get it.

Ted and I look at each other.

"So, how do you know Sam?" I say.

"I met him through Al, the guy out on the deck. Sam sells me pot."

"Oh. You too, huh?"

"He sells to everyone here."

"Really? You're all his, uh, clients?"

"Yeah. There's a couple of us missing. He has us all for dinner every month."

"Is that industry standard?"

"Um, not exactly. Not much about what Sam does is standard. He charges more, but we get security, and a superior product. He buys from his cousin, who's an organic farmer, and he only sells to married people with families—people with a lot invested in not getting caught. Plus he hosts these dinners, so we can get to know each other, and feel less like a bunch of sketch bags."

"So is everyone getting high after supper, then?"

"I'm not. Neither will most of the others. I smoke at home, personally. I have esophageal cancer, but with the limit my doctor's set, I'm not able to get enough of the medical stuff to completely kill the pain."

Sam doesn't eat meat, so I wasn't expecting supper to be very exciting. But it's not bad. He made vegetarian lasagna, and it disappears quickly. Compliments and approving grunts come from all around the room.

As Last Suppers go, it's actually pretty good.

*

I get up shortly after 10 and ride my bike to the grocery store.

Standing before the Customer Service counter, I raise my 1-page résumé into the air. "To whom should I give this?" I say.

The woman behind the counter looks at me with one eyebrow cocked. She's wearing a bright yellow t-shirt with "Spend Easy" scrawled across the front. Her nametag says "Betty." She's chewing gum, and the piston-like motion of her jaw is hypnotic. "Give what?"

"This." I hold my résumé higher, and it bends over until the tip of the page tickles my forearm.

"Here," Betty says, holding out her hand.

I pass it to her, and she drops it into the garbage bucket behind her. "Thanks."

I blink. "That was my résumé."

"Yep."

"You just threw it in the garbage."

"That's the résumé bucket."

"There's a Pepsi can in there."

"It's also the recycling bin."

I frown.

"Listen," she says. "You don't want to work here."

The phone sitting near her splayed hand begins to ring, and she snatches it up. "Customer Service, Betty speaking. Oh. Yes. He's an applicant." I follow her gaze across the store and up, to a tinted window that overlooks the cash registers. Behind the glass is the silhouette of a head talking on a phone. I get the feeling it's staring right at me.

While Betty's on the phone, a lady walks up to the Customer Service counter with her son, five bottles of detergent piled in her arms. "I'm in a rush," she says.

Betty glares at her. Into the phone she says, "I'll send him up." She replaces the receiver and instructs me to take the stairs behind the last cash lane.

"Can I have my résumé back?"

She fishes it out of the trash.

"Thanks."

For a moment, I consider heading for the exit instead.

But I walk past the cash registers. Behind the last one a staircase awaits, just as Betty said. It's narrow and black. At its top I find a short hall with three doors. The one on my right stands open, and a voice calls for me to enter. Inside, a man is sitting in a swivel chair, facing the tinted window. He swivels.

"Hi," I say, "I'm Sheldon Mason, I'm here to—"

He isn't looking at me. He's looking at the single page dangling from my hand. "I need that."

I hold it out, but he swivels again, and pushes himself backward with his feet until he's sitting behind his desk. He looks across the room, at a filing cabinet in the corner. "Place it on my desk."

His eyes don't leave the filing cabinet until the résumé is in his hands. He glares at it. I learn from a placard on his desk that his name is Frank Crawford.

His eyes flick to the empty air two feet to my right. He has yet to make eye contact. He reminds me of a horse just escaped from a burning barn, eyes rolling madly. "The uniform consists of black pants, black shoes, a yellow Spend Easy t-shirt, and a nametag. We strive to maintain a professional appearance. Shirts tucked in. Nametags worn at all times. Facial hair neatly trimmed."

"Are you offering me a position?"

He doesn't answer. He picks up the phone on his desk, presses a button, and says, "Eric Andrews to the store office please." His voice comes out through a speaker above my head.

I stand awkwardly, and Frank returns to his study of the filing cabinet. We wait. Soon, I hear footsteps ascending the stairs. I feel them, too. A large mammal approaches.

Indeed, the person who appears in the doorway is among the biggest, hairiest men I have ever encountered. His eyes are small, but I can feel them measuring me—weighing me. Contemplating how I would look, drawn and quartered and marked down for purchase. He extends his hand, and I have the fleeting impression he is going for my jugular. Then I recall the ritual, and we shake. He doesn't try to impress me with his grip. He doesn't need to.

"Eric Andrews."

"Sheldon Mason."

He motions to the chair behind me. "Why don't you have a seat?"

I sit.

Frank folds his hands and gazes down at them. "Eric is the Meat manager. We have openings in both the Meat and Grocery departments. The Grocery manager is Ralph Thompson, who isn't in today."

"I could really use him in Meat," Eric says. "I'd work him hard." He grins down at me with a mouth full of teeth.

"Both positions are full-time," Frank says.

"There's a chance of getting promoted, in the Meat department," Eric says. "If you work out, I'll make you a meat cutter. There's a pay increase."

I swallow. Eric is standing very close.

"It's up to you," Frank says.

"I'm a good boss," Eric says. He places a hand on my shoulder, so sweaty it soaks through my t-shirt.

"I'm sure you are," I say. "But—"

Eric raises his eyebrows.

With his hand still on my shoulder, I try not to breathe too deeply. I cannot work for this man. He freaks me out.

"I'm a vegetarian," I say.

Eric's smile vanishes. "What?"

"I don't eat meat."

"You don't have to eat it."

"I can't work with meat. It's against my principles."

"There's meat in the Grocery department, too."

For a moment, I hesitate. "It's in cans. It's different if you can't see it."

Eric looks at Frank, who shrugs. Eric looks back at me, eyes narrowed.

"Well. Enjoy yourself in Grocery."

Chapter Two

I find a Spend Easy guy in Aisle Two. He's a little taller than me, with shaggy black hair, and scruff shadowing his cheeks. I wouldn't say he looks messy—at least, he's the kind of messy I imagine girls finding attractive.

He's slowly taking cans of dog food from a cardboard box and arranging them on the shelf. The box sits on a metal trolley. As I draw near, he glances at me with bored eyes.

"Working hard?" I say.

"Depends. By the standards of Bangladesh, definitely not. But by this country's standards? I'm overtaxing myself. Soon time to take a break."

A middle-aged man approaches us holding a can of carrots. "I don't need this many carrots," he says. "Do you have a smaller can than this?"

"Beats me," my new co-worker says.

"Aren't you even going to look?" the man says.

"I'll look," I say.

"You stay out of this," my new co-worker says. He's wearing a gold ring on the middle finger of his left hand. He's twisting it with his right.

The customer furrows his brow. "Could one of you please do your job?"

"My job, old man," my new co-worker says, "is to put these cans on this shelf, and to remain sane despite incessant customer bitching."

The man's face is turning red, and so, I think, is mine. "What's your name, you little brat?"

"Can you read?" He points to his nametag, which reads "Ernest."

"Okay, Ernest. You'll regret your treatment of me. I'll be having a chat with your manager, and you'll be out a job if I have anything to say about it."

"Go right ahead." Ernest takes something from his pocket. "Here's his business card." Ernest flicks it. The card spins through the air and hits the man in the chest. He flinches. "Say hi to him for me," Ernest says.

The man picks the card off the floor, glowers at Ernest, and storms out of Aisle Two.

"Um," I say.

"What an asshole," Ernest says. He nods at the yellow shirt I'm holding. "So, you're the new Grocery boy?"

"Yeah."

"Wow. They're getting quick."

"Sorry?"

"I said they're getting quick. They just sacked John two hours ago, and now they've hired his replacement already."

I wonder what John had to do to get fired.

"Frank said to find a stock boy to show me around," I say. "He said there's a video I should watch?"

"What's your name?"

"Sheldon."

"I'm Gilbert."

"I thought your name was Ernest."

"What gave you that idea?"

"Your nametag says Ernest."

"That's because this is Ernest's nametag."

He turns and starts walking toward the rear of the store. He pauses, and glances back at me. "Were you recently a patient in a psychiatric ward?"

I struggle to keep my shock from registering on my face. "No. Why do you ask?"

"You're wearing Velcro sneakers."

*

When Sam brought me the Velcro shoes, I asked him how he got to the hospital. He doesn't have a car—at least, I've never seen one in the driveway.

It turns out he walked.

"Why did you walk an hour to visit someone you don't know? Why'd you buy me this stuff? I was going to kill myself in your shed."

"Our shed."

"Why are you doing this? I can't repay you."

"You will repay me. For the book, the sneakers, and the ambulance ride. But don't worry—I can wait till you find a job, and my interest rates aren't that high."

My debt mounted quickly. Sam was feeding my cat, and he said in a couple days, rent day, he intended to pay it for me. He'd tell the landlord I was out of town, which was technically true. The hospital's in the city—we live in the next town.

It's occurred to me a couple times that maybe I should find it weird that Sam is helping me so much.

*

The girl in the video wears a t-shirt with Spend Easy written across it, but it's bright blue instead of yellow. She's walking past shelves filled with canned goods, and she speaks with the kind of enthusiastic condescension you can only get away with in safety videos.

"Hey there! My name is Sandy. I'm a Grocery worker, just like you! My experience with the Spend Easy chain of supermarkets has been both enjoyable and rewarding, and I just know you'll feel the same. But don't get carried away! Every job has its potential safety hazards, and Grocery is no different. The last thing we want is for you to end up with a fractured skull!"

The scene switches to a warehouse, where a tall, gangly guy is reaching up to place a cardboard box on a shelf.

Enter Sandy. "This is my co-worker, Stan. Say hi, Stan!"

"Hi, there."

"Stan is about to help me demonstrate an important safety rule."

Stan scratches his head. "I am? What rule is that, Sandy?"

The camera zooms in on the box Stan just put on the shelf, which tips forward, dumps three packages of macaroni noodles on his head, and settles back onto the shelf.

"You're never supposed to place product above eye level, Stan!" Sandy says, and skips away, leaving Stan rubbing his head.

Next, Sandy's in a parking lot, pushing shopping carts past rows of parked cars. A truck screeches to a halt a meter away from her. The driver leans out his window and shouts, "Why don't you watch where you're going, lady!"

Sandy wags a finger at him. "Why don't you watch where you're going, mister! I'm wearing a bright orange safety vest with yellow reflectors, as per safety regulations!"

Gilbert steps forward and turns off the TV. "Anyway. You get the idea, right?"

"I guess."

"Sandy is a lie, by the way. There are no girls in Grocery."

"Why not?"

"There just aren't."

The warehouse is accessed through a set of red swinging doors. We're in a tiny office to the right of them. The warehouse has walls and floor of cracked concrete. Towers of cardboard boxes sit on wooden pallets all around, and still more boxes sit on carts like the one Gilbert left in Aisle Two. A metal rail runs along the walls, low to the floor, and the space between is overflowing with litter.

"Is Ernest working today?" I ask.

"Nope."

"So, what if that customer calls Frank and says 'Ernest' mistreated him today? Won't Frank figure out what really happened?"

"Oh, are you concerned for my welfare? Trying to save me from myself?"

"I didn't—"

"Frank never knows who's working. If he gets a complaint about Ernest, he'll do what he always does—call the fat fucker to the office and tell him off."

Gilbert directs me up a staircase farther into the warehouse, to the washroom for male employees, where I change into the Spend Easy shirt. Then we head back toward the sales floor.

"So," I say. "How long have you been working here?"

"What?"

"How long—"

"I'm not interested in making small talk with you."

We walk to Aisle One. Gilbert takes a box of plastic bags near the back of the shelf and slides it to the front. "Fronting," he says. He places a second box behind it, and then stacks another atop each one. "For the first three months, every rookie fronts. Nothing else. Aisles One through Five, Dairy, and the freezers. It all gets fronted. Makes the shelves look neat and full—for a time. But as you front, the customers will slowly pick apart your work behind you. Usually, by the time you get to Aisle Five, Aisle One will look like you never touched it."

I reach into the shelf and bring a box to the front. Then, another. I create a wall like Gilbert's—two high and two deep. "This doesn't seem so bad."

"Sure thing, Sisyphus." He walks away.

I grab another box.

I finish the plastic bags and start on dish detergents. After those, scrub pads. Then light bulbs—incandescent and fluorescent. Scented candles. Air fresheners. Household cleaners. I stand back and study my work: a solid wall of product. Tidy. Sort of calming, actually.

Taking Stock31# Taking Stock31# Taking Stock31

A woman pauses to my left, takes two boxes of plastic bags, and drops them into her cart.

There's a hole in my wall.

I dig for two more boxes.

The assistant manager of Produce drops by while I'm fronting dryer sheets. He's skinny, with curly red hair that sticks out from underneath a black baseball cap. "I'm Merridan," he says. "Jack Merridan. I've been working here since the store first opened, eight years ago."

Jack tells me Spend Easy has a theft problem, and Frank is certain the culprits work in Grocery. He's asked Jack to discreetly investigate the matter. Jack wants me to help—to let him know if I catch anyone taking stock without paying for it. My cooperation will be rewarded. Raises, promotions, hours tailored to my liking. All I have to do is snitch.

"I don't know," I say.

"Sorry?"

"This is my first day—it feels a little early to get involved in, um, politics."

"Are you planning to steal food, too, then?"

"No. I'm just not comfortable spying on people."

"Okay. I'll find someone else to do it. And I'll tell him to keep an eye on you."

"I'm no thief."

"I recommend you keep all your receipts. You may be asked to produce them at any time." He maintains eye contact for another few seconds, then looks down. "Your forearms are skinny, like a T-rex's."

He faces the front of the store, puts his hands in his pockets, and walks away.

Jack's threats don't scare me.

What scares me is that Spend Easy is my first taste of what's commonly referred to as the 'real world', and so far the real world reminds me of high school. I didn't do so well in high school. My best memories are of the times I managed to make myself invisible. I graduated friendless. Soon after, my Mom died.

Two years after that, I searched the internet for how to tie a noose.

*

Gilbert returns as I'm fronting the last section in Aisle One, his hair shorter.

"What happened to your hair?" I say.

"I got a haircut. You're still fronting Aisle One?"

"Good afternoon, gentlemen," someone calls from the other end of the aisle. He's a tall, athletic-looking guy wearing a Spend Easy shirt. He nods at Gilbert. "Nice haircut."

"Hey, fat-ass. Meet the rookie."

"Hi," he says. "I'm Paul."

Gilbert heads toward the warehouse, and I follow Paul to Aisle Two, which affords me the opportunity to evaluate Gilbert's claim regarding his ass. It's true: despite an otherwise muscular frame, Paul's ass is enormous. We begin fronting canned vegetables.

"Are employees normally allowed to go for haircuts during work?" I ask.

"Only employees named Gilbert."

"Why?"

Paul shrugs. "He just gets away with stuff."

Fronting goes much quicker, with two. Paul tells me I'm being too meticulous—the product doesn't need to be lined up perfectly.

"Good word," I say.

"What?"

"Meticulous—that's a good word."

"Thanks."

It turns out I know someone who works here: Ernie, a guy I went to high school with. He's Gilbert's 'Ernest', I guess. He walks past as we're fronting dog food.

"Hey, Paul," he says. "I'm just popping in to check the schedule."

"Okay."

Ernie makes it to the end of Aisle Two, and then he turns around and stares at me. "Holy shit."

I raise my eyebrows.

"Sheldon?" he says. "Sheldon Mason?"

"Yeah."

He rushes back to us, hand thrust forward. "Holy shit! I haven't seen you in like three years! What have you been doing all this time?"

"Nothing."

He shifts his weight from one foot to the other. "No, really—what have you been doing?"

"Really. Nothing."

Whereas most people ignored or ridiculed me in high school, Ernie constantly pestered me to come hang out with him at his house. I learned to have an excuse prepared at all times. I felt bad, but the truth is, I think he's disgusting. His house smells bad, and his personality makes me nauseous. After I graduated I started using a different email account, and whenever Ernie called, Mom told him I wasn't home.

"Are you still writing?" Ernie says.

"No."

"Oh. Right on. Well, I'd better go, then."

"All right. See you."

"Hey—we should hang out some time."

"Uh. Okay."

Once Ernie's gone, Paul glances at me. "Is he a friend of yours?" His face is blank, and his tone is neutral, but I sense there's some silent judgment being passed. Of course there is.

"Yeah," I say. "I guess."

He nods. "I'm glad. He needed one, here."

Paul's pocket emits a brief, 8-bit melody. He takes out his phone and starts texting. "Not supposed to be doing this," he says.

"Was that the 1up sound, from Mario?"

"It was indeed." He puts away his phone. "So, you're a writer?"

"Used to be."

"Anything published?"

"No."

"What did you write?"

"Fiction."

"Cool. I write a blog. About video games."

"Good for you."

"I've been thinking about trying a novel. This place is actually pretty inspiring."

For some reason, this really irritates me.

"What, you mean Spend Easy?"

"Maybe. I think it could be good."

"What would the conflict be?"

"I don't know yet."

"The characters need to want something. What would they want? Food?"

"I don't really know."

I replace a bag of dog treats and stop fronting. "Can I take my break now?"

"Sure, man."

Paul leads me into the warehouse, where a punch clock hangs on the wall near the entrance, flanked by two racks filled with punch cards. He searches them.

"Looks like you don't have one of these yet. Oh well. Just come back in 15."

"Fine." I start to leave.

"Hey—Sheldon, right?"

"Yeah."

"Can you recommend some good writing books?"

"Listen, Paul, writing fiction is nothing like blogging."

"I'm aware of that."

"It takes years of practice. Writing every day. You need stamina, especially when it comes to novels. Trust me—I wrote for years. I even won a short story competition. But I never got through a novel."

"All right, then. I'll see you in 15."

I start to leave, but hesitate on my way out the red warehouse doors. "*On Writing* is good," I say. "By Stephen King."

"Thanks."

I haven't eaten today, but even my ravenous hunger is given pause by the sheer variety that now confronts me. I walk aimlessly along the freezers until the TV dinners catch my attention. I mouth their names. "Salisbury Steak." Intriguing. "Chicken Parmagiana." Captivating. "Roast Duck with Orange Sauce." I think I'm getting aroused.

I grab the Roast Duck and take it to the cash registers. Lane One's lineup is kind of long, so I go to Lane Two. The cashier has short, dark hair and glasses. Her nametag says "Lesley-Jo."

"Hi," I say. I have a thing for girls with glasses. My brain is devoid of things to say.

"Hey. You the new Grocery boy?"

"Yep. Sheldon."

"I'm Lesley-Jo." She scans the dinner: beep. "That's $3.89, Sheldon."

I pay her. "Bon appétit," she says.

I turn around and find Eric staring down at me. His eyes are narrowed.

"What's that?" he says.

"It's a microwavable dinner."

"What's in it?"

Slowly, I turn the package till the duck's gleaming breast is in view.

He points at the picture. "You're supposed to be a vegetarian."

"Um, I am."

"This is meat."

"It's not mine. It's—it's for Gilbert."

"Well, let's go give it to him, then."

We walk past the aisles. Eric's damp hand rests on my shoulder again, and I feel like I'm being escorted to the gallows. We find Gilbert in Aisle Five, sitting on his cart, restocking boxes of popcorn. He notices us before we reach him.

Eric holds up the Roast Duck. "Is this yours?"

Without moving his head, Gilbert glances at the dinner, at Eric, and at me. He's expressionless, and his darting eyes are almost too quick to follow. He stands up and plucks the dinner from Eric's hands. "Yep."

Eric blinks. "He bought this for you? Why?"

"I told him it's tradition for the rookie to buy lunch for whoever trains him in."

"I haven't heard of that before."

"That's because I made it up."

Eric studies Gilbert's face a moment longer. Then he looks at me. "For a second I thought you might be a liar, vegan."

"Damn, rookie," Gilbert says once Eric's out of earshot. "You make friends quick." He puts another box of popcorn on the shelf.

"How did you know what was going on?"

"He looked pissed, and you looked worried. I figured you lied to him about something."

"What's his deal?"

"He got back from Afghanistan two years ago, and he's worked here ever since. That's his deal."

"What will he do if he catches me eating meat?"

He scratches his scruff-shadowed cheek. "Have you fired, probably."

"Great."

"It could be worse."

"How?"

He takes the Roast Duck from his cart and walks toward the warehouse. "You could be working for him."

Chapter Three

Home, I take two steak burgers from the freezer and put them in the microwave. I only had enough break left to grab an apple after my encounter with Eric, and now I'm craving meat. Once they're done I place them in buns, squirt some ketchup on, and eat them standing in the kitchen.

Marcus Brutus comes in and gazes up at me with wide eyes. "Meow."

"Shut up."

"Meow."

"Shut up. Go away."

Marcus Brutus licks his paw and sneezes. He looks back at me. "Meow."

I visit Sam later, and he asks about my day. I consider telling him about Gilbert's mid-shift haircut, or the meat manager's strange interest in my diet. But Sam got me the job, and I don't want to seem ungrateful.

"It was pretty good."

"How are the other workers?"

"Nice, I guess."

"Talk to them much?"

"A little. I don't really know what to say to them."

"Say anything. Life's not like fiction, you know."

"What do you mean?"

"I mean I think you read too many books. Stop worrying about finding things to say, and stop assuming every silence is awkward."

"I—"

"Shut up for a minute. You need to stop being so afraid. Just don't say anything for a while."

*

They let me out of the psych ward because, despite diagnosing me with clinical depression, they no longer thought I was in immediate danger of killing myself. This was after three weeks on Zoloft, of course.

They also assigned me a therapist, and I have my first session with her the morning after my first shift at Spend Easy. The receptionist invites me to take a seat, and when my therapist enters the waiting room to escort me to her office, I see they've made a big mistake. She's beautiful. I can't 'open up' to her. I'll be as talkative as a dead clam.

I follow her into the office and sit down.

"So," she says, her legs crossed, a clipboard perched on her knee. She has bright blue eyes, long eyelashes, and thick brown hair. "I'm Bernice, you're Sheldon. How is Sheldon?"

"Fine," I say. I try not to wipe my sweaty palms on my pants. "Nice weather."

"Wouldn't this be more efficient if you just asked me why I wanted to kill myself?"

She jiggles her pen, tapping it lightly against the clipboard. "Is that what you're interested in discussing?"

"No. Of course not."

"Then let's not."

"But—"

"Being a decent therapist is really easy, Sheldon. If all I do is listen to you talk about the things you're ready to talk about, then I've done my job pretty well. If I manage to say a few things that help you reach some insights about yourself, then I've been an excellent therapist. And that's about all there is to this."

"What if I'm not ready to talk about anything?"

"Then I would say that's pretty typical for a first session. Why don't we try again next time?"

I stare at her.

"Go on." She makes a shooing gesture. "Go talk to the receptionist about scheduling your next appointment."

*

I forgot *Crow* at Spend Easy, and I need to find out when I'm working, so after I leave Bernice's office I bike to my new workplace.

When you first enter Spend Easy, you're facing the section with the Bakery, Deli, and Produce departments. Across the store, just out of sight, is Meat. Hang a right. Now you're walking between the aisles and the cash lanes. With only five aisles and six cash registers, Spend Easy isn't a very big grocery store.

If you look at Lane Two, you'll see Cassandra, the current record holder for breaking my heart the most, checking in a bag of frozen peas. She works here, too.

She sees me. Her eyebrows shoot up, and she raises her hand. "Hey, Sheldon," she says.

Look away. Make a quick detour down Aisle Two.

I met Cassandra in junior high. She was attractive, and willing to talk to me, which is a rare quality among females. In fact, girls were so uninterested in me, I assumed Cassandra was a fluke. I assumed that this was the first and last time a girl would ever have time for me.

We became close. We laughed a lot. She thought it was cool I liked to write, and I thought it was cool she was hot.

She has large brown eyes, and a way of smiling with half her mouth that always made my heart race, back then. Whenever she was thinking about something she would brush her hair over her right ear. I noticed every time.

We spent a lot of time together. I told her everything about myself, except that I loved her. She told me a lot, too. About her Mom walking out on her and her Dad when she was a kid, and never coming back.

Once, she told me I wasn't like other guys. I didn't treat her like a 'girl' as distinct from a 'boy'—I just treated her like another person. She liked that.

That same day, I told her I loved her. After that, the hanging out stopped. So did the late-night IM conversations. In the halls at school, she smiled and looked away.

That was grade nine. In grade 10, around Christmas, she messaged me to say she missed me. I was the only one who understood her. She wanted to hang out again, so we did. We went skating, and skiing, and when summer came, we did summer stuff. One day, in August, she reached out and took my hand while we were walking. I didn't let go till we reached her house.

When I did, she locked eyes with me and said, "You know, Sheldon, one day you're going to hate me."

She got a boyfriend the first week of grade 11. We stopped talking again.

I made friends with Sean that same year. He wanted to be a writer, too. He was well-liked—not an outcast, like me. I'm not sure how we were friends, actually.

In grade 12, it happened again with Cassandra. I told myself I didn't feel anything for her anymore. But I was wrong.

One night, surprising even myself, I asked if I could kiss her. I asked her permission. She said no.

And, when I heard a couple weeks later that she'd kissed Sean at a party, it crushed me. They started dating, and I haven't talked to either since. Presumably their love attained breathtaking heights, and they went on adventures together to distant lands, bringing back stories they'll recount again and again to their grandchildren. Hell, I don't have a Facebook account—she might have married him, for all I know.

Meanwhile, I attempted suicide.

Yesterday Frank said the Grocery manager is named Ralph, and there's a blond-haired man wearing a Ralph nametag in the warehouse, toting a futuristic black gun. I'm guessing that's him. He and a delivery guy are circling a pallet stacked high with dairy products held together with plastic wrap. The guy rips the plastic, exposing a yogurt container's barcode, and Ralph points his gun, a blinking red light playing over the product. There's a beep, and Ralph presses some buttons on the gun's interface. They repeat this several times. I wait patiently, a spectator to their awkward, shuffling dance.

They finish. The delivery guy moves the pallet into the walk-in dairy cooler, and exits through the back door. Ralph and I are alone.

"You're the new guy, right?" he says. "Sheldon?"

"That's me."

He offers his hand, and we shake—firm but brief. "I'm Ralph. You worked your first shift yesterday, with..." He checks a schedule lying next to a computer. "Gilbert and Paul. What was your impression of them?"

"They appear to know what they're doing."

"How much work did Gilbert do?"

"Not sure—I wasn't with him, much."

"I know for a fact Gilbert did very little last night. And I think you know it, too."

"Really?"

"So, I know you're not a tattler. Which is fine—I don't need a spy to know what's going on in my department. Besides, I already have a tattler. Do you consider yourself a hard worker?"

"I've never had a job before."

"Well, I'll tell you something. Almost every new employee that comes through those doors is a hard worker. Pretty much everyone hauls ass when they're first hired on. Yet Grocery is full of slackers. You, the new guy, you'll put out a 100 cases of stock on order night, and they'll put out 45. You'll answer pages for carryouts and price checks, and they'll relax in the warehouse. They'll even make fun of you for working so hard. Eventually, you'll start asking yourself why you should work any harder, when you're only getting paid minimum wage, just like everyone else. Are you asking yourself that?"

"I think so."

"Well, I'll tell you why. A decent person isn't comfortable sitting on his ass and collecting a paycheck for it. A decent person knows that if someone's paying you to do a job, you do it. Otherwise, it's stealing." Ralph turns and takes a clipboard from the desk. "We hired you to replace John. He was supposed to work today, 5-10. Can you work that shift?"

"Sure."

"Great. I'm in till five, so I'll see you as I'm leaving."

The store got busier while I was in the warehouse, and leaving involves navigating around pushy customers wielding carts. I leave through Aisle Two, grabbing a few cans of cat food on my way—Turkey Giblets in Gravy, the only thing Marcus Brutus will eat. I take them to the Customer Service counter (Eight Items or Less), where Betty awaits. She scans the cans without speaking.

"That's ungrammatical, you know," I say.

"What?"

"It should say Eight Items or Fewer. Not Less."

"You owe me $5.37."

Frank rushes past to my right, then backs up and scrutinizes the metal flaps that conceal the cigarettes behind Betty. Does he ever make eye contact?

"Mason," he says. "Got a minute?"

"Sure," I say.

"Do you want to change the outside garbage for me? Thanks." He turns on his heel and marches down Aisle One.

"I haven't started my shift yet," I call after him.

"You'll need rubber gloves," he shouts back. He's already past the dryer sheets. "You can get them from the Meat department."

I'm not sure Ralph's pep talk prepared me for this.

But this is the only job I have, and I'm not likely to get another. So I head for the Meat department.

There are two entrances into Meat—one from the sales floor, and one from the warehouse. It has three rooms. The first room features a window through which customers can speak to employees working inside. I peer through. Eric's not there. I go in and start searching for the gloves.

The double doors that lead to the next room swing open, and Eric emerges, holding a long, blood-spattered butcher knife. Tiny rivulets of red trickle down his plastic apron. I begin inching backward.

"Hi," I say.

"Morning, vegan. What brings you to my den of sin?"

"Rubber gloves. Frank said they were in here."

Eric takes a step closer, without lowering the knife. I take a step back. "This is my department," he says. "Frank has no idea what I keep in here. For instance—" He turns abruptly, and I jump. He grabs a box from a shelf. "We have latex gloves. Not rubber."

He takes two from the box and throws them at me. I catch one, the other bouncing off my chest and onto the concrete floor.

I pick it up, keeping my eyes on him. "Thanks." I back through the door.

"They're disposable!" he says. "You throw them out when you're done."

Betty supplies me with a big black bag, and I bring it outside. When I find the garbage disposal, I realize I'll need more bags. The disposal consists of a concrete cylinder cemented to the sidewalk, and at this point, throwing trash here is a purely symbolic act. There isn't room for any more.

I put on the gloves and pick up a coffee cup. It's half full, and some coffee spills out, narrowly missing my sneakers. I drop it into the bag and grab a burger wrapper. I can feel the grease through the latex—it's like I'm not even wearing gloves.

A guy walks by wearing the trademark yellow shirt. He notices me, and stops. "Whoa, dude. Are you new?"

I drop a half-eaten slice of pizza into the bag. "I was hired yesterday."

"Where's your uniform?"

"Home. My shift doesn't start till five."

"Looks like it started early to me, bro. I'm Brent, by the way. I work in Grocery."

"Me too. I'm Sheldon."

"Why are you digging around in that trash if you're not in till five?"

"I came in to find out when I'm working, and Frank asked me to do this."

"He told you to scour that disease pit, when you're not even on?"

"Yep."

"You know why he asked you, right? You, and not someone else?"

"Not really."

"Because no one but the new guy would go near that. Look at it. It's disgusting."

I nod. "Yeah."

"It needs to be done, though, so who better than the rookie? And during his off-time, no less." Brent shakes his head. "I wouldn't do it, bro."

"You wouldn't?"

"I'd refuse. You're not even on shift right now, and that isn't sanitary. Go home."

"But he's my boss."

"He's your boss during working hours. And even then, I'd tell him to go screw himself. You're allowed to refuse unsafe work, you know. There are probably things living in there." With that grim prophecy, Brent enters Spend Easy, leaving me with a barely diminished mound of waste. Now that I've disturbed it, flies are buzzing peevishly around, landing on my shirt and skin. I fight an urge to vomit.

Brent's right—this is bullshit. I'd be well within my rights to abandon it, at least until my shift starts, and probably then, too.

I consider whether Mom would have continued cleaning out this garbage. I'm thinking yes. Not because she was the sort of woman to put up with bullshit, but because she was such an idealist. I'm pretty sure she would have been nodding right along with Ralph's pep talk. She wouldn't have just earned her paycheck—she would have gone way beyond that.

It turns out nothing larger than a fly lives in the garbage. There is, however, a congealed mixture of coffee, melted ice cream, and soda waiting for me at the bottom. I return to the Service counter and ask Betty for paper towels. She tears off a few sheets. I tell her I'll need the whole roll.

*

I never knew my father. He contributed his sperm, and not much else. Mom never spoke about him, except once, when I asked if he was alive—yes—and if she knew where he was—no. After that I decided I didn't care to learn anything else about him. If he gave up my mother, then he wasn't very interesting to me.

Mom studied business and philosophy in university. Business helped her navigate the world as a single mother. Philosophy helped her die.

Her favourite philosopher was Plato. I didn't learn to read till I was nearly seven, but even as I struggled with kindergarten readers, I knew the principles behind Plato's *Crito* backward and forward. It was one of my bedtime stories, and Mom would do the voices—calm and wise for Socrates, slow and dumb for *Crito*. I knew why it was Socrates' duty to drink the poisonous hemlock, even though he felt his sentence was unjust. He did it to uphold the laws of Athens.

Socrates believed we should obey the law simply because we're citizens—because the law keeps us safe. That's called a social contract. 2000 years later, I think Mom assumed everyone had signed the contract. She would leave her things unattended in public places, since, you know, theft is against the law. And guess what? Her stuff was always waiting when she came back. Purse, laptop, shopping bags—nobody ever stole them.

I wish they had.

My mother would walk across crosswalks with her eyes straight ahead, heedless of traffic, since, you know, pedestrians have the right of way. This is how she lived. Cars would screech to a halt, inches away, horns blaring, and she would just smile.

She lived in a better place. It wasn't until she was 37 that disillusionment came.

Two years ago, on June 30th, my mother was killed by a drunk driver while crossing the crosswalk two kilometres from our apartment. It was 5:37 PM.

*

My bedroom floor is a sea of white, grey, and black, with a single patch of bright yellow near the bed, which I pick up and pull on. I dig a pair of black pants out of my closet, as well as some old black shoes—not Velcro, this time. I'll never wear those again, if I can help it.

In the kitchen, I hit the microwave's RESET button and the time appears: 4:50 PM. 10 minutes to get to work. I go outside and get on my bike.

I enter the warehouse a couple minutes to five. Gilbert is sitting on a big box of toilet paper, doing something on his smartphone, and Ralph is standing at his desk, using the computer.

I have a punch card, now. I drop it into the punch clock, which makes a sound like a strangling robot.

Ralph walks over. "Evening, Sheldon. I want you to keep an eye on the cart corrals outside. Bring in the carts when you see the corrals getting full." He turns to Gilbert. "Hey. You've been sitting there for an hour. Time to do some work."

Gilbert doesn't look up. "I have been working."

Ralph raises his eyebrows. "I think we're operating under different definitions of the word."

"Think so? Mine is 'anything you're paid for'."

Tonight I'm fronting with Matt, who was hired the week before I was. He's short, with greasy black hair and a lot of pimples.

"I'm practically a midget," Matt says, "and my face is covered in pimples. I smell, because I don't shower enough, because I'm lazy. And I'm too old to be working here."

"You're not that short," I say.

There are a lot more guys on in Grocery than there were yesterday. Gilbert, Brent, Ernie, Matt, a guy I haven't met yet, and me. Ernie happens by occasionally with a cartload of product to stock, but the guy I don't know is the only one I see frequently, and he doesn't stop to chat. He goes as fast as his towering cartloads will allow. He turns corners quickly, his tower wobbling, and he only pauses long enough to rip open a box and cram its contents onto the shelf. Then he throws himself against his cart and speeds away.

Matt and I have fronted our way to Aisle Three when the store intercom emits two beeps. "Grocery personnel to Aisle Two for a cleanup."

"I should probably go get that," Matt says. He runs a hand through his greasy hair, and fronts a stack of tuna cans.

"It's fine. I'll get it."

There's a box of spaghetti noodles on the floor of Aisle Two, the majority of its contents scattered around it.

Lesley-Jo is behind the Service counter today, looking bored, but she grins when she sees me coming. "I hear I accidentally sold you contraband, yesterday."

"The roast duck?"

She nods, and adjusts her glasses. "Rumour has it you turned down Eric when he offered you a position. He told the cashiers to alert him if you buy anything containing meat. He's pretty pissed. Vegetarians might as well worship Satan, as far as he's concerned."

"Well, a lot of people don't understand the lifestyle, you know."

"You're not really a vegetarian, are you?"

"No. No, I'm not."

Her grin widens. "Your secret's safe with me." She passes me the broom and dustpan. "It's probably safe with most of the other girls, too. But I'd still be careful." Her gaze drifts up and over my shoulder. "Frank is watching."

I look. A head-and-shoulders silhouette stands at the tinted window.

The spaghetti noodles group together as I sweep them into the dustpan, resembling some sort of mutant porcupine. I dump them into the garbage near the cash registers. Glancing out the big window, I see that both corrals are pregnant with carts. Like, really pregnant. Oops.

I go to Aisle Three, but Matt isn't there. The guy I don't know is, though, yanking bottles of canola oil out of a box, two by two, and putting them on the shelf. I clear my throat. He doesn't turn. "Excuse me?" I say.

He cries out and drops one of the bottles. It's glass, but miraculously doesn't break. He whirls around. "Jesus Christ!"

"Sorry."

He's staring at me like I'm frothing at the mouth. "You need to not sneak up on people when they're in the middle of something."

"I'm sorry. Ralph told me to keep an eye on the carts, and it looks like they're ready to be brought in. I'm Sheldon."

He studies me a few seconds more, his eyes wide. He doesn't introduce himself, but his nametag says Casey. "This God damned order is never getting put up," he says. He marches past me toward the front end. "Come on."

I follow him to a coat rack that sits against the wall near Lane Five. He tosses me a flimsy orange vest with yellow reflectors, and takes one for himself. Mine is tangled up, and I have a hard time finding the arm holes. "Why do we have to wear these?"

"Regulation," he says as he walks briskly toward the exit. "If we're struck and we're not wearing them, we can't sue the bastards."

An elderly cashier glares at Casey's back from Lane Three.

Casey takes the corral on the left, and directs me to the other. On my way across the parking lot I almost have an opportunity to sue the bastards, but the black SUV stops just in time, the driver leaning on his horn and scowling. I make my way to the carts and start fumbling with them. Almost immediately, I squat my thumb.

Across the parking lot, Casey is moving with superhuman speed, swinging the carts from the stall and swiftly assembling them into a line at least 12 carts long. That done, he leans forward so his head is nearly level with the first one's handle, and pushes with all his might. I can see the tendons on his neck from over here. He's a regular cart cowboy.

He makes quick work of his corral, and comes over to help with mine. He puts together some carts, but before bringing them in he points at a sign hanging from the corral's roof. I didn't notice it before. "CARTS ARE PROVIDED FOR YOUR

CONVENIENCE. PLEASE BRING THEM TO THE CART
CORRAL WHEN YOU'RE DONE WITH THEM."

"Now tell me this," Casey says. "See if you can explain this
one to me. Why would they put a sign asking customers to bring
carts to the corral right on the God damned corral? Isn't that
sort of preaching to the fucking choir?" He spins around and
starts pushing his carts toward the entrance. "Morons!"

Matt's back in Aisle Three when I return, and I tell him I'm
taking my break. I grab a bag of chips—Sour Cream and Bacon—and bring them to the Service desk. Lesley-Jo glances at
the flavour. "You're walking a fine line," she says as she scans
the barcode.

I take my chips to the break room, which is upstairs from the
warehouse. Gilbert, Brent, and Ernie are all sitting around the
table. "He kept asking me if I like rain," Ernie is saying as I enter. "Apparently he loves it. Wouldn't shut up about it. Rain!"
Ernie chuckles. "Seriously, though. I always feel bad when I
meet a mentally challenged person."

"I don't," Gilbert says. "I think of them as angels, sent by
God to help us be thankful for what we have."

"Wow. Really?"

"No. I don't believe in God."

I sit down and open my chips.

"So, Sheldon," Ernie says, "I hear you're a vegetarian now. Is
that true?"

"Yeah."

"I'm sorry, but I find vegetarianism so stupid. Like, why are
animals more important than plants? Why the plant discrimina-
tion?" Ernie chuckles. "And what about bacteria? Isn't it a sin to

kill them, too? Maybe we should all lie in bed and not move, to avoid killing bacteria."

Silence.

"The problem with good jokes," Ernie says, "is no one knows what to say afterward." He gives a half-hearted laugh. "What are you doing tomorrow evening, Sheldon?"

"Um, not sure."

"Would you like to grab a beer?"

"I'd have to check the schedule, to see if I'm working."

"I already checked it. You're working John's shifts, right?"

"Yeah."

"Then you aren't working tomorrow."

"Oh. Great."

"So, do you want to?"

"Sure."

Gilbert says, "He doesn't actually want to, Ernest. He's only saying yes to preserve the tattered remnants of your self-esteem."

"Nice haircut, Gilbert," Ernie says. "I heard you got it in the middle of your shift." Ernie turns to me. "Gilbert takes slacking off very seriously."

Gilbert glances at the microwave clock. "You've been up here five minutes longer than your sanctioned break, Ernest."

Ernie leans back. "The order tonight isn't that big. There's no need to kill ourselves out there."

"That's debatable, in your case."

Ernie stands up. "Want to meet at the bar across the street, Sheldon? Tomorrow at 6:00?"

"Six it is."

"See you, then." He leaves.

Brent coughs. "Have fun with that, bro."

Chapter Four

Socializing is like a job. You work to make money, and you socialize to accumulate social currency. In both cases, you give up some freedom. Where you go, what you do, what you eat—these are things you negotiate with the person paying you. If the pay isn't high enough, you quit.

Agreeing to hang out with Ernie doesn't feel like a very good deal. That wouldn't matter to me, if I thought Ernie had redeeming qualities. But I don't. I'm frustrated with myself for humouring him. He's a bastard, and now my co-workers will probably associate me with him.

Not that I care.

I find Ernie sitting at a corner table, as far away from the bar as it's possible to get. He has his chin stuck out, and his hands are folded over his stomach. He's wearing a smug little smile.

"Thought you'd get here sooner," he says. "I ate a burger while I waited."

There's an empty plate in front of him, smeared with grease and ketchup. At my seat, a Caesar salad awaits. I sit.

"I bought that for you," he says.

"I can't eat it. It has bacon bits."

"Oh. Shit. I'll have it, then." He slides it over. "Can I buy you a drink?"

"I'll buy my own."

Ernie's urge to pay for everything always made me slightly uneasy.

We walk to the bar in silence, and order a beer each. Ernie leaves a tip equal to the price. We make the long walk back to our table.

"So," Ernie says once we're sitting again. "How do you like Spend Easy?"

"It's all right. Eric kind of creeps me out."

"Eric's a good man. Did you know he hires mostly under-privileged youth to work in Meat? He teaches them meat cutting—a marketable skill. He's been on the news because of it." I can tell Ernie really enjoys telling me this. His expression is getting smugger.

"I didn't know that."

"Are you aware that Cassandra also works at Spend Easy?"

"Yep."

"Is that hard for you?"

"Why would it be hard?"

"Well, everyone knows you're in love with her."

"Everyone?"

"You know. People we went to school with."

"I don't talk to anyone we went to school with. Do you?"

He shrugs. "Not really."

"Then who are you talking about?"

"Me, I guess."

"Well, for your records, I'm not in love with Cassandra."

"That's probably for the best," he says, "because she's still with Sean. You're finished your beer already?"

"Looks that way, doesn't it?" I stand up. "It's been great chatting, Ernie."

*

I was grateful when Sam brought my MP3 player to the psych ward, because I thought I could use it to avoid conversation with the other patients. I was wrong. My second day there I was sitting in the common area, listening to "Bohemian Rhapsody", when a man walked over and picked up my MP3 player from the coffee table in front of me. He was short, balding and wiry. I took out an earbud. "Hi."

"This device contains components made from cassiterite, wolframite, niobium, and tantalum. These minerals were almost certainly bought from rebel groups in the Democratic Republic of Congo, who used the money to arm themselves. Your purchase not only helped sustain the conflict there—in which nearly 6,000,000 have died since 1998—but also contributed directly to femicide, the systematic raping, beating, and killing of women."

I took out the other earbud.

"Do you think karma exists?"

I shook my head.

"I hope you're right. Because our society conducts itself on land acquired by murdering the original inhabitants. We pretend we're much more civilized than our ancestors, but we finance suffering around the globe. We wear clothes made in sweatshops, we dump our waste on poorer countries, and we buy electronics bathed in blood. So I hope you're right."

He put down my MP3 player and walked away.

Another patient came over and offered his hand. It was very large. I only hesitated a little.

"How ya doin'? I'm Fred."

"Sheldon Mason."

"I see you met the Professor."

"He's a professor?"

"He wishes he was. He doesn't even have a degree. Want to sit with me during lunch? The food's gonna be here, soon."

We walked to one of the cafeteria tables in the middle of the room. The second we sat down a woman wearing purple appeared, pushing a metal trolley taller than she was. "Wasn't she an extra in *The Hobbit*?" Fred whispered to me. She left the trolley at the end of our table, and Fred pointed at it. "Let's go there and back again."

Patients trickled in. There was little conversation, and a lot of shuffling. I found a tray with my name on it and followed Fred back to our spot.

"Hey," he said. "Isn't she about your age?"

"Who?"

"The girl sitting on the couch over there, staring at you like you're the last man left on Earth."

I looked, and she looked away. She was very thin, but attractive all the same. "This is the last place I'd look for a girlfriend," I said.

"Suit yourself." Fred picked up a slice of turkey between two thick fingers and inserted it into his mouth. Next, a hard ball of mashed potato. He finished his meal in fewer than 10 mouthfuls.

Then he looked at mine, untouched. "The nurses check your tray to make sure you're eating, you know."

"I'm not hungry. You want it?"

Fred pulled my tray toward him.

*

For the first 15 minutes of my shift, I front alone. Then Matt shows up.

"I'm 20 minutes late," he says.

"Doesn't concern me."

He looks down. "My shirt should be tucked in, too. We're supposed to tuck them in."

I loosen my belt and stuff my shirttail into my pants.

Other than volunteering the occasional piece of self-criticism, Matt is fairly untalkative, and as we front Aisles Two and Three I'm mostly left to contemplate myself.

He does ask me what I think of the décor.

"What?" I say.

"Spend Easy's colour scheme. Red, white, green?" He grasps his shirt with both hands and pulls it outward. "Yellow." He grins.

"It's fine."

"So natural, isn't it? So vital. The yellow of sun. The green of trees. The red of blood."

Cassandra comes by and asks if I'd like to take a break with her. I tell her I wouldn't, particularly—but she's already purchased me a salad. It's difficult to refuse free food, especially when it conforms to one's newfound dietary restrictions. So I follow her to the break room. It's what anyone would have done.

"You didn't wave to me, the other day," she says. "You didn't wave back."

The first forkful of salad is already being masticated. This was a bad idea.

"Are you upset with me?" she says.

"Why would I be upset?"

"You don't have to snap. Ernie said you were upset last night, when you two were hanging out."

I stop chewing. "Ernie?"

"He said he brought me up, and you looked like you were going to cry."

"What the fuck?"

"He told me you stood up and left."

"I left because he makes me nauseous. I needed to go home and vomit."

"It's okay to have feelings, Sheldon. It doesn't make you weak. I'm sorry you're hurting."

"I'm not hurting!"

"I do have a boyfriend, though, Sheldon, and I love him. You need to come to terms with that." She sighs. "I think you and I should avoid seeing each other. I don't think it's good for you."

"I don't want to see you."

Someone is stomping down the hall toward the break room. Cassandra and I exchange looks. I try to think of who I would least prefer to walk through the door right now, but I can't decide.

The door swings open, and Matt stomps in. He places a two-litre bottle of pop in front of a chair and sits down.

"Why were you making so much noise?" Cassandra asks.

"I wanted to give you enough time to stop talking about me."

Her brow furrows. "We weren't talking about you."

"Thank you for saying that. That's really nice."

*

Bernice the therapist attempts neither to conceal nor draw attention to her attractiveness. But that just makes her more attractive. I wonder if this is an issue with many of her patients.

Today, her brown hair is swept back and held in place with a purple clip. She's wearing a white shirt with black buttons, and a patterned skirt. She looks at me with an expression that isn't quite bored, but isn't quite interested, either. If I want interest, I will have to earn it.

"So," she says.

"So," I say.

"Since our last visit, have you given any thought to what you'd like to discuss?"

"I haven't given thought to that, or anything else."

"No thoughts."

"None."

"Nothing's on your mind."

"It's very Zen."

"I'll bet. Do you socialize much, Sheldon?"

"Not much, no."

"Do you work?"

"I got my first job last week. At a grocery store."

She raises her eyebrows. "Your first job? How old are you?"

"Mom earned enough for us both to live, so I kind of just...lived off her."

"Where's your Mom now?"

"She died."

"I'm sorry." She writes something on her clipboard. "Why didn't you want to work, before?"

"I was afraid my co-workers would end up being people I went to high school with. I didn't want to spend any more time with them than necessary."

"Why not?"

"Because they didn't like me and I didn't like them."

"It's improbable they all disliked you."

"Well, I had two friends. But even they didn't invite me to parties, or anything. I think people were wary of associating with me too much—afraid it would hurt their status, I guess. Their brand." I give a dry chuckle. "I mostly felt invisible in high school. Except—that's not exactly right. More like, I felt like a book with the covers ripped off."

"And there's been no one you've connected with since high school?"

"Well," I say, and pause. "I did meet Theresa—she was in the hospital, too."

"Have you spoken with her since?"

"No. She didn't want to keep in touch. But I confided in her." I take a breath. "I told her why I wanted to kill myself."

Bernice raises her eyebrows. "You did?"

I nod.

"Would you like to tell me?"

"No."

"Okay. Why didn't Theresa want to keep in touch?"

I shrug. "Maybe she didn't like me enough."

Bernice thinks I "overgeneralize" when it comes to others' opinions of me, and that I "magnify negatives". She suggests that, next session, we start Cognitive Behavioural Therapy, which is supposed to help overcome such "maladaptive behaviours".

I tell her I'm all for it.

*

Paul takes a box of Borax off the shelf. He hands it to me. "Check that out. It's called the Droste effect."

"Huh?"

"See how the girl is holding a box of Borax, which features another girl, holding another box of Borax? The idea is that it goes on forever—there's an infinite number of girls, holding an infinite number of boxes. The Droste effect."

"If there's a purgatory," I say, "I bet it looks a lot like Spend Easy."

"I could have been working on the order, tonight, you know. But I volunteered to go fronting with you instead."

"Why would you do that?"

"I've been reading the book you recommended. My Dad already owned it. You were right—it's good. But I want to ask you something. King says to be a writer, you have to read a lot. So, can you recommend some stuff I should read?"

"You mean, stuff that will help you write a book about a grocery store?"

"Sure."

"I have no idea."

"Does he know yet?" someone says from behind us. Paul and I turn to see a guy with wide eyes standing near the end of the aisle. He's clutching a tattered magazine against his chest. "Have you told him, Paul?"

"Go away, Tommy. You need a hobby."

"He deserves to know. It concerns everyone." Tommy appears to be in the process of going bald, though I'm sure he must still be in high school.

"Know what?" I say.

"Jesus, Tommy," Paul says. "Why are you here? You aren't even working tonight."

"I'm quitting." He takes out a piece of paper tucked between the magazine's pages and holds it up. "This is my letter to Ralph, notifying him of my resignation, effective immediately. I'm leaving it on his desk."

"What about two weeks' notice?"

Tommy shakes his head, a sad smile on his lips. "You don't get it, do you, Paul? Nobody needs to worry about their record of employment, anymore. It doesn't matter how neatly the shelves are fronted. You don't have to waste any more of your time doing society's busywork."

Paul sighs.

Tommy opens the magazine and holds it in front of my face. He points at a headline, which is printed in bright yellow block letters: "SUN TO EXPLODE JANUARY 12TH!"

"That's in 178 days," Tommy says. "The sun will go supernova in 178 days, a lot sooner than science predicted—thousands of years sooner."

"Billions, actually," I say.

"Exactly. Thousands and thousands of years. Anyway. There was an archaeological dig in Greece a few years ago, and they found one of the Bible's lost books. It's all in there. It matches up with Revelations, too, if you consider recent world events. The government's trying to cover up the whole—"

"Tommy."

Tommy's eyes go even wider. "They wouldn't publish it if it wasn't true, Paul!"

"That article isn't even mentioned on the cover."

"They didn't want to start a panic, duh. They say that in the article."

"It's a tabloid, Tommy. They'll print anything."

Tommy puts a hand on my shoulder. "Get right with God. Put aside old grudges, and contact those you've lost touch with. Tell your family you love them." He rolls up the magazine and stuffs it in his pocket. "I gotta get going. I'm late for paintball."

Paul and I are silent for a moment after Tommy leaves.

"Anyway," I say. "Do you know Cassandra?"

"Yeah, cashier, right? Hot?"

"She's all right."

"She's sexy as hell. Pretty sure she's taken, though—I'd ask her out if she wasn't. What about her?"

"Never mind." I wanted to see how far Ernie's gossip has spread, but I've lost all desire to talk about her.

I find a banana rotting behind some boxes of baking soda, and I take it back to the warehouse to throw out.

Eric is standing next to the garbage chute with one of the Meat workers—Joshua, I think. The chute's door is open, so I guess they were throwing some stuff out, but that's not what they're doing now. Eric's face is red, and blood streams from Joshua's nose. Eric is gripping Joshua's shoulder with his left hand.

"What happened?" I say, and Eric stares at me, blank-faced. Joshua stares at the floor.

"I opened the door too fast," Eric says finally. "I didn't realize he was standing there." He shakes him lightly. "Joshua?"

Joshua nods, eyes still on the floor.

Chapter Five

A shift at Spend Easy imparts an odour difficult to describe—not revolting, but not too agreeable, either. It's the smell of product that's been handled several times, packed into boxes, left sitting in warehouses, shipped long distances. The skin of the hands and forearms becomes papery. The odour is strongest, there.

After a long, hot shower, I walk around the house to Sam's apartment, where he's playing Super Nintendo in his pajamas. He's in the middle of a Grand Prix in Mario Kart, but once he snags first he switches over to Battle Mode, and we play till after midnight. He kicks my ass, repeatedly.

I'm about to request we switch games when he gets a customer—Al. I recognize him from the dinner party. We go out on the deck, and Sam produces a joint. Al has a couple puffs and holds it toward me.

Sam takes it from his hand.

"That's not for Sheldon."

Al lifts an eyebrow. "Getting stingy, Sammy?"

"That's not it."

"What, then?" I say. "Out of curiosity."

"I don't sell to 20-year-olds."

"Okay then, Mom."

We go inside, and Al plays video games with us for a few hours, until he feels all right to drive home.

"Not sure why you're so uptight about me smoking pot," I say when Al leaves.

"It's not good for you."

"That's such shit. You smoke it."

"I mean it's not good for you. You, specifically."

"What's that supposed to mean?"

"What do you think the Zoloft's for, Sheldon? I didn't want to talk about it in front of Al. But we already know your brain chemistry's volatile. They prescribed you Zoloft to try and balance it out. Do you really want to add THC, and risk throwing it off again?"

I stare at the TV, stuck on the game's victory screen—Sam's victory. I know he's making sense, but I'm pissed off, so I don't say anything.

"I've smoked for years, Sheldon—I know I'm fine with it. Plenty of people are. For some it's a painkiller, others use it for anxiety. Most smoke for fun, and never have a problem with it. But I've also seen a couple people go right off the deep end. I don't want to see that happen to you."

"All right."

"No offense, Sheldon, but you're already pretty paranoid. You don't need pot."

"All right, Sam."

"Okay."

I sigh. "Can I ask you a question?"

"Shoot."

"Why didn't you want me to mention your name to anyone at Spend Easy?"

He doesn't answer for a couple seconds. "Let's just say the person I know at Spend Easy would prefer my name didn't come up."

"Is it a client of yours?"

"You know I don't discuss that."

I want to tell him about seeing Eric and Joshua near the trash compactor—about Joshua's ruined nose.

But clearly Sam stresses out about me enough, as it is. And anyway, I'm probably being dumb. The security cameras can see where they were standing. If Eric had done something to Joshua, there'd be a record of it.

We play a few more rounds of Mario Kart, but I'm not really in the mood for it anymore. I tell Sam good night and walk around the house to my place.

*

Tonight I'm fronting with Brent, who spends most of his time in the warehouse. Meaning I need to move twice as fast if I'm going to front the whole store. I'm not worried, though. I'm getting pretty quick at it. Plus, there's something calming about looking back at a wall of product you've assembled—a temporary bulwark against entropy.

Ernie finds me in Aisle Two and asks if I've seen his nametag anywhere. "It keeps going missing," he says.

"Maybe you shouldn't leave it lying around."

"I guess. Hey, are you free to hang tomorrow night?"

"No, I'm not."

"What about Saturday?" He's holding a white coffee cup, and as he sips from it he peers at me over the lid.

"No."

"Well, maybe Sunday, then. I'll have to see if I'm working. I think Ralph is posting the schedule tomorrow."

"Yeah, Ernie. You'll definitely have to get back to me about that."

"I'm really glad we got the chance to spend time together, Sheldon. When we were in high school, I used to sometimes think you didn't like me. Every now and then, I even got the feeling you looked down on me."

"Don't be silly."

"Well I'm glad to learn it isn't true. At least, if it was true then, it certainly shouldn't be now. You have no reason to look down on me."

"You mean, other than being taller than you?"

Ernie takes another sip, and then raises his coffee a few inches into the air. "This looks disposable, doesn't it? It looks like your everyday disposable cup."

"Sure."

"It's not, though." He taps on the side of the cup with his fingernail. "It's made of porcelain, and it's reusable. My mug looks disposable, but, in actual fact, it's saving the planet."

"That's—"

"Why were you wearing Velcro sneakers on your first shift? And why haven't you worn them since?"

The tightness in my chest returns. I didn't realize it was gone.

"Well?" Ernie says.

"I hate shoelaces," I say at last.

Ernie grunts. "The carts need to be brought in," he says. "Gilbert and Brent already called 'not it', and I'm on break. Wanna go do that for me?" He turns and struts in the direction of the warehouse.

I don't know when Ernie discovered environmentalism. Sometime between high school and now, I guess. He's made it his mission to make sure every cardboard box gets broken down and put in the cardboard compactor, where it'll get recycled, instead of in the trash compactor, where it won't.

Earlier tonight, he tried to prevent Gilbert from wasting cardboard by locking up the garbage chute. Gilbert grinned, and 20 minutes later the padlock had disappeared. Ernie confronted him.

"What did you do with the lock?" he said, his face getting red. "Our species doesn't own this planet, Gilbert. We've only borrowed it. You need to recycle. We all need to."

Gilbert laughed. "Let me tell you about recycling, Ernest, you waste of ejaculate. Unless 100 percent of everything gets recycled—and it doesn't—resources will run out. You can reduce and reuse all you want. Society depends on several key resources, and when just one of those is gone, there goes society."

Saturday comes, and I'm working then, too—6:00 to 10:00. Just as I'm beginning to wonder who's helping me front, Tommy shows up, wearing a uniform. Without speaking, he reaches into the shelf for a bottle of dish detergent. He doesn't make it, though. His hand drops to his side. He sighs.

"I thought you quit," I say.

"My parents wouldn't let me. They called Ralph and told him to ignore my resignation." He runs a hand through his sparse hair. "I don't want to die fronting."

"You don't have to worry yet. The supernova's not till after Christmas, right?"

He nods. "174 days."

*

The psych ward was plastered all over with inspirational messages.

"If a window of opportunity appears, don't pull down the shade."

"He who seeks rest finds boredom. He who seeks work finds rest."

"The only job where you start at the top is digging a hole."

One afternoon, Sam made up his own: "It's better to lead a life filled with failure than one filled with apathy."

When I felt over-inspired, I sat in the TV room. There weren't any inspirational messages in there. This particular evening, there was a patient I hadn't seen before. He was sitting cross-legged, and bouncing up and down. He met my glance with a wide smile. "Hi."

"Hi."

He looked back at the TV, still bouncing. I tried not to stare, but it was hard to avoid looking out the corner of my eyes. He caught me, and said, "Can I help you?"

"Um, I don't mean to be rude, but why are you bouncing like that?"

His smile didn't change. "Why not bounce? Life is too short. There should be more bouncing." Continuing to bounce, he picked up the remote control from a nearby table and changed the channel. *America's Next Top Model* was on. "Those people want to be models," he said.

"Yep."

"Have they made reality TV out of your dream yet?"

"Sorry?"

"I always wanted to be a chef. Then they made a reality TV show about becoming a successful one, and now I don't want to do it anymore. What do you want to be?"

"Nothing."

"Come on. If you could be anything."

"A writer, I guess. I don't think they've made one about that."

"They will. Soon. You'll watch aspiring writers do treacherous things to each other, and endure unspeakable humiliation on national television, in order to achieve their dreams. You'll realize you aren't willing to do any of those things. Then you'll just give up."

He changed the channel, still bouncing. "When you're insane, everything makes such perfect sense. Would you agree?"

"Oh, I don't—I'm not—"

"Everything seems to just add up, you know? Little things you never even thought about before you were nuts, they all seem to fit together. Do you want to be alive?"

"I—"

"Sane people want to survive. Humans are hardwired to survive. If everything upstairs is ticking along smoothly, you want to be alive. But it's funny, you know. The most successful people are risk takers. When you take a risk, you jeopardize your security—your finances, your relationships, your personal safety. It's downright suicidal. But the most successful people take risks.

It's insane. Know what else is funny? In order to be really good at something—in order to be a truly world class whatever—you have to be obsessive about it. You have to want to do it all the time. You have to be a little insane."

He changed the channel. He bounced.

The Professor walked in. He said, "Global warming is like finding out the entire human race has terminal cancer."

I couldn't handle them. Not both of them. I got up and left.

*

One of the challenges of working around food is wanting to eat all of it. Case in point: as I'm fronting rice chips, I get an acute craving for rice chips, which is followed by the realization that now would be a fine time for my break. I grab the rice chips and bring them to the cash registers.

On my way through the warehouse to the break room, I'm accosted by Eric, who puts out an arm to block my path. "Hey there, vegan. What are we eating, today?"

"Rice chips. Do you want to read the ingredients?"

He doesn't lower his arm. It's pressed against my chest. I stay where I am.

"I need to get by," I say. "My break is running out."

"Don't whine, vegan. Tell me, do you think you're better than me?"

"What?"

"The way you act, when I'm around—I'm starting to get the impression you think you're better than me."

"Why would—"

"I had command of a unit in Afghanistan, you know. And I had a soldier, once, who thought he was better than me. In fact, he thought he was better than everybody. It made him insubordinate, and so I had to discipline him. Now, I could have gone through the chain of command to do this. They would have given him a slap on the wrist, and probably he'd have continued behaving the exact same way. But I didn't do that. Do you know what I did?"

I don't want to know what Eric did. I want to take my rice chips up to the break room and eat them. I try to maintain a bored expression.

"I took him out behind the barracks," Eric says, "where no one else could see. And I dealt with him. I dealt with him in much the same way alpha lions are known to settle disputes. We didn't have any issues, after that."

"Will you let me pass, now?"

He lowers his arm. "Sure, vegan. Enjoy your rice chips."

Gilbert and Brent are already in the break room, sitting across from Jack, the assistant manager of Produce. Jack is observing Gilbert and Brent sternly—though, as I understand it, that's how he does most of his observing. Even while on break, he's still wearing the black cap Produce guys wear, red curls sticking out underneath.

"Look, Jack," Gilbert says. "Sheldon's here. Now we outnumber you."

"You outnumbered me before he came. Idiot."

"Right, sorry. I suck at math. I guess that's why I've been working in a grocery store for eight years."

"You've only worked here two years."

"Damn. Right again. You're the one who's been here eight years."

I sit at the end of the table with my rice chips.

"Do you have a receipt for those?" Jack says.

"Yeah," I say. "Hold on, I'll—"

"He's not talking to you," Gilbert says. "He's asking about my Ringolos. And yes, Jack, I do have a receipt."

"Where is it?"

"Up your ass."

Jack stands up, glaring at Gilbert. "Your eyes are bloodshot. Yours too, Brent. Are you stoned?"

"No, dude," Brent says.

Jack stares at them a few seconds longer, and for a moment I expect him to spit on the floor. But he just leaves.

Brent's phone rings, and he fishes it from his pocket.

"Hello," he says. "What? Who is this? Oh. All right. Um, sorry."

He puts it back in his pocket.

"Who was it?" Gilbert says.

"Frank."

"Really? What did he say?"

"He said employees aren't supposed to have their phones on at work."

They look at each other, and burst out laughing.

*

Some kid threw a tantrum, tossing a pack of crackers on the floor and stomping on them. I'm the one cleaning up the aftermath. To make matters worse, I'm pretty sure the kid got whatever he was screaming for.

As I sweep, Gilbert happens by, and takes a can of coffee from the shelf. "See this?" he says. "This container can hold a pound of coffee, and one time it did. But they slowly reduced the amount, and now it's just 11 ounces. They also shrunk the text that tells you that. The only thing that has increased is the price." He puts the can back on the shelf. "It's not just coffee. Grocery stores are full of rip-offs. Diluted bleach. Chicken plumped with salt water. Fruit juice with only 10 percent actual fruit juice. Crab cakes with zero crab."

I shrug. "Pretty dishonest."

"It's theft. Plain and simple." He's twisting the gold ring he wears.

They have other techniques for manipulating people, Gilbert tells me. They put candy and sugary cereal at kids' eye level. Also, the sole reason to have a bakery, he says, is to create the aroma of baking bread, to make customers hungrier. "What else is freshly made, in-store? It's not like they can't get enough bread from suppliers. They're crafty." He taps the side of his head.

I return to Aisle One and continue fronting where I left off. Every now and then Casey rockets past with his cart. The third time I see him, he yells for me to move out of the way. I back up six feet or so, and he tears open a case of laundry detergent, packing the bottles onto the shelf.

Tommy's supposed to be fronting, too. Tonight's order turned out to be bigger than expected, though, and Casey recruited him to help out with it. When I walk through the warehouse on my way to the washroom, Tommy is sitting on a box of strawberry jam, bent over his tabloid. He has a bald spot on the top of his head.

On my way back out, I find Casey standing over him.

"What are you doing?" Casey says.

"Reading," Tommy says.

"There's work to do."

"Calm down, Casey. Have another coffee."

"There are five pallets left, and it's almost 6:00."

Tommy looks up, his eyes getting wide, like they always do when he's about to start prophesying. "You're a fool. You assume your corporate masters are the ones you should be pleasing, when really you should be on your knees, praying for—"

Casey grabs Tommy by the front of his shirt, pulls him to a standing position, and slams him against a pallet of product nearby. "You work in a Grocery store. You tried to quit, but your Mommy wouldn't let you. Remember?" He lets go. "Get to fucking work."

Tommy quickly exits the warehouse.

Casey walks to Ralph's desk, picks up a large coffee, and sips from it noisily. He puts it down and faces me. "I need you on the order."

"Yes, sir."

"Gilbert's nowhere to be found, as usual. If it's just me and Tommy, we won't come close to getting it put out."

"There is one minor detail."

"What?"

"I haven't worked here three months—I'm not supposed to work orders yet. Oh, and I don't have a box cutter."

"I don't care when you were hired. There's an extra box cutter in the desk. Put it back at the end of the night."

He begins sorting through the order, pulling out products that go in Aisles Two, Three, and Four. Soon, he's stacked my cart as precariously as he stacks his own, with at least 20 cases piled on.

The store intercom beeps, and Gilbert's voice comes out. "Attention shoppers. You are all mindless drones—victims of instant gratification. You buy your groceries, you slither back to houses you can't afford, and you stuff your wobbling maws. The thrill of the hunt has been robbed from you. You disgust me. Have a nice day."

Casey and I look at each other. "Just go," he says.

I push the cart out onto the sales floor. God, it's heavy.

*

I'm tired of eating crackers and salads and carrot sticks on every break, so Sam takes it upon himself to tutor me in the art of cooking delicious vegetarian meals.

"Remember my lasagna?"

"Yeah," I say. "It was legendary."

"You can be legendary, too. You can make big batches of lasagna, or spaghetti, or whatever, and freeze it in portions. Then you can take it to work and heat it up in the microwave. You'll never eat carrot sticks again."

He gives me a stuffed green pepper wrapped in tin foil to eat on tonight's shift. There's a mini fridge in the break room, and when I arrive I stick it there for safekeeping.

Later, as I'm fronting syrups in Aisle Four, some guy walks up and says, "Have you heard the Good News?"

"Toilet paper's on for half price?" I say.

"Not that. I'm talking about God, and his son, Jesus. He died on the cross, so that no man need go to hell."

"What about women?"

"Them neither."

Behind him, Gilbert is walking toward us, eating a bag of Cheezies.

"Is he applying for a job, Sheldon?"

"I don't know."

"He's holding a résumé in his hand."

I look down. It's true. The guy is holding some stapled-together papers that very much resemble a résumé.

He faces Gilbert and holds out the hand that isn't holding papers. "My name's Donovan. I'd like a job in Grocery."

Gilbert pops a Cheezie into his mouth. "Frank doesn't accept applications for specific departments. You have to apply and hope for the best."

Donovan's hand drops to his side. "I'm applying for a Grocery position. I've prayed about it—that's where I'm needed."

"You take orders from God? Heavy."

"Indeed."

"Does he have email now, or is he still rocking the whole angelic messenger thing?"

"The Lord's servants are no strangers to mockery. I don't need you to take me seriously. I just need you to give this to your manager." He hands his résumé to Gilbert. "God bless."

He walks toward the front of the store. Then he stops. "I'm about to smoke a joint in the parking lot. Would either of you care to join me?"

Gilbert, who was in the process of crumpling Donovan's résumé, straightens it out again and studies it. "You don't mention your religion here."

"I didn't think it relevant."

"It is to the store manager. Print off a new copy that includes it, and give it to Frank yourself. His office is upstairs. Don't tell him we spoke. Can you give a good interview?"

"Anyone with more than two brain cells can give a good interview."

"Very true. Be sure to bring up religion a lot."

"I will."

"Welcome to Spend Easy, then. Let's go smoke that joint."

My shift ends not long after that.

Ernie's standing next to the desk when I punch out. "Sheldon," he says as the punch clock ejects my card. "Can you come here for a second?"

I walk over.

"I bought you something. I couldn't help but notice you were drinking coffee from a disposable cup, the other day." He reaches under the desk and takes out a white reusable mug. "It's made from porcelain, just like mine. I think you should use it." He holds it out to me, smiling.

I take the mug, walk across the warehouse, and open the trash compactor door. I throw it as hard as I can. It shatters against the back wall, and the pieces land among the rest of the garbage waiting to be compressed and sent down the dumpster chute.

I turn back to Ernie. "Thanks."

I walk out of the warehouse.

Chapter Six

Rodney, a heavyset guy who scowled constantly, made up for how quiet most of the psych ward patients were. Once, as I was leaving the TV room, I heard a loud noise to my right. I looked and saw Rodney stomping around the corner, eyes bloodshot. "Hey. Sheldon, right?"

"Yes."

"Do you smoke?"

"No."

"Come into the smoking room with me."

"Okay."

Once inside, we each took one of the plastic chairs that ringed an ashtray on a pedestal. He lit a cigarette, which looked tiny against the thick black beard that covered his face. He told me that in a couple months, there wouldn't be a smoking room in the psychiatric ward anymore. They were closing it down. "Big mistake, that is," he said. "Big mistake." He showed me his fist. The first three knuckles were bloody and torn. "See this?"

"Yes."

"I was on the phone with my girlfriend. She pissed me off. I punch things when I'm pissed off."

"Really?"

"Go to the kitchen and get me some orange juice."

For a few seconds, I just looked at him. He didn't break eye contact.

"No," I say.

He held up his bloody fist. "See this?"

"Yes."

"Go get me some orange juice."

"No."

"Do you see the blood?"

"Get it yourself."

He stood up and pointed at me. "I know where you sleep." He threw the half-smoked cigarette at the ashtray, missed, and left the room. I picked it up and put it in the tray. Then I stood and followed Rodney out. He stomped off toward the rooms. I started walking toward mine.

A nurse intercepted me before I could go in. "Is anything wrong?"

"No."

"Did Rodney say anything to you?"

"He said things."

"Do you feel safe, Sheldon?"

"Yes."

"Okay. Let me know if you need anything. I'll be at the Nurses Station."

"Thank you."

I didn't know whether Rodney was a threat—and to be honest, I didn't care.

A couple weeks later, not long before I got out, I was sitting on a cushioned bench near the Nurses Station and watching a few of the patients walk laps around the ward. The Professor was one of them—he walked with his hands folded behind his back, gazing at the floor tiles, muttering. He rarely ever stopped pacing, actually.

I glanced down the hall and saw Rodney, wearing a white and blue checkered dress shirt with black jeans. His hair was gelled, his beard trimmed, and he was smiling. When he reached me, his eyes were clear. He put out his hand.

I shook it.

"I'm out of here today," he said. "My girlfriend's picking me up, we're going out to dinner, and then I'm going home to sleep in my own bed. Sleep for a week, if I can get away with it."

"That's—that's great. Good for you, Rodney."

"Hey, sorry if I said anything strange over the past few days. The meds really had me screwed up. I was jumping at shadows."

"Don't mention it."

"Few months ago, I fell off the roof of a house I was helping build. Landed right on a pile of bricks. My insides were pretty mashed—I'm lucky to be here. I had four operations, and I've been having trouble getting off the pain meds. They put me in here till my mood swings levelled out."

"What will you do now? Are you still going to work construction?"

He nodded. "Getting right back on that horse."

*

With just 91 days left before the human race is seared from the universe like a gnat caught in a wildfire, I go into Spend Easy to work my first eight-hour shift. Ralph is waiting in the warehouse when I enter, and the moment I punch in, he hands me a green box cutter in a leather holster. I clip it onto my belt, within easy reach of my right hand.

"You've been here three months, now. Time to start working the order. Welcome to Grocery."

Our uniforms changed recently—no longer the yellow of sun shining down on sizzling steaks bought on special from your local Spend Easy. Now we're wearing long-sleeved, collared shirts, the white of snow, with Spend Easy's red and green logo scrawled in tiny script over our hearts. Now is the time for customers to stock up, solemn-faced, for winter, in case it doesn't end.

I'm not convinced giving us white uniforms was such a good idea. Mine is already the kind of dirty washing won't get out.

The order gets here before five. Ralph and I grab a pallet jack each and start hauling it off the truck—eight pallets in total. Afterward, he shows me a black binder with 40 or 50 spreadsheets inside. He marks my name on one of them, explaining that for each trip to the aisles, we're supposed to record how many cases we bring out, and how long it takes to put up the whole cartload.

Ralph helps me load my first cart with 14 cases, and then he punches out. I sneak a glance at Casey's case count. His cartloads all number between 15 and 20. Glancing through his sheets, I estimate he averages around 48 cases an hour.

"I reserve the right to continue calling you rookie," Gilbert says when he sees me with a cart and a cutter.

Casey's working the order tonight, along with Gilbert, Brent, and me. It takes me a half hour to put out my 14 cases. Next trip, I try taking just nine. This way it's easy to find only products that go in Aisles Two and Three—meaning less distance I have to travel. Plus, with less weight, I'm able to move faster.

I can appreciate now why I was made to front for three months. I've learned where practically everything goes, so I'm able to stack the boxes on my cart according to where they're shelved, for easy access. This cartload takes just 15 minutes.

On my third trip, I try taking five cases. And it's perfect. It takes me seven minutes to put them on the shelves.

When I return to the warehouse, Gilbert's lounging on the pallet we're currently working. He watches me throw my empty boxes into the cardboard compactor, scribble down my case count, and grab five more cases from behind him.

"Damn, rookie," he says. "Are you breaking a sweat?"

"Not yet. When I do, I'll let you know what it feels like, okay?" I roll out onto the sales floor.

Next time I go to the warehouse I'm alone, and I take a moment to scan Casey's count. I'm catching up.

Casey and I are bringing out most of the order. Brent's count is abysmal. And on the single sheet marked "GILBERT RYAN," nothing is written.

When the order's finished, Casey's average is 50 cases an hour; mine is 46. I didn't begin the night taking out five cases, though. If I'd been using my method from the start, I might have tied Casey. Maybe beaten him.

*

Other than choosing to cooperate, I didn't have much input into the decision to try fixing my brain with Zoloft. My doctor in the psych ward concluded I had insufficient serotonin, so he prescribed me a "selective serotonin reuptake inhibitor".

So, when Bernice asks me what I think should be my Cognitive Behavioural Therapy's main focus—what I think my biggest challenge is—it catches me off guard completely.

Finally, I tell her I'd like to work on my confidence. I want to be able to navigate social situations without second-guessing everything I say, and without wondering whether some hidden meaning lurks beneath what others say.

I tell her about a few examples—like worrying that my co-workers know I was a psych ward patient—and we start working through them. In the middle of that, though, I blurt out with: "I feel like I am making progress at work."

She raises her eyebrows. "How so?"

"I'm not sure what it is exactly I'm making progress with, but—well, I'm actually enjoying stocking the shelves, and stuff. I never would have expected that. It just feels great, you know? Having something to focus on."

Absurdly, a lump forms in my throat, and I'm in danger of crying.

"I think...I think Mom would have been proud."

I have to take a few moments, then. A few deep breaths. Bernice waits.

I tell her I'd like to return to writing. I think that's also a confidence issue. Since Mom died, I've been too afraid of screwing up to even start writing anything. Without someone to tell me I do good work, my fear is more effective than any writer's block ever could be.

*

The second time I work the order Ralph is on too, taking cartloads of frozen overstock out of the walk-in freezer and checking to see if there's room for it on the shelves. He finds some frozen pizzas that are past their sell-by date, and he's about to throw them out when I say, "Wait. How far past the date are they?"

"A little over a week."

"Well, don't throw them out. I'll take them."

He shakes his head. "Store policy. Gotta chuck 'em. Sorry." He tosses all four in the trash compactor.

I push a cartload out to Aisle Five. Gilbert is there, perusing the chip selection. "Have you seen Ralph?" he says.

"In the warehouse."

I restock taco kits, three different brands of popcorn, and ice cream cones. I turn the cart around and head back for another load. Gilbert's still near the chips, and as I pass he grabs a bag and tosses it onto the bottom level of my cart.

"What are you doing?"

"Shut up. I need to sneak it past the cameras."

"I'm your accomplice, now?"

"Don't flatter yourself. You're more an accessory."

The first hour of using my new method goes well, but after that I get a few cases that take a while to stock. The little cans of tomato sauce, for instance—they don't fit into each other like other cans do, and I keep dropping them.

Ralph notices I'm taking only five cases at a time, and asks me why.

"Well, it's working for me."

"I know. I saw your case count. But why five?"

"Five cases don't weigh you down like 10 do, so you can move faster. It's also easier to find five from the same aisle, which reduces the distance you travel. Plus, fewer boxes to flatten."

"But you're making twice as many trips back and forth to the warehouse."

I shrug. "I think the benefits outweigh the one drawback."

"Come with me."

We walk to his desk in the warehouse, and Ralph finds a calculator. He adds up my cartloads. "You've put out 110 cases so far, and it's been two hours. 55 cases an hour—nearly a case a minute. That's good work."

"Thanks."

He picks up the phone and presses the intercom button. "All Grocery personnel to the warehouse, please." He hangs up.

Within a couple minutes, Gilbert, Ernie, and Brent are standing with us around Ralph's desk.

"We're trying something new," Ralph says. "Sheldon's been experimenting, and he's found that bringing out five cases at a time is faster than taking 10. He's totaled 110 cases since we started tonight."

Brent stares blankly back at Ralph. Ernie's hands are balled into fists, and he's not looking at anyone. Gilbert starts slow clapping.

"I want everyone taking out five cases for the rest of the night," Ralph says. "Understood?"

*

It becomes known, with some derision, as the Sheldon Mason Five Case Approach. It doesn't become standard procedure or anything—Ralph just gets everyone to try it for a shift. After that, Casey returns to his mountainous cartloads, and Gilbert sticks to 10 cases or so, when he brings out any. Almost everyone else uses my method, though. Once perfected, the Five Case Approach doesn't require much work to produce a moderate result. But with sincere effort, the results are impressive. There are hours I put out 70 cases. One night I total 315 over five hours, which, I'm told, is a store record.

I'm getting a lot more hours than I did during my first three months. Whenever someone calls in sick, I'm one of the first Ralph offers the shift. I have a nametag now, too.

"Congratulations," Gilbert says one night. "Grocery's increased its productivity, Ralph is beating Produce in the suck-up war, and Frank still ignores you completely. Think you're going to get a raise?"

"I'm not looking for one."

Later, Jack shows up as I'm restocking lima beans and asks me to take a break with him. For once, he isn't wearing his cap. His red hair sticks up in all directions.

Not wanting to appear as uninterested as I feel, I say, "Sure."

While my homemade lasagna is heating up in the microwave, Jack tells me there's been a lot of talk in Produce this week about the work I've been doing. He says everyone's impressed—especially Vince, the Produce manager. A position recently opened, and Vince is wondering if I would consider filling it.

"You mean, like, switch departments?"

"Exactly. We checked with Frank, and he gave us the go ahead."

"No thanks."

"Sorry?"

"I like working in Grocery."

Jack shakes his head. "Grocery is full of slackers. In Produce, you'll be working with employees of your calibre."

"Um, I like where I am, and I like working for Ralph. I don't want to switch."

He stands up. "Frank is planning to wipe out the entire staff in Grocery, and replace them with non-slugs. I hope you don't think you're safe. He's been suspicious of you since you refused to help eliminate employee theft." Jack smirks. "Grocery's a sinking ship, and you just blew your last chance to get off." He leaves the break room.

I eat another mouthful of lasagna. I don't think Jack's very good at persuading people.

*

The day before Halloween, a Tuesday, I go into Spend Easy to discover the only other person scheduled to work is Gilbert. On an order night. The order gets here shortly after I arrive, and it's huge—10 pallets. After we finish taking it off the truck, we stand in the middle of the warehouse and stare.

"We are badly undermanned, here," Gilbert says.

"So it would seem."

"No, seriously. I don't think you can do all this by yourself."

Suddenly, miraculously, three new Grocery employees arrive, already wearing uniforms.

"That's funny," Gilbert says. "Grocery is understaffed for six months, and then, one Tuesday, we get three new hires all at once, as if Ralph ordered them along with the beans and tampons."

Our new co-workers remain silent.

"Why do you all have box cutters already?" I say. "Who gave you those?" I stroke the holster of my own box cutter lovingly. Jealously.

"Ralph did," one of them says. "He said for us to help you with the order."

"Who gave you permission to speak, rookie?" Gilbert says.

"He asked me a question. And my name's Randy."

"For the next three months, your name is Mud. Incidentally, that's also how long rookies are supposed to toil in the aisles, fronting their brain cells away. Are you sure Ralph said you're starting the order tonight?"

"I don't know, Gilbert," Randy says. "Why don't you call and ask him yourself?"

Well, that's interesting. Gilbert isn't wearing his nametag tonight—he's wearing Ernie's.

Gilbert moves closer to me, cupping a hand to his mouth.

"Something is seriously amiss."

Chapter Seven

On Halloween, I'm fronting with Donovan in Aisle Three while Gilbert sits on a cart behind us and twists the gold ring on his finger.

"I can't believe the new guys started the order on their first night," I say. "I had to tell them where a million things were. They don't know where anything goes."

"They will learn," Donovan says.

"They suck."

"We can't all be restocking prodigies."

I'm growing used to this sort of sarcasm. Brent's started calling me Ralph's golden boy.

I say, "Jack asked me to work in Produce, the other day."

Gilbert looks up. "He asked you to quit Grocery?"

"Yeah."

"What'd you say?"

"I said no. He told me I'll regret it." I consider telling them about Frank's supposed plan to fire everyone in Grocery, but I don't want to get involved.

Gilbert's eyes are narrowed. He goes back to twisting his gold ring.

Donovan glances back at him. "Where'd you get that ring?"

"Found it. When I was a kid."

"Where?"

"Under a tree, actually. They tore down the woods near my house for a subdivision, and left the fallen trees lying there for months. I found a hollow in the ground with a metal box, and inside it there was a bronze horse sculpture, a G.I. Joe, and this ring."

Gilbert is highly suspicious of our new co-workers. It turns out one of them, Randy, is Frank's son. Another is named Patrick, who's deaf, which he indicated by writing "I'M DEAF" on a piece of paper. But Gilbert didn't believe that until he spent two minutes screaming into Patrick's ear as he restocked popcorn.

A couple hours into his first shift, I encountered Randy near the case count binder and tried to make small talk. I asked if he was attending school, and he said no, he's taking a year off before going to college. I asked if he's worked Grocery before, and he said yes, but the store layout is different and he'd probably need help locating product.

And then we sort of looked at each other for a few seconds.

"Wow," said Gilbert, who was loading his cart nearby, "Do you feel that? You guys just completely ran out of things to say to each other. It's palpable."

For most of today's shift, Gilbert sits behind us on his cart, which he pushes along with his feet as Donovan and I front our way up and down the aisles.

The store closes at five on Sundays. Six minutes before that, two prepubescent boys wearing Halloween costumes walk past us carrying four cartons of eggs each. They're almost past the bottles of pop when Gilbert shouts, "Hey!"

They freeze, and slowly turn around.

"What do you think you're doing?"

"Sorry," one of them says.

"Put those eggs on my cart. Right now." They do. "Now come with me."

He brings them to the Dairy section and puts the eggs back where they were. "Those were medium-sized eggs," Gilbert says. "You guys are going to want extra-large. They're in the blue cartons."

Two abashed frowns are replaced by two devilish grins. They grab the eggs and run toward the front end.

"Happy Halloween!" Gilbert calls after them.

*

"Hey, Sheldon," Fred whispered once the purple-clad lady was gone, having wheeled in the trolley holding all the patients' lunches. "You want your lunch today?"

"No. You have it."

"You're a good guy, Sheldon."

"Thanks." He walked over to collect it.

Another patient was sitting on the couch next to mine, staring at me. I stared back.

"What do you do?" he asked. "What's your job?"

"I don't have a job."

"You must get one. If you don't, they'll crucify you. Quickly—what do you enjoy doing?"

"I used to like writing."

"Writing what? Poems? Essays?"

"I wanted to write novels."

His eyes went wide. "God. You're not going to put me in a book, are you? Is that your plan? Put me in a book? People would think you're a real ass, putting a mental patient in a book. I don't want to be in your book. I'd be upset."

"I can't put you in a book if I don't know your name."

"I'm Methuselah."

"You don't seem very old."

"You don't need to be old for your name to be Methuselah. You just need a nutcase mom. Isn't that right?"

"I guess so."

Sam arrived, holding a takeout bag in one hand. "Thought you could use a second lunch. You're looking skinny. What are they feeding you, in here?"

"I'm not hungry."

"I'll have it," Methuselah said.

Sam said, "I bought it for you, Sheldon."

"Fine."

He took out a burger and onion rings and set them in front of me. "I came up with another inspirational message."

I unwrapped the burger while chewing an onion ring. "Yeah?"

"The secret to life is shut up, look, listen."

"Not bad."

"I thought you'd like that one. Do you like the burger?"

"Can I have an onion ring?" Methuselah said.

"Sure," I say. "Go ahead."

He stood up, took three, and walked away. Sam watched him go.

"The burger's tasty," I said.

"You like it? It's veggie."

"Really?"

"I don't eat meat, so I can't justify buying it for others."

"You're a vegetarian?"

"I am."

"Why?"

"It's a long story."

"It's a long day."

"Well, when I was a kid, my uncle lived in the country, and he owned two pigs. I loved visiting, because it meant I got to see them. I named them Oink One and Oink Two, and I spent hours playing with them. Pigs are extremely intelligent. They're like us, in a lot of ways. One day, in spring, my uncle had the whole family over—aunts, uncles, cousins, grandparents, the whole clan. I spent the afternoon searching for the Oinks, but couldn't find them anywhere. During supper, I asked my uncle where they were. There was an awkward silence. And I looked down at my plate."

"Oh my God. What did you do?"

"I didn't do anything, at first. I stared at it with a lump of masticated pork still in my mouth. Then I spat it onto the table. I ran to the bathroom, and threw the rest up. And I never ate meat again."

A woman standing at a nearby bookshelf looked over. "Hey," she said. "If vegetarians eat only vegetables, then what do humanitarians eat?" She chuckled, and walked away.

Sam looked at me, frowning slightly. I shrugged.

*

Five guys are scheduled in Grocery tonight, which seems like a lot for a Monday. We're gathered around Ralph's desk, in the warehouse. "He left instructions," Gilbert says. He picks up a piece of paper covered with neat cursive writing in blue ink, and clears his throat. "'Ernie: continue working the overstock racks.'"

So much for that—Ernie went home at four, complaining of a stress headache.

"'Tommy: front the store 100%—two deep.' He underlined 'two deep.'" Gilbert says. "And he wrote it in capital letters." Tommy snickers, and heads toward the warehouse doors. "'Brent: work the freezer and the dairy cooler.'" Brent groans. "'Gilbert and Sheldon: decorate the store for Christmas.'"

"What? Let me see that."

Gilbert passes me the note.

"He seriously wants us to decorate for Christmas," I say. "Me and you."

"Seems that way."

"But Halloween was last week."

"Yes. Now it's time to remind consumers that another holiday approaches, and if they want to avoid social tension, they should start purchasing gifts for their family, friends, significant others, co-workers, and acquaintances."

"This is a grocery store. We sell food."

"We'll start selling toys, shortly," Gilbert says. "The first shipment comes in tomorrow."

The decorations are stored on the top shelf of the overstock racks, so we need an extension ladder. When it's time to decide which of us will go up, Gilbert cites his seniority, and I start climbing.

The first thing I find is a sign that says "ONLY 50 SHOP-PING DAYS LEFT", with a bag of digits stapled to the back. The numbers are coloured like candy canes. I drop it down to Gilbert, and grab a plastic snowman.

We travel around the store, plastering wrapping paper and Christmas banners onto every available surface, in every department except Produce. Gilbert explains that the entire Produce department will gather an hour before the store opens tomorrow, for hot cocoa and decorating and plotting the demise of every Grocery employee.

We leave the ledge above Frozen until last. We're supposed to place some fake snow there, and a glowing Santa. We get the ladder. I climb up, and Gilbert starts passing me decorations. Once they're all on the ledge, he comes up, too. I start arranging some of the snow.

And then, the step ladder falls with a crash onto the frozen goods bunker.

"Shit," Gilbert says.

I turn around. "What happened? Did you knock it over?"

"No. It just fell."

"How could it just fall?"

"I suspect gravity was involved."

I walk to the edge and look down. "Think we could jump?"

"You can try, if you want. But if you break your ankle it'll be your own stupid fault, and you won't qualify for workers' comp. You're probably that dedicated. I'm not."

I decide I'm not that dedicated. There are a couple folded-up lawn chairs left up here from a summer display, and we put them to use. I can't see a single customer anywhere.

"Someone should come by soon," I say. "Isn't Brent supposed to be restocking the freezers?"

"In theory, yes."

I glance toward the cash registers. I'm surprised none of the cashiers heard the ladder fall. They'd probably hear me if I called out, but I'm not going to. Cassandra's on Lane Four, and I'd rather be stuck here all night than talk to her. A customer will come by soon enough. Brent will be out with a cartload. Eventually.

"Do you plan to procreate?" Gilbert says.

"What?"

"Babies. Will you make any?"

"Why are you asking me that?"

"I'm going to make one. A daughter."

"You'll be able to choose, will you?"

"I'll wait a few years," Gilbert says. "Embryo manipulation should be sufficiently advanced, by then."

"Fair enough."

"Her name will be Melaena."

"You picked out a name already? That's so sweet."

"Guess what it means."

"What?"

"It's a medical term for blood found in stool samples."

"Melaena means bloody shit?"

"Yes."

"And you're naming your daughter that?"

"Certainly. Think about it—all my parenting problems will be solved. 'Eat your peas, Melaena,' I'll say, 'Or I'll tell all your friends what your name really means. Clean your room, Melaena. Time for bed, you steaming pile of diseased feces.'"

"Oh my God."

"Eventually one of her classmates will look it up anyway. That will be character-building."

"Someone's coming," I say. There's a guy strutting past the freezers, wearing an oversized hoodie and a backward baseball cap. He looks kind of short, though that might be a function of my current perspective.

Wait. I recognize him.

"Hey," Gilbert says.

"Don't. He won't help us."

"Hey!" Gilbert shouts. "Little help?"

Rick Chafe peers up at us, sitting on lawn chairs 10 feet above the floor.

"Is that Sheldon Mason?"

"It might not be," I say.

"Shelly! Long time no see. Looks like you've really moved up in the world."

"Ha, ha."

"Are you still a virgin?"

"I don't have time to discuss my sexual history right now. I'm busy."

"Yeah, looks like it. Strange place to have a date with your butt buddy, though."

"Hey," Gilbert says. "He isn't nearly good looking enough to be my butt buddy. If you're interested, though, we might work something out once you fetch us that ladder."

"Fat chance." He grabs a frozen pizza from the bunker, and leaves.

"Way to blow it," Gilbert says.

"Me? I'm not the one who agitated his homophobia." I get up and walk to the end of the ledge, for a better view of the Meat department. "I'm surprised Eric wasn't over here the second the ladder fell," I say. "Normally he's breathing down my neck."

"Maybe he has a crush on you."

"Have you ever noticed how antisocial his workers are? Most of them will barely even make eye contact."

"You know he hires all poor kids, right?"

I look at him, my brow furrowed. "So? Just because they don't have money doesn't mean—"

"What are you guys doing up there?"

Brent is slouching over a cartload of ice cream, squinting up at us.

Two hours later, at the end of the shift, we're all standing around Ralph's desk.

"Do you guys think Frank will watch the cameras?" I say. "Will he be pissed we sat up there for so long?"

Brent laughs, and walks a little deeper into the warehouse. "Dude, I show these cameras my middle finger all the time." He demonstrates. "I took a nap this shift. Shit, Gilbert stands in front of the computer there almost every night and jacks off stale-faced to gay porn. The cameras are always rolling, but no one ever watches."

*

When a customer needs help locating a product, I try to provide the best service I can.

But it can be trying, sometimes.

One afternoon, I'm accosted in Aisle Five by a man holding a phone to his ear. He says, "Hold on, I think I see an employee. Hi! Excuse me. You work here, right?"

"I do."

"Hold on, honey."

"Sorry?"

"I was talking to my wife. Listen, do you carry chopsticks? We're hosting a Chinese night for some relatives."

"Sorry, sir, we don't have them."

"They don't have them," he tells his wife. His face falls at her answer, which is so loud I can hear it. "She says she bought them here before."

"I don't see how that's possible. I've never seem them."

"He doesn't see how that's possible, honey," he says, like a man defusing a bomb. The shouted reply makes him wince. He covers the phone with his hand and whispers, "She wants to know your name. I have to tell her your name." He removes his hand. "His name is Sheldon, honey." He covers the phone again. "She wants to speak to your manager. I'm sorry." He uncovers the phone. "She says she wants to speak to your manager."

"Um, it's okay. Follow me."

I tell him to wait outside the warehouse doors. Ralph is inside, working on the computer.

"Someone wants to speak to you," I say.

He follows me out to the floor. "Good evening, sir. How can I help you?"

The man hands over the phone, and we both watch as Ralph takes it.

"Yes?"

The woman on the other end shouts something. Her husband is thin, but I imagine her overweight, sitting in an overstuffed armchair-throne. I picture her leaning forward, jowls wobbling, staring sternly into space.

"I find that hard to believe," Ralph says.

She shouts again.

"Ma'am, I highly doubt Sheldon refused to find a product for you. I've seen him deal with customers, and he's polite. But even if he did refuse, I wouldn't reprimand him, because I can't afford to lose him. He's my best worker."

The lady is shouting again, but Ralph gives the phone back to her husband, who wears a resigned expression. "Sorry, sir," Ralph says. The man nods, and walks away. His wife's shouting recedes with distance.

"Thanks for saying that," I say.

Ralph shrugs. "Chopsticks are in Aisle Three, by the way."

He tells me there's a Frozen order coming in tonight, two pallets, and that Brent will be in at six. Which means I'll be the one actually putting it on the shelves.

Ralph goes home at 5:00, and when 6:00 rolls around, Brent doesn't even show up. He still isn't here a half hour later, but by 7:15, I have the first pallet finished. At this rate, I'll have time to sweep the warehouse after I'm done. Maybe work the overstock a little, too.

I won't rat Brent out. I'm not a snitch.

On one trip to the cardboard baler I encounter Jack, standing near the trash compactor. He's taking garbage out of a shopping cart and throwing it down the chute.

When he sees me, he stops. "Are you working alone, tonight?"

"Yeah."

"Why?"

"No one showed up."

"Do you regret turning down my offer yet?"

"No, actually. I don't."

"You'll get there."

He leaves the warehouse, and I go into the freezer.

As I'm stacking frozen juice onto my cart, the big, white door slams shut behind me, and I jump. There's a safety knob on this side. I walk toward it.

The lights go out just as I lay my hand on the cold plastic. Between my fingers, the knob is a luminous green. Turns out it glows in the dark. I press it, but it doesn't budge. I can't open the door. Something's lodged underneath the handle on the other side.

"Hey!" I shout, pounding on the door.

No one opens it.

Chapter Eight

One of the nurses, chuckling, told me how lucky I was to have a friend like Sam. He clearly cared a lot about me, she said. He'd been asking them all lately whether I'd been eating. "I assured him you have. I told him we check the trays after every meal. I think he's a bit of a worrier." She winked.

I don't know why I wasn't eating. I wasn't rebelling, or anything. Like everything else, food simply held no interest. Fred certainly didn't complain.

I felt pretty crappy after I ate the burger Sam brought me. Having eaten nothing for days, it was like a stone knocking around in my stomach.

During another of Sam's visits, we were sitting in the common area when the same nurse unlocked a glass door to our right. The door let out onto a small garden surrounded by a chain-link fence. She smiled at us. "It's a beautiful day."

"It sure is," Sam said. "Want to go out, Sheldon?"

"Okay."

We stepped out into the sunlight. The other patients stayed inside.

"I bet I could get over that fence," I said.

"Maybe. They'd bring you back, though."

I looked back through the windows. They'd served lunch about a half hour before, and now the others were getting up from the tables and shuffling to their rooms. "You know, my Mom didn't believe in mental illness," I said. "She only believed in strong opinions. A psychiatrist might diagnose you with a superiority complex, but Mom would say you just have a bad case of 'I have the answer to everyone's problems.' I've met a lot of people with strong opinions. I've met some afflicted with 'I have nothing worth saying,' others with a touch of 'My morals are so inconsistent, I'm two people.' During my stay here, I've even met someone with 'Everyone around me is secretly working for the CIA.'"

"And what's your strong opinion?"

"A self-diagnosis?" I paused. "I think I have 'I don't need other people.'"

"What if you had to diagnose the entire human species?"

"That's easy. OCD."

"Can I ask you a question?"

"Sure."

"Did you think that if you died, you'd get to see your Mom?"

I shook my head. "Mom is gone. She's not anywhere. She doesn't know about what's happening with me. She doesn't know how I felt after she died. She doesn't know anything. I envy that. I don't want to know anything, either."

"You're jaded."

"Is that what I am?"

"Yep. Like the rest of your generation. Nowadays, the average age for becoming jaded is around 20. Humans grow accustomed to high levels of pleasure fairly quickly, and these days, young people are inundated with pleasure. Binging is the order of the day. If you binge enough, on food or media or whatever, you become desensitized. Nothing satisfies anymore."

"What about, like, my Mom dying? Think that might have something to do with it?"

"It's just an excuse. You're jaded, Sheldon. Nothing unusual. It's sort of boring."

"Whatever."

"Yeah. Whatever." Sam stood up. "I'm gonna go home and feed your cat. At least he eats the food that's put out for him."

*

The temperature drops immediately.

Jack. He must have snuck back after he left the warehouse. How long does he plan to leave me in here?

There's a camera that points right at the freezer door. All I have to do is ask Frank to watch the recording tomorrow, and Jack will be fired. Maybe even charged.

It's so dark.

For some reason, this reminds me of standing on that stool, in the shed I share with Sam. I was able to see in there, of course, and I could have left if I wanted. But I was trapped all the same. In a sense, Sam came and let me out. I don't think he's coming, this time.

I knock on the door again, and yell. I knock for at least five minutes. My knuckles begin to hurt, and I switch to my left, but it becomes sore even quicker. My throat feels raw. I'm already shivering. I stick my hands in my armpits, and start kicking.

Eventually, someone will walk by and see whatever's keeping the door shut. Someone will hear the banging.

I don't know who, though. I'm the only one on in Grocery, and other than Produce the only ones with any reason to come into the warehouse are Meat employees. And who's working in Meat tonight?

Eric.

Could he and Jack be in on this together? Maybe. Or maybe this wasn't Jack at all—maybe Eric saw me enter the freezer, and acted alone. He seemed to be trying to send me some sort of message, with the story about the soldier in Afghanistan. Perhaps this is another message.

Jack, or Eric? Or both?

Will they let me out? Would either of them actually let me die in here?

The longer I'm trapped, the more likely it seems. My teeth are chattering. When I try to knock it's like 1000 needles being driven into my knuckles. I feel like I'm standing outside in the middle of January with no coat on.

I fumble in the dark until I find my cart, and I slam it against the door. I bring it back, and slam it again. I have to stop—my fingers are sticking to the cart's handle. Normally there are gloves in Ralph's desk, but I couldn't find any earlier. Maybe Jack took them.

"Help!" I scream, but I'm hoarse.

I'm crying, now. Sobbing. The tears leave frigid trails down my cheeks, and every breath feels like I'm inhaling ice.

"This is your chance, Sheldon," I say out loud. "This is your big chance to die and not know anything, ever again."

But I don't want to die.

I say that out loud, too: "I don't want to die."

I start running on the spot. Stamping my feet. Rubbing my hands up and down my arms, my legs.

I try kicking the door again, but it's too painful.

I try to yell: "Let me out!" It comes out a whisper. I sob again.

My heart is beating very quickly. In the dark, I see a parade of detailed images. I try shutting my eyes, but it makes no difference. Casey, heaving product onto his cart, slurping coffee, jittering. Jack, smirking. Tommy, eyes wide, ranting about impending apocalypse. Gilbert, wearing Ernie's nametag, his head thrown back, laughing. Eric, standing with Joshua near the trash chute.

Blood dribbling from Joshua's chin.

How long have I been in here? A long time. The store's closed, now, I bet. Everyone is probably already home. Asleep.

Sleeping is the last thing I should do, right now.

But I could sleep.

I try running on the spot again, and stop. Moving requires such effort.

Sleep would mean escape from the cold.

I'll have to, eventually. Everyone gets tired.

I sit down, just for a moment.

I try to stand.

I lay my head on a case of juice cans. Something crunches under my ear, and I realize it's frost.

I fall asleep. And I know nothing.

*

"Sheldon," someone says. "Wake up!"

"Mm." I open my eyes, and see Cassandra.

"Get up. Come on!"

She's leaning over me. Her eyes are wide.

"Hi," I say.

"Sheldon, you need to move. Your lips are blue."

It's still dark in the freezer, but there's light coming from the warehouse. Cassandra crosses her arms and hugs herself.

With Cassandra's help, I stand and walk out of the freezer. There's a cart nearby, and I sit.

"Is this what was blocking the door?" My voice still isn't very loud.

She nods. "Someone wedged it under the handle." She glances toward the punch clock.

I look, too. A few cashiers are gathered, peering over at us. An elderly lady, Marilyn, drops her punch card, and it flutters from her hand. She walks over and touches my forearm.

"Like ice," she says. "Are you all right?"

"I guess I am."

Cassandra touches me, too. "Are you sure? Maybe you should go to the hospital."

I pull away, and stand up. My limbs are stiff. I shuffle past the desk, to where my coat hangs from a nail.

I pull it on, walk to the clock, and try to grasp my punch card. I can't.

"Sheldon?" Cassandra says.

Marilyn takes my card and drops it in for me. "Cassandra noticed the cart blocking the door. Thank heaven she did."

"Thanks," I say.

"You don't drive, do you?" Marilyn says. "My husband will drive you home tonight."

"My bike is locked up out front."

"You can come back and get it tomorrow. You're in no shape to bike home. You need to get home and wrap up in some blankets. Who will answer my pages if you lose your fingers?"

I smile. Marilyn reminds me of my grandmother.

"You'll tell Frank about this, won't you?" she says.

"I will."

I glance at Cassandra, who's still standing near the open freezer door. She returns my gaze, blank-faced.

"Bye," I say.

*

Frank's office door is slightly ajar, and I push it open the rest of the way. He's sitting at his computer. "Can I speak with you?" I say.

He looks up at me—looks me in the eye, for the first time—and then his gaze flits back to his computer screen. There's a flurry of clicking. "Don't they train you to knock in Grocery?"

"Um, I think that would have been my mother's job."

"She didn't do it very well." More clicking. If I were to guess, I'd say Frank is using his work computer inappropriately.

"I need to speak with you," I say.

"That's convenient. Because Ralph and I want to have a talk with you." He picks up the phone and punches a button, making the store intercom beep. "Ralph Thompson to the store office please. Ralph Thompson to the store office." He hangs up.

"Did you watch the camera footage from last night?" I say.

"I didn't need to. It's pretty clear what happened."

"So you know who did it?"

He looks out the narrow window overlooking the cash registers. "Nobody did it. When we got here this morning, it wasn't done."

I decide to wait until Ralph gets here.

"Sheldon," Ralph says when he arrives. "You're not scheduled to work today. Why are you here?"

"I came to speak with Frank."

Frank emits a dry hybrid of a cough and a laugh. His eyes swivel to the floor. "I hope you brought your letter of resignation, after last night."

"Easy, Frank," Ralph says.

"Wait," I say. "What do you think happened last night?"

Frank laughs again. "Not very much."

"The frozen order was only half done this morning," Ralph says. "It wasn't much work—between you and Brent, there should have been time to spare."

"Slackers aren't tolerated," Frank says, which is so funny I could puke.

I recount the events of last night, which doesn't take long.

Ralph's brow is furrowed. "Where was Brent during all this?"

There's no covering for him. They'll see he wasn't there on the cameras. "He didn't come in for his shift."

"Then we need to know why." Ralph picks up Frank's phone. He calls down to the Customer Service counter and gets Brent's number from Betty. But there's no answer when he dials it. He hangs up and tries again. This time, after a couple seconds, he says, "Brent? This is Ralph. Why weren't you in for your shift yesterday?" He listens. "I see. All right, then." He hangs up. "Brent says he called to see whether he was scheduled for last night, and Donovan told him he wasn't."

Ralph calls Donovan, who says he must have misread the schedule.

"It happens," Ralph says once he hangs up. "Sometimes people look at the wrong day. It's just bad luck." He shakes his head. "You should have called Brent, and then called me if you couldn't reach him. You should never be the only one working in Grocery."

I nod. "Next time, I will."

"Let's check the video feed," Ralph says. "That's the next step. There's a camera pointing right at the freezer door."

Frank looks down at his computer mouse. "That won't be possible."

"Why not?"

He clears his throat. "The cameras weren't on last night."

Ralph speaks slowly: "Why wouldn't they be on?"

"The cameras are never on." Frank pauses. He looks across his office, at the wall. He clears his throat again. "The cameras are fake."

*

As I exit Spend Easy's sliding doors, a yellow Hummer pulls into the nearest parking spot—a handicapped spot. Gilbert sits in the driver's seat. I walk over, zipping my coat as I go. It's getting cold.

"Is this yours?" I say.

"I'm driving it, aren't I?"

"Wow. You sure know how to make a stock boy's salary go far."

"I have multiple income streams." His left hand is resting on the steering wheel, and he's twisting his gold ring with his right. "I hear you chilled out for once last night."

"Oh, that's really good. You definitely don't deserve to be punched for that."

"Thanks."

"Who told you?"

"Cassandra. How long were you stuck in there?"

"Almost three hours. You talk to Cassandra?"

"Occasionally," he says, shrugging. "Guess I can't call you a rookie anymore. If almost getting hypothermia isn't an appropriate initiation, I don't know what is. Who do you think did it?"

I hesitate. "Well, I saw Jack before I got locked in—less than a minute before. But there's no way to know for certain. Gilbert, the cameras are fake. They don't work."

He raises his eyebrows. "Are you sure?"

"Frank admitted it. Me and Ralph asked to see the footage from last night, and he told us there is no footage, because the cameras don't work. Ralph didn't know. He was pretty pissed when he found out, actually."

"Jack is Frank's golden boy—maybe the cameras do work, and Frank is lying to cover Jack's ass."

"You think he'd cover up attempted murder?"

"Sure."

I shake my head. "I don't even know for sure it was Jack."

"Who else would it be?"

Eric. But that's little more than a hunch.

"I don't know."

"It was definitely Jack," Gilbert says. "He hates Grocery—
and he hates that we have someone now who outshines anybody
in Produce. He's afraid you'll usurp him as Frank's favourite."

"So he locked me in the freezer?"

"He's a zealot, man. A crazy person. He wanted to intimidate
you into quitting."

I pause. "He did say something weird, recently. When he
asked me to work in Produce. He said Frank's planning to replace the entire Grocery department, and that switching to Produce would have been my last chance to keep my job."

"Jesus Christ. We need to stand up to them, Sheldon. Jack
and Frank. We need to give them a taste of what they've been
dishing out."

Suddenly I'm concerned someone from Spend Easy is within
earshot. I check behind me, but see no one. I turn back to Gilbert.

"What do you have in mind?"

He opens the glove compartment, takes out a pen and note-
pad, and scribbles a number. He tears off the sheet and gives it
to me. "That's my cell number. Call me tonight, after 10:30."

"What are you planning?"

"Just call."

He starts the car, and the Hummer's engine roars. He drives
away.

*

I'm standing by the side of the road with my hand in my
mouth, wiggling a tooth. It's a molar, and it's loose.

It comes out. I look at it, lying in the palm of my hand. I try to fit it back into my gums, but it won't stick there.

I look up, and see my mother standing across the road. She's watching me with a hand over her mouth, her head tilted to the right. She walks toward me.

Out of nowhere, a yellow Hummer appears and runs her down.

I wake up to the phone ringing. I walk out to the kitchen.

"Hello?"

"You didn't call." It's Gilbert.

"I fell asleep on the couch. How'd you get my number?"

"I called the store before it closed, and Cassandra gave it to me. She said it's so nice of me to hang out with you. She thinks you really need a friend right now."

"That sort of makes me want to vomit. Listen, what sort of revenge are you planning? I'm having second thoughts."

"You don't think they deserve it?"

"I'm not even sure who 'they' are. And I'd like to know what 'it' is."

"'They' are Frank and Jack. And you'll find out the other thing shortly. I'm coming to pick you up. What's your address?"

I sigh. "Foresail Road. 37a."

"On my way."

Gilbert screeches into the driveway around 11. I get in, and he glances in the rearview, slams the gearshift into reverse, and darts into the road. We take off.

We park next to a Cart Corral, which is the same yellow as Gilbert's Hummer.

"How do you expect to get into the store?" I say.

"With my key." He holds up his key ring, jingling it.

"How do you have a key to Spend Easy?"

"I borrowed it from Ralph's coat, one time. Got a copy made and put it back a couple hours later."

"We could get arrested."

"We won't, though. Spend Easy doesn't have security guards. And no one checks up on the store during the night. Anyway, if they did, we'd tell them Ralph called us in for an emergency overnight shift. They'd believe it—how else would we have gotten in?"

"Tell me what you're planning."

"It's a surprise. Come on." He opens his door.

"But what are we doing?"

"You'll see. This is our one opportunity, Sheldon. Frank might have working cameras installed as early as tomorrow."

When we left Frank's office, Ralph said he planned to stop posting the schedule in the warehouse, where anyone can read it. He's going to get everyone's email address, and start sending it electronically. From now on, only Grocery employees will know when Grocery employees are working.

Gilbert and I walk to the sliding doors, which don't slide open, of course. He inserts the key into a lock halfway up the door. We enter. Something starts to beep, and my heart rate speeds up.

"Shit. The alarm. We forgot about the alarm!"

"We didn't forget about anything." Gilbert walks to the panel and punches in four numbers. The beeping stops. He looks at me, eyebrows raised.

"All right, then," I say.

He leads me past the cash registers. With only one strip of fluorescent lights on, and no customers, the store seems larger.

It's quiet, too. I didn't realize how noisy Spend Easy gets until now that there's no music, no talking, no cash drawers opening and closing.

We walk up the stairs and enter the room next to Frank's office. Near a computer monitor sits a row of four black scanning guns, all nestled in a battery charger. I remember them from my second day at Spend Easy, when Ralph used one to scan Dairy products. Gilbert grabs the one labelled "PRODUCE," and we go back down the stairs.

"Jack is responsible for placing the Produce orders," he says. "He placed one just this morning, using this order gun. We're going to make a little adjustment."

We walk a couple meters into Aisle One. Gilbert taps a few buttons on the gun's interface, and then takes a box of condoms off the shelf. "Lubricated," he says. "Jack will appreciate that." He points the gun at the box and pulls the trigger. A blinking red line of light falls on the barcode. There's a beep. Gilbert presses a few more buttons.

"How many are you ordering?"

"A fuckton. Come on."

We walk back to the warehouse, and Gilbert accesses the computer. I watch the entrance while he works, as well as the doors that lead to the Meat department's back room. I'm petrified we'll get caught. Why did I agree to this?

"There," he says after a few minutes. "Now the Produce order for Monday consists of all condoms, and no veggies."

Gilbert turns the alarm back on and locks the doors, and we get back in the Hummer. He drives out of the parking lot as fast as he pulled in. I don't speak, and neither does he.

In my driveway, with my fingers on the door handle, I say, "Why did you need me to come with you tonight? I didn't actually do anything."

He doesn't answer for a moment. Then he says, "I wanted you to enjoy your vengeance. I could have done it myself, but then watching Jack haul all those condoms off the truck wouldn't be as satisfying for you—just funny."

"Oh. Well, thanks, I guess."

"Do you mind if I smoke in your driveway?"

"Go ahead."

We get out, and he opens the Hummer's back hatch. We sit.

Gilbert takes an apple out of his pocket. "Behold," he says. "I made a pipe out of an apple."

He's carved a little bowl where the stem used to be, and lined it with tin foil. After a couple puffs he holds it out to me. The thick smoke wafts on the crisp November air.

"No, thanks."

*

My next shift is Monday afternoon. I wake up around 10, and for once Marcus Brutus isn't crying for food, or water, or his kitty litter to be changed, or release from an existential crisis. He's just lying on the coffee table, on his back, with four paws up in the air. He tracks me with his eyes as I walk by. I stop. "What? Are you completely at peace with the world today, or something?"

I have an appointment with Bernice before work. I don't tell her about getting locked in the freezer. I do tell her what's resulted, though—that I think I've moved past any thoughts of suicide. She asks how, and I give a true answer. I say I no longer feel so alone.

But that's only part of the truth.

The possibility that someone wants to kill me has made me realize there's nothing I want more than to live

.

Chapter Nine

One day, the Professor approached me in the common area. "I hear you're writing a novel," he said.

"No, I'm not," I said. "I don't write anymore."

"Tell whoever reads your novel that they aren't going to learn anything from a novel. Fiction doesn't properly represent cause and effect—it's just what the author thinks would happen. Tell them they should be reading non-fiction."

"Sure. I'll make that my epigraph."

"I used to want to be a professor, you know. Before my...issues."

I considered this for a moment, and said, "I think you'd make a good one. I've learned a lot from you already."

The Professor smiled—for the first time, that I'd seen. "Thank you." He walked away.

I glanced across the room and saw Rodney sitting on the other side, glaring at me. He was drinking a can of something. He held it up so I could see it, then chugged it in one go.

He smashed the empty can against his head, and roared. I had to try pretty hard to keep a grin from forming. He got up and stomped away.

*

Brent calls my name as I wheel my bike toward a 2-10 Monday shift. He's standing near the corner of the building, motioning for me to come over. I hold up a finger—I need to lock up my bike, first.

I snap the padlock shut and walk to meet him. He's smoking a joint. "Hello," I say.

"Hey, dude. I heard what happened on Friday, with the freezer. Sorry I wasn't there."

"It's fine."

He holds out the joint. "Want some?"

"No, thanks. I don't smoke. And I'm about to start my shift."

He pulls back one side of his unzipped jacket, revealing the Spend Easy logo on his breast pocket. "So am I. We're working together."

I shrug. "To each his own."

"Don't act so superior. The way you're looking at me right now, it makes me want to punch you in the face. Seriously." He tosses the roach onto the ground. "You think I shouldn't be working here, right? You think they should fire all the stoners."

"Think what you want, Brent."

I walk into Spend Easy, expecting Frank to summon me to his office at any moment. I glance up at his tinted window as I walk past the cash registers, but there's no looming silhouette there.

The first three hours of my shift are devoted to bringing overstock out to the sales floor and checking to see if it will fit on the shelves. At 5:37, a frozen order comes in. There are three pallets. I take them off the truck and put them in the middle of the warehouse.

The truck leaves, and I go to the coat rack at the front of the store, where two heavy, padded coats are hanging. I take one. I brought a pair of gloves from home, and I put on those, too. And a hat.

Standing in the warehouse, bundled up enough to weather a blizzard, I stare at the pallets and avoid looking toward the freezer.

I could ask Brent to do the frozen order alone. But that would almost guarantee it wouldn't get done.

This is part of the job. I need to be able to work in the freezer.

I look around to make sure no one else is in the warehouse. Then I take a deep breath, as though about to dive deep underwater, and haul the first pallet into the freezer. Then I bring in the second.

I'm about to move the third inside when Jack appears. I close the freezer door and wait. I won't go in there with him here.

But the door buzzer goes off, and he lets in a delivery guy. He won't trap me in again with a witness present. Right? My heart beating rapidly, I shove the third pallet into the freezer and get out as quickly as I can, slamming the door shut.

Jack is watching the delivery guy pull a pallet of condoms off the truck. His eyes are as wide as Tommy's. The guy hands Jack a piece of paper, and he stares at it like he hopes what's written on it will change. I grab a broom and start sweeping.

"There aren't any vegetables listed here," Jack says. "There are just 500 boxes of condoms."

"Yep," the guy says. "That's the whole order."

"I didn't order condoms. I ordered vegetables. For the Produce department."

"That's not what the invoice says."

"Didn't you know you were delivering a Produce order? You made a mistake."

"I didn't make any mistake. This is what they gave me."

"Then the warehouse made a mistake. You have to take them back there."

"Call them, if it'll make you feel better. But these condoms travelled hundreds of miles. For a special trip, just to return them—that would cost more than the amount on the invoice. The supplier will refund the condoms, but Spend Easy would have to pay for their transport."

Jack crumples the invoice in his hands. "This is $1800 worth of condoms."

"Yep."

"What am I supposed to do with $1800 worth of condoms?"

The guy shrugs. "Help solve overpopulation. Listen, I have more deliveries to make. I gotta go."

"What about the vegetables?"

"Sorry, man. You won't find anyone to bring you produce at this hour."

He leaves. Jack looks at the crumpled invoice in his hand, and straightens it out again. He walks to the desk and picks up the phone.

He doesn't dial anything, right away. He puts the phone down, leans his forehead against the wall, and takes deep breaths. "Oh my God," he says in a high-pitched whimper. "Oh my God."

He picks up the phone and punches some numbers. "Sir," he says, "we have a bit of a problem here, sir. It seems there was a mistake with the order. I don't know how it happened, but it would seem the order has been replaced with 500 boxes of condoms. Condoms, sir. Yes. He said the amount we'd spend returning them is greater than the refund. Yes, sir. I'm so sorry. I'll wait for you here."

He hangs up, and finally sees me. His eyes narrow. "Do you know anything about this?"

"About what?"

"Do you not see the pallet of condoms?"

"I just assumed you Produce guys were planning a staff meeting."

I don't go back into the freezer until Frank turns up. While I'm in there I keep my eyes on the door as I fumble products onto my cart.

I hear Frank ranting to Jack about "the Robertsons' order", and it soon becomes evident that a customer has placed an order for a large number of fruit baskets, which they are coming to pick up tomorrow.

I take a break around seven. Frank's son, Randy, is already sitting in the break room, chatting with Lesley-Jo. Randy looks a bit annoyed when I enter. He isn't wearing a uniform.

"Hey, Sheldon," Lesley-Jo says.

"Hey." I take my vegetarian spaghetti from the fridge and put it in the microwave. I look at Randy. "Why are you here? You're not working tonight."

"He brought me supper," Lesley-Jo says. A burger and fries sit on the table in front of her. She's cleaning her glasses with a tissue.

"How nice," I say.

Randy excuses himself soon after that, claiming he has an essay due tomorrow. After he's gone, Lesley-Jo offers me a fry, and I accept. "I think he likes you," I say.

"Oh, I'm not the first cashier he's given food to. He's looking for a date. Any date."

"Will you go on one with him?"

She shrugs. "He's not bad looking. I might, if he wasn't going for three other girls at the same time."

I nod. "If you chase two rabbits, you will not catch either one. Or four rabbits, in this case. That's a Russian proverb." The microwave beeps, and I get up to collect my dinner.

"I'm not a rabbit."

"That's not—"

"You know, Sheldon, if you wanted a date with a cashier, I bet you could have one, easy. They all seem to adore you."

I glance back at her, eyebrows raised. "Is that an invitation?"

"I was thinking of Marilyn, actually. Are you into older women?" She stands up, laughing. "That's the end of my break. Have a good shift, Sheldon!"

*

Jack manages to buy enough produce from other stores to satisfy the Robertsons. Gilbert says it's a lucky thing he did. According to him, Spend Easy is already a few million dollars in the hole. If the store lost another big customer, and Frank blamed Jack, who knows where Jack would be working right now.

The next day, Frank has working cameras installed. Men with ladders make their way around Spend Easy, taking down the fake ones and replacing them with black globes.

"It doesn't matter," Gilbert says. "No one's going to watch the footage. Even on fast forward, real life is incredibly boring."

Frank orders Ernie to move the pallet of condoms next to the Dairy cooler, where I assume they'll sit until he figures out what to do with them. Jack doesn't seem to have taken much heat from Frank after all. It makes sense, really. How could he have accidentally cancelled the entire order, walked to Aisle One, and ordered 500 boxes of condoms instead? It must be obvious to Frank that the order was tampered with.

So the question is, whom does he suspect?

*

Gilbert was wrong. Frank really enjoys footage of real life. Ralph claims Frank is able to access the feed from his computer, at home, and it soon becomes clear this isn't mere propaganda.

One night, Frank calls the warehouse and asks for Brent. He tells him that if he and Gilbert don't stop putting cardboard in the dumpster, they will be written up. Company policy dictates cardboard go in the cardboard compactor, to be recycled.

"Looks like surveillance footage isn't so boring after all," I say to Gilbert after Frank's call. "Looks like Frank could watch real life all day."

Gilbert shakes his head. "This doesn't prove anything. Ernie's working tonight too—Frank's tree-hugging informant. He probably called Frank to rat us out, and then Frank pretended to spot it on the cameras. To hide the fact he has a big fat mole in Grocery."

Nevertheless, Gilbert starts putting cardboard in the cardboard compactor.

On another shift the intercom beeps, and Frank's voice comes out: "Gilbert Ryan, tuck in your shirt, please. Gilbert Ryan, tuck in your shirt." We're both in Aisle Two. Gilbert stuffs his shirt into his pants, frowning.

I haven't heard about anyone from other departments getting reprimanded. Eric and the Produce guys have started wrestling each other in the warehouse. Doesn't that show up on camera? Isn't roughhousing a violation of company policy?

Eric always wins these wrestling matches. He's huge, and military trained. It's not serious wrestling—just a playful way for Eric to express his physical dominance. For the Produce guys' part, they appear to love it. They emerge from Eric's arms red-faced and beaming. I think they enjoy submitting to authority.

Two weeks after I was locked in the freezer, Frank calls a staff meeting.

Ralph tells us the purpose of the meeting is to discuss new store policies, and to refresh employees on some existing ones.

Attendance, he says, is mandatory.

*

I didn't realize how many people work at Spend Easy. That is, there are fewer than I expected. We're holding the meeting in the front end, and I estimate about 60 people gathered around the cash registers.

Frank called this meeting, but he doesn't speak. That's left to Ralph, who picks up the Service counter phone and taps a button. His voice emanates from the ceiling speakers.

"All staff to the front end, please."

Matt and Paul emerge from Aisle Five. Unlike almost everyone else, they're wearing uniforms. The Produce employees are standing near the mouth of Aisle Two, and they're also in uniform. Grocery is scattered throughout the crowd.

The sun set over an hour ago, and it's dark outside the big windows.

Ralph sits on two upside-down milk crates, one stacked on top of the other. He surveys the crowd.

Silence, now. Ralph is still holding the phone receiver, cradled in his lap. The milk crates don't look very comfortable. His feet aren't quite touching the floor, which gives him something of a boyish look. He glances to his right, toward the parking lot. Ernie is leaning against the Service counter beside him.

Ralph clears his throat.

He raises the receiver.

"This is a grocery store, and we serve the public. Everything we do here—in the Grocery department, in the Bakery, in the Produce department, at the cash registers—is for the customer's benefit."

Jack interrupts.

"That's right! And when you break store policy, you do the customer a disservice!"

"True, Jack. We work in the food industry, the most important sector of the economy. We have a lot of responsibility."

I glance at Jack. He's exchanging grins with another Produce worker.

"You've all been given the Employee Handbook," Ralph says, "and you're expected to know the policies." He lowers the receiver for a second and looks around at everyone. He raises it again. "None of us are children. We're all getting paid to do a job, and we owe it to ourselves to do it well."

Murmured agreement—from the cashiers, mostly.

"The store has to be kept neat and tidy. We all need to make sure our uniforms are tucked in. And if you don't know the policies, you need to learn them, or you won't be able to do your job effectively. Earlier this week there was an altercation over prices, between an employee and a customer. The customer found a price tag for a product that was on sale the week before. The tag should have been changed, but our policy is that if the customer sees a product listed for a reduced price, they get it for that price. The customer knew our policy, and the employee didn't. If the employee had known the policy, that argument could have been avoided."

Ernie whispers something in Ralph's ear. Ralph hesitates, then hands him the receiver, looking uncertain. Ernie stares into the crowd. At first I think his gaze is on me, but then I realize he's looking behind me, to my right. At Brent.

"We also have a policy against throwing cardboard in the dumpster."

"Shut up, Ernie," Brent says.

Frank is standing a couple feet into Aisle Four, staring out the windows. "Quiet down," he shouts.

"When you throw out recyclable material, you do the public a disservice," Ernie says. "You actually do the planet a disservice. No one is coming to save humanity, you guys. We have to look out for ourselves. We're running up against all kinds of environmental limits, here, and if we keep going the way we're going, we won't have any home left to live on. Earth will become just an empty ball of dirt, circling the sun forever."

Ernie lowers the phone to his chest and looks at us, solemn-faced. The silence is complete.

Ralph takes the phone back. "So, um, some of us need to catch up on store policy, but it isn't all doom and gloom. Spend Easy's a good place to work, with employees who are lots of fun. Obeying store policy doesn't mean we can't have a good time together."

Jack walks over and holds his hand out for the phone receiver.

"There are cameras now," he says. "Working cameras. Breaking store policy will carry consequences, sometimes severe ones. You may have heard about the recent incident with the Produce order. Such transgressions will now warrant immediate termination."

He hands the receiver back to Ralph and walks back to the group of Produce workers.

Tommy comes forward and whispers something in Ralph's ear. Ralph shakes his head. Tommy goes back to where he was standing.

Ralph lifts the receiver again. "There's only one more thing to mention before we can all go home. Employee theft is becoming a big problem. We knew it was happening before, but it's really escalated in the last year or so. Like Jack said, we now have the means to document it. If any employee is caught stealing, he will be fired immediately. No second chances. We will also consider showing the footage to the police." He smiles. "Thanks for coming, everyone. You're a great crew, and I look forward to working with you well into the future. Brent: Frank and I need to speak with you in the store office."

The employees start to disperse. I glance at Brent, who hasn't moved. He's frowning.

I look down Aisle Three. A couple meters in, Gilbert is sitting on a cart, expressionless. He meets my gaze until I look away.

*

"It's going to rain in your living room," Sam says, leaning with a hand on the door frame. He has no coat on. His top three shirt buttons are undone, and his hair sticks every which way. He reeks of pot and liquor.

"Aren't you cold?" I say. "Come in."

"Can't. Your cat will agitate my allergies."

"Are you drunk?"

Sam grins. "Yeah."

"It's Monday."

"When you sell dope, the weekend never ends." He burps. "You should really check your living room. You're going to need buckets. Lots of buckets."

"What are you talking about?"

"Been asking the landlord to replace the toilet for months."

"Okay..."

"It overflows."

"Do you own a plunger?"

"Yeah, but I didn't realize it was happening until it already happened. Normally, I check the bathroom a couple minutes after I flush. I didn't this time, because I'm drunk. Sorry."

"It's fine."

He rests a hand heavily on my shoulder. "Get the buckets. Hurry!"

I get garbage containers from my bedroom and bathroom, emptying them into the big kitchen garbage. But there are more leaks than I have buckets. I'm going to need the dish pan too, and the new litter box I bought Marcus Brutus, and the margarine container from the fridge. Luckily there isn't much margarine left.

Sam is still standing outside my open door. "We have contained the crisis," he says. "Now we must go to the source."

'We' didn't contain anything.

I follow him to his apartment. He reaches underneath the steps and drags out a flower pot filled with rocks. He holds up one of them. "This is a fake rock, with a key inside. If this happens again and I'm not here, use it."

I follow him up the steps. "Leave your shoes on," he says. We walk through the living room, past a multitude of empty beer bottles, and through his bedroom, stopping short of the bathroom, where the flooding is a couple centimetres deep. "Wait here," he says. "We need the mop."

I wait in his bedroom, feeling a little weird about being here. It's not as cluttered as the living room. In fact, I'd call it downright Spartan. The twin-sized bed is the only piece of furniture. I wonder where he keeps his weed. Maybe in the closet.

Once the mopping's finished, Sam insists on compensating me for my trouble with several beers and assorted other alcoholic beverages. The landlord will take care of any water damage to my apartment, he says. We end up on the couch playing video games.

He beats me in a couple rounds of Super Smash Bros. I put down the controller. "I need a breather." I pick up my beer, and we drink in silence for a few minutes.

"Today's my birthday," he says.

"It is? Sam, you should have told me."

"Maybe if I had a Facebook account, you'd have known. That's how you 20-year-olds remember birthdays nowadays, right?"

"I don't have Facebook either. I'm sorry I didn't know."

"It's fine. I was just making a dumb joke."

I sip from my beer.

"So, did you do anything today?" I say. "To celebrate?"

He holds up his drink. "Just this."

"Did anyone call?"

"My customers don't know it's my birthday, and I don't talk to my family, other than my cousin. They're closed-minded people." He tosses back the rest of his drink. "My cousin probably forgot."

"How old are you?"

"37."

That's how old Mom was.

I stay until it isn't his birthday anymore, and a few hours past that, since I don't have work tomorrow. I'm about to leave when Sam puts his arm around my shoulder, and slurs something about what a good friend I am. He invites me to crash at his apartment, but I tell him I can make it to mine. I'm not that drunk, I say, trying to make a joke out of it.

His arm is still around my shoulder. He shakes me, and calls me a good friend again. I thank him. He asks if I want to stay and smoke some pot. I tell him he's drunk. He wouldn't offer that to me, sober.

He puts his hand on my thigh, and says it's time for me to try some weed. He says to sit right here and he'll go pack his pipe.

I tell him I'm going home.

*

My mother and I believed in chance, not fate—coincidence, not design. So when we began to notice the number 37 appearing in our lives again and again, we made a joke of it. "God is trying to tell us something," she would say. "We need to start going to church."

I was born at 3:37 AM. My grandmother's house was 3700 square feet. There were 37 entrants in the short story contest I won in high school. 37 appeared in both our social insurance numbers. You got 37 when you added our birthdays together. 37s seemed to appear on license plates an unusual amount, and when we looked at clocks, it always seemed to be the 37th minute.

It's a classic example of confirmation bias, of course—the tendency to favour information that supports a pre-existing belief. In this case, the belief was that a number appeared in our lives with unusual frequency. Subconsciously, we probably ignored the numbers that weren't 37.

Over the last few months, I've been noticing a lot of 37s.

It was 12:37 when patients started showing up for the information session in the TV room. The nurses held these on Tuesdays right after lunch, and this was the second I'd attended. They usually filled up early, because most of us had nothing better to do. This particular session was about getting enough sleep.

At 12:40 they brought in extra chairs to form a circle around the room. It didn't start for another 20 minutes, yet there were already seven people there. Fred sat across from me, on a couch with room for no one else. Rodney was to his right, scowling at nothing in particular. The Professor sat in an armchair to my left. Methuselah walked around the room, asking everyone if they'd ever had sex with a man.

"Have you ever had sex with a man?" he asked the Professor.

"I have not."

"Have you ever had sex with a man?" he asked Fred.

"Nope."

"Have you had sex with a man?" he asked Rodney.

"Do you wanna get punched?"

"Is that a yes?"

"Get out of my face."

"Have you ever had sex with a man?" he asked the skinny girl Fred pointed out to me my second day here.

"That's really none of your business."

Two nurses came in before Methuselah got to me with his query, and he sat down. One nurse introduced herself as Brianne, the other, Margaret. "Today, we'll be talking about getting enough sleep," Brianne said. "Proper sleep habits are important, especially for those dealing with mental illness."

The Professor raised his hand.

"Yes, Richard?"

"True statements are merely those consistent with the dominant paradigm."

"Thank you, Richard. But that's not what we're discussing today."

"I only mean to suggest that perhaps we're patients here because we don't share your worldview."

"I'm not really qualified to comment on that."

Methuselah raised his hand.

"Yes, Gregory?"

"I had a bad dream last night."

"Was it about boning a dude?" said Rodney.

"That's inappropriate, Rodney," Margaret said. "If I have to say that again, I'm going to ask you to leave."

"Dreamers are a dime a dozen," the Professor said.

When I left the meeting, I found Sam waiting at one of the cafeteria tables, talking to Methuselah, who'd reached him first.

"Have you ever had sex with a man?" he asked Sam.

Sam placed a hand on his shoulder. Methuselah's whole body went rigid, and he grimaced, but he didn't pull away.

"It doesn't matter," Sam said.

Chapter Ten

I'm three hours into an eight-hour shift when Gilbert finds me in Aisle Two and asks me to take my first break. "I need to talk to you. Away from here."

I punch out, and he drives me to a nearby cafe. He gets us both coffees. We sit next to a window.

"They fired Brent," he says.

"For theft?"

"Yeah. Ralph practically announced they were going to do it at the staff meeting. Without actually saying it, since that would be illegal." He sips his coffee. "They're crafty. They're using scare tactics."

I clear my throat. "I guess Frank really does watch the cameras."

He shakes his head. "I'm telling you, Sheldon, no one's able to stomach security footage long enough to find anything useful. It's all Ernie. Yes, they caught Brent stealing a bag of Ringolos. But Ernie was working that night."

"Maybe the answer is not to steal."

"Okay, Sheldon, yes. Getting caught stealing is a bad idea, we can both agree on that. But is it right, the way Frank's going about this? Spying on us? Barely investigating when you told him Jack locked you in the freezer?"

"I didn't tell him it was Jack. I don't know who—"

"The point is, it's pretty clear what Jack said was true. Frank really is planning to fire the entire Grocery staff. And in some cases, yes, he has cause. A lot of us have been slacking. I know I have. And stealing—he's right about that, too. But what reason does he have to fire a worker like you?"

I shake my head, saying nothing.

"And what about Paul?" Gilbert says. "Or Casey?"

"It wouldn't make any sense."

"Exactly. But Sheldon, I don't want to get fired either, and like I said, I know Frank has cause. I'm planning on working harder. And from now on, I'm going to pay for everything I eat."

"You are?"

"I think we all should. For some reason, Frank's chosen to demonize Grocery. We should stand up to that."

I work with him the next order night—the night he begins a case count, and uses the Sheldon Mason Five Case Approach for the first time. He beats my records, both for cases per hour and total cases in one night. Casey, who I've never seen slow down, actually stops working and stares the first time Gilbert speeds past him.

Ernie's on tonight too, and once the initial shock of Gilbert's newfound industriousness passes, he tries to catch up, piling boxes onto his cart as fast as he can and throwing his weight against it. 10 minutes later, he's sweating and panting. For the rest of the shift he's even slower than usual.

I think Gilbert may be right about Ernie. He doesn't actually work very hard—his value to Frank must stem from his willingness to sell out his co-workers. He still gets called to the store office, but I doubt it's to answer for wrongdoings Gilbert committed in his name. No, I suspect Frank and Ernie discuss other things.

The next night Donovan is fronting, and he's working at least twice as hard as I've ever seen him work. I ask him about it, and he says that after speaking with Gilbert, and praying, he's found that working harder just feels right. "Jack thinks Produce has a monopoly on hard work," he says. "But the only true monopoly is God's."

Another shift, I push my empty cart into the warehouse to find Gilbert, Casey, and Paul gathered around a pallet stacked waist-high with product. There's a broken-off broomstick stuck into a box of toilet paper, with a rotten watermelon skewered at the top. There are little half-moons carved out for eyes, and a thin slash for a mouth. Stinking juice runs down the broomstick. Chunks of the melon's scooped-out innards are scattered all around the pallet.

"Is this shit for real?" Casey says. "We gotta clean this up?"

"We should tell Frank," Paul says.

Gilbert shakes his head. "That's what Jack wants us to do. There are no cameras covering this part of the warehouse. We can't prove anything, and nothing would satisfy Jack more than for us to run crying to Frank."

I speak up. "There would be footage of Jack bringing the melon to the warehouse."

They all turn. "There are ways of doing it undetected," Gilbert says. "Jack might have hidden it in a box, which he brought here under the guise of throwing in the dumpster. He's too clever to be caught so easily."

"What are we going to do to him, then?" Casey says.

Gilbert looks around at us. "This isn't just about Jack being an asshole. Frank supports Jack in pretty much everything he does. They think we're untrustworthy, and they want us all fired. Jack said so, to Sheldon."

Paul and Casey look at me, and I give a reluctant nod.

"But if we work hard," Gilbert says, "to front the shelves, reduce the overstock, and get orders out quickly, there's nothing they can do to us. If we work hard, and Frank tries to fire anyone with the case counts and the cameras proving we're working hard, we can sue him for wrongful dismissal."

Gilbert's on a mission: outperform Produce, he says, and keep our eyes peeled for them to slip up. If we're lucky, maybe it will be our hard work that gets Jack fired.

He convinces Tommy that some things are worth working hard for, even if the sun is going to explode in 37 days.

He tells Matt that everyone's been talking about what a slacker he is.

"But I know I'm lazy." Matt says. "I said that already!"

"It doesn't matter," Gilbert says. "People are still talking."

"Christmas is coming," Gilbert tells us, "and Frank won't want to rock the boat at such a busy time. We should make a pact. If Frank fires a guy in Grocery, we all threaten to quit unless he hires him back."

Something unexpected happens, too. A customer finds a shrew baked into bread she bought from our store. It's on the local news, and a newspaper runs a picture.

But the news doesn't mention our store by name, and Ralph quietly asks us not to discuss it outside work.

"We're untouchable, now," Gilbert says. "Frank won't want to piss us off."

Gilbert warns us not to repeat anything he says to the new guys—especially not Randy. They work hard anyway, and Gilbert is convinced Randy was hired to spy for Frank. They might all be spies, he says.

"I think Randy's more focused on looking for a girlfriend than spying," I say. "Lesley-Jo says he keeps bringing the cashiers food."

Gilbert says nothing, but a couple hours later he finds me in Aisle One, restocking Javex. "You were right about Randy," he says.

"Yeah?"

"For sure. Come see who he's hitting on now."

He leads me to the end of the aisle and points to the first cash register. Randy's leaning against the counter near the shopping bags, laughing about something with Cassandra. She pushes him lightly. Randy's grin widens.

"Something wrong?" Gilbert says.

"No. Why?"

*

Casey is moved by Gilbert's newfound work ethic. After witnessing Gilbert's success using the Five Case Approach, he reduces the number of cases he takes out, and seems pleased with the results. It's getting him more miles per gallon of coffee. He zooms around even quicker than before.

Everyone's surprised at Gilbert's turnaround—including Ralph. He asks me if I think it's for real, or if Gilbert will start slacking off again in another week.

"Seems sincere," I say.

Ralph turns back to the computer, shaking his head. "And I thought I'd seen it all."

One night, I enter the warehouse to find Casey standing at the desk, shaking even more than usual, trying to hold a pen steady with his left hand while blood streams down his right.

"God, Casey, what happened? Let me see."

"Wait!" He motions with his injured hand for me to stay back, and screams.

"Jesus." The top of his index finger is split wide open, and blood pulses out. I glance at Casey's cart, which sits nearby, and I know what happened. Casey put up half a case of cereal, and he was cutting off the empty half so the box would fit better on the overstock racks. I picture him in Aisle Four, moving in his jerky, caffeinated way, not paying attention, and then—

"Why'd you bring your cart back after you cut yourself?" I say.

"I couldn't leave it there fucking covered with blood!"

I pick up his box cutter, which is lying on a case of pancake mix. "Casey, this is razor sharp."

"I sharpen it every shift." He sounds close to tears. He picks up his coffee from the desk, chugs from it, and slams it down, spilling some. He continues trying to use the pen.

"What are you writing?"

"Took a bandage from the First Aid kit. Supposed to record everything we take."

"Go to the bathroom and wrap your finger. I'll take care of this. Give me the pen. Is there anyone who can drive you to the hospital? You're gonna need stitches."

He gives me his roommate's cell number and heads to the washroom. I dial, and the phone rings six times. I'm about to hang up when someone answers.

"Yeah?"

In the background, the buzz of conversation.

"Hi, my name's Sheldon. I work with Casey at Spend Easy, and he needs someone to drive him to the hospital. He cut himself pretty bad."

"Why don't you drive him?"

"Me? I don't drive."

Casey's roommate sighs. "Well, I don't feel like driving him either."

"You don't feel like it?"

"I'm not his chauffeur, okay? I'm his roommate. Is he dying, or something? Can he still pay rent?" Someone laughs in the background. "If he bleeds to death, I'll have to post another ad."

"He's going to need stitches."

"I can't drive. I'm drinking. Mitch, pour me a shot of that. Pass that here." There's a slurping sound. "I'm drinking, dude."

I hang up.

Casey comes down the stairs, cradling his hand. "What did he say?"

"Uh, he's busy. Is there anyone else?"

Lesley-Jo walks through the red doors and comes around the corner. Her eyes widen when she sees Casey. "Oh my God, are you okay?"

"He needs stitches."

"Do you have someone to bring you to Emergency?" she says.

Casey's bottom lip is quivering.

"You poor thing! Come with me, I'll take you. It's not very busy. They can do without me for a half hour. Sheldon, can you tell them where I'm going?"

I nod. Casey gets his coat from a pallet and gingerly pushes his injured appendage through a sleeve. He follows Lesley-Jo through the red warehouse doors.

*

Paul says he's halfway through his first draft, and he asks me to come to his house and have a look at what he's written. I'm not sure how he knows he's halfway without having finished the book, but I decide not to ask.

He lives in a large two-story house with his parents. "They're vacationing, right now," he says. "I'm having a Christmas party while they're away—gonna invite people from Spend Easy. Doesn't seem like Frank's throwing a staff party, so I figure I might as well. You should come."

"Sure." It will be my first party ever, but I don't tell Paul that.

He offers me a drink from the bar he says his dad installed last year. I take a beer, and he leads me to what used to be his video games room. "It's my writing room, now. All the time I used to spend gaming—probably six hours a day—I write fiction instead. I gave up my blog, and my journal, too."

"You write six hours every day?"

"Yeah. I tend to get obsessive about stuff."

There's a tiny desk, in the shape of a quarter circle, shoved into the corner. His manuscript's the only thing on it. I walk over, pick it up, and settle into an armchair.

Paul sits across the room, watching me read. I pretend not to notice. After a couple pages, I chuckle, and he says, "What made you laugh?"

I clear my throat. "Um, the part with the employee who's told he looks like Toby Maguire, so he starts acting like him. I like what Saul says—that the guy basically copied and pasted Maguire's personality."

Paul smiles. "Cool. Thanks."

I try to continue reading, but I'm having trouble concentrating. Paul's manuscript feels so bulky in my hands. How many words is this? Have I written this many words in my life?

I told Bernice I wanted to improve my confidence, in order to write more. I feel like I'm doing a bit better, socially, but I haven't written a word. Seeing Paul dive straight into novel writing, unflinching, and get this far this fast...something about that makes me angry.

I pretend to read a few pages more and then I toss the manuscript back on the desk. "I'm impressed, Paul. It isn't complete garbage."

His smile falters.

I head for the porch. As I'm putting on my coat and sneakers, he thanks me for coming over.

"Sure," I say. Before I leave, I get the urge to say something nice. I feel sort of lousy. But I can't think of anything. "I'll see you at the party."

Chapter Eleven

I stand on the sidewalk in front of Paul's house for at least 5 minutes, hidden from view by a big leafy maple, holding a half case of beer. I can hear the party from out here.

I'm not sure I can exactly call anyone at Spend Easy my friend. Will they be glad to see me, or indifferent?

I take a deep breath and step into the driveway.

Someone left the door open. I enter the porch, and find Casey leaning against the wall, eyes closed, a bottle of wine dangling from his hand. As I'm untying my shoes the wine starts to fall, and I catch it. Casey glances down at me.

"Sheldon Mason," he says, pronouncing each syllable with great care. "Here's a man with a high case count."

"Thanks."

"There's slackers in there." He jerks his thumb toward the hall. "They should be thrown out!" He shouts this, and swings his arm around to point at the door, nearly swiping me across the face in the process.

"Think so?"

"I need a coffee." He walks outside, not bothering with shoes.

"Do you want your wine?"

He points back at me without looking. "Keep it secret. Keep it safe."

I put it in the corner and take off my other shoe. Jay-Z booms from deeper inside the house. As I walk down the hall, a door opens to my right, and Donovan emerges. "Sheldon! Follow me." He leads me to Paul's gaming/writing room and lifts a cloth draped over an end table. "Hide your beer here. There's a Produce employee skulking around this party. He'll probably try and steal our beverages."

"Won't they get warm?"

"Yes, so drink three or four right away. After that, you won't care."

"Okay. Thanks."

"When you drink all your beer, come find me. I have a couple shots of tequila with your name on them." He heads farther down the hall. The Scissor Sisters pick up where Jay-Z left off.

Gilbert, Matt, and a guy I don't know are sitting on the couch, and Paul is in the armchair. The three on the couch are holding Nintendo controllers. They're playing Bomberman.

The current match ends, and Matt says, "I suck at video games."

Gilbert notices me standing in the doorway. "Hey."

"Hey Sheldon," Paul says. "Have a seat."

"I'll stand. Who's winning?"

"Gilbert. For now."

Paul challenges Gilbert in Call of Duty, and for a while I watch them vie for supremacy. They seem pretty evenly matched. Eventually I decide to explore the rest of the party, so I grab another beer and head into the hall.

There are three people lined up to use the washroom. Lesley-Jo's one of them, and she asks if I've seen Casey.

"He went to get a coffee. He's not back yet?"

"I haven't seen him. The nearest place to get coffee is a half hour walk. Oh my."

"How many stitches did he end up getting?"

"Seven."

In the living room, they're playing a drinking game at the bar, and in the kitchen, they're playing Poker. The guy from Produce is leaning against the counter by himself. I walk over.

"Hey," I say. "Vern, right?"

"Yeah. You're Sheldon."

"Do you know many people here?"

"Well, from work."

"You probably wish there were more here from Produce."

Vern glances sideways, toward the Poker game. "Actually, I'm not here as a Produce employee. I'm here as Paul's friend."

"Of course."

"That said, it's been a real honour, rubbing shoulders with you Grocery guys. Excuse me. I need another drink." He leaves the room.

I remain leaning against the counter, watching money change hands around the table. After a few minutes, Casey enters the kitchen and stumbles over to me, clutching the counter with both hands.

"Lesley-Jo was looking for you," I say.

"I know. I just escaped her."

"Why'd you want to escape?"

He doesn't reply. He stares into the sink and belches. God, he's drunk.

Someone sitting on this side of the table is holding four kings. "All in," he says.

Casey looks at me and says, "Know what bothers me about people?"

"What?"

"Their annoying tendencies. Where's my wine?"

"Porch. How was your coffee?"

"Couldn't find a store." He turns on the water and drinks from the tap, gargles, and spits. "She asked me to add her on Facebook."

"Lesley-Jo?"

"Wants to keep tabs on me. Browser tabs."

"Are you going to add her? She seems nice."

"She'll want me to change my relationship status, next."

"She asked you out?"

"Not yet." He turns around, his back to the sink. "She will, though. She'll want me to say I'm 'In a relationship' on Facebook, so that once we have kids, other women will know to stay away."

"What?" He's making me not want to be near him. He's making me want to avoid him for the rest of the party.

His voice is getting louder. "She's trying to turn me into a vegetable. I won't have it."

Everyone sitting at the table stops playing and looks at Casey.

"Don't fall in love," he tells them. "It's a trap!" He stomps out of the kitchen.

They look at me. If they want an explanation, I've got nothing for them. "I need another drink," I say.

Walking down the hall, I become aware that I'm grinding my teeth.

Other than Gilbert and Matt, the game/scribbling room is empty. I grab a beer and walk toward a chair.

"You can sit by me, Sheldon," Matt says. "There's lots of room on the couch."

"The chair is fine, thanks." I sit.

Matt says, "That was kind of gay, wasn't it? I don't know why I asked you to sit with me. It doesn't really matter where you sit."

Gilbert and I exchange glances.

"You know, I could be gay," Matt says. "I don't find girls all that attractive. And I have these dreams, sometimes."

"Look, Matt," Gilbert says. "See the blank expression Sheldon is wearing right now? Take a few seconds and study that expression. Learn to recognize it. And the next time you see it on someone's face, just stop talking."

"I haven't seen Brent," I say. "What's he doing tonight?"

"No clue," Gilbert says.

"Was he invited?"

Gilbert shrugs.

I finish my beer and grab another. The second I sit down again, Donovan comes in and points at me with the hand holding a drink. "That your last one?"

"It's my fourth."

"Whatever. Follow me."

I follow him to the kitchen, and he lines up a couple tequila shots on the counter. "I hope you're not about to ask me for a slice of lemon, or some shit," he says.

"I'm not."

"Good—I only have enough for myself." He opens the fridge and takes a lemon slice from a little plate on the top shelf. He licks his hand, shakes some salt onto it, and picks up the shot. "Ready?"

"Ready."

He licks the salt, takes the shot, and sucks on the lemon. I throw mine back and fight to keep a straight face. Donovan gags. "Delicious," he says. He sips some beer, and I do too.

Cassandra comes into the kitchen, sees me, and squeals. "Sheldon!" She runs over and hugs me, pressing her head into my chest. "We finally get to party together."

"I think this is my cue to leave," Donovan says.

"I just came from another party." Cassandra says. "I'm already drunk."

"That's awesome. Where's Sean?"

She lets go of me. "I don't know. He doesn't tell me where he goes."

"I need to use the washroom."

"Okay. Talk to you after?"

"Maybe."

Entering the washroom is like stepping into another world. Music and conversation become muffled once I shut the door, and I'm left alone with my thoughts, as well as the taste of tequila in the back of my throat. It's like a brief intermission where I realize how drunk I am.

When I leave the washroom, I find Casey waiting to use it.

"Hey."

"Did you wash your hands?" he says.

"Uh, yeah."

"I didn't hear the water running."

"I washed them."

"Did you use soap?"

"Yes."

"Did you pay special attention to your wrists and fingertips?"

"No. I didn't."

His mouth turns downward at the corners. "You disgust me." He goes in and slams the door.

I grab another beer and make my way to the living room. Paul calls out to me from the bar. "Sheldon! Come have some Gladiators with us."

I walk over. "Some what?"

"Gladiators. Half a shot of amaretto mixed with half a shot of Southern Comfort, dropped in a mixture of 7UP and orange juice."

"Are you sure that's what gladiators drank?"

"You'll love it." He makes me one.

Gilbert, Cassandra, and Paul are all standing around the bar. "Cheers!" We all drink.

Silence.

"That was anticlimactic," Gilbert says.

"Ooh, that's a big word," Cassandra says. "Did they teach you that in your Philosophy degree?"

I look at Gilbert. "You have a Philosophy degree?"

"No. I don't."

"He would have a Philosophy degree," Cassandra says. "If he did one more course." She holds up a finger, to indicate 'one'.

"Why don't you, then?" I say.

"I'm not sure I'm ready for the vast riches that await me."

Casey drinks even more, and is soon so drunk that he shuts down the party. He ends up in the backyard with an armful of drinking glasses, smashing them one by one against the fence. Paul's already called a cab to come collect him, but until then he asks me and Gilbert to help restrain him. Gilbert tells Cassandra to watch for the cab, and we put on our shoes and head out back.

"Casey," Gilbert says. "What are you doing?"

"Don't worry," Casey says. "It's under control. I'm breaking all the glasses, and then I won't be able to drink any fucking more."

"You were drinking from a wine bottle, earlier," I say.

"Wine's gone. All I have left is Lamb's."

"Paul has plastic cups too," Gilbert says. "You can't break those."

Casey falters. "We could melt them."

"Do you have a lighter?"

"No. Do you?"

Gilbert shakes his head.

"Damn it."

Casey puts the glasses down on the grass. We get him into the house and onto a couch. He's passed out by the time a cab arrives. Gilbert takes Casey's phone from his pocket, looks through the Contacts, finds "Mom", and calls her. He gets her address, and says her son is on the way. We carry him out to the taxi.

Most of the guests are gone by now, and the rest of us gather in the living room to watch TV. I sit on the floor against the wall, and after a few minutes Cassandra sits beside me and takes my hand. She holds it in her lap and strokes it.

I don't talk to her, and I don't look at her. But I don't pull away, either.

Chapter Twelve

Gilbert and I are at the coffee shop again, at a table near the window, with drinks he purchased sitting between us. He just finished his shift, but he offered to take me here on my break before he went home.

I have a fierce headache.

"You and Cassandra were getting pretty cozy last night," he says. He sips his coffee and peers at me over the rim.

"I didn't do anything. She came over and took my hand."

"Doesn't she have a boyfriend?"

"Probably."

"Did you hook up after the party?"

"No. God, no. And I only let her take my hand because I was drunk."

"Sure."

"Can we change the subject?"

"Only if you have something more interesting to talk about."

"I can't think of anything."

"Didn't think so."

"Wait. I have something. I think Frank smokes pot."

His coffee halfway to his lips, Gilbert puts it back on the table. "What are you talking about?"

"The guy who lives in the apartment above me is a dealer. I saw Frank leaving there this morning. Pretty funny."

"Does Frank know you saw him?" Gilbert says.

"I don't think. Why?"

"Just curious."

*

Bernice says I should be proud of the progress I've made with Cognitive Behavioural Therapy.

She thinks I'm pretty quick picking up the techniques. There are four steps: identifying problematic situations; becoming aware of thoughts, emotions, and beliefs about these situations; identifying negative or inaccurate thinking in response to the situations; and challenging the negative or inaccurate thinking. There have been worksheets and exercises for each step, and we've already progressed to the last one.

Once I've 'mastered' CBT, I'll be able to mentally apply all four steps, in a matter of seconds, during the actual situations. In theory, anyway.

During each session with Bernice, I come up with examples from my life where the techniques I'm learning might have come in handy. I figure the first party I've ever attended should provide an excellent source for today's session.

"Casey was at the party," I say. "A guy I work with. He was super drunk—he kept ranting about how women use Facebook to keep track of their boyfriends, or something. It was embarrassing."

"How did it make you feel, listening to that?"

"Well, embarrassed, like I said. I tried to change the subject a few times, but he wouldn't quit it—it was like he was intentionally trying to piss me off. There were people at the kitchen table playing cards, and I was worried they'd think I'm Casey's friend. Not to say I'm not his friend. But I was afraid they'd associate his behaviour with me."

"Do you think any of your perceptions were negative or inaccurate?"

"Um," I say, and take a moment. "Probably my assumption was, that the others would associate me with what he was saying."

"What about the perception that Casey meant to anger you?"

"Yeah."

"Can you tell me why those thoughts were negative or inaccurate?"

"I guess there was no reason to think Casey wanted to piss me off. He was just really drunk."

"Anything else?"

I shrug.

"Do you think it was rational to assume the others would connect you with Casey's actions?"

"No—it's pretty common, I guess, for people to say weird stuff like that when they get hammered at parties."

Bernice prompts me for another example, and I use Cassandra taking my hand at the end of the party. But I'm not sure this is a good example for CBT. After all, my perceptions of a situation won't always be negative or inaccurate. What am I supposed to take from her holding my hand, except that she was making some sort of move?

I have mixed feelings. Cassandra still goes out with Sean, and she's broken my heart so many times my default instinct is to avoid her.

But it felt good—my hand in hers.

*

On Christmas Eve, Casey and I are the only ones working in Grocery. Everyone else requested the day off—even Gilbert. I wonder what he could possibly be doing. I try to picture him going door-to-door carolling, or reading the Bible to seniors.

For the entire month of December, we've been subjected to the same jazz versions of Christmas songs over and over. "Jingle Bells" is especially grating. Paul told me that last year, Gilbert kept sneaking up to the control room and switching the CD for one filled with death metal. He hasn't done it this year, but I wish he would. And I hate death metal.

If you're buying your kids' gifts from a grocery store on Christmas Eve, I'm not sure what that says about you. But there are a lot of those people here tonight, and they're tipping well. The carryouts are constant, netting me $35 in four hours. Christmas loosens everyone's purse strings.

When we're not carrying stuff outside for customers, Casey and I are working a Dairy order. Shortly after six, Donovan visits with gifts for both of us. Casey turns red, and takes his to the warehouse without unwrapping it.

"I think that means 'thanks,'" I say.

"Of course."

"What did you get him?"

"Beer glass."

I tear mine open. It's a box that contains an expensive-looking pen, with my name embossed near the clip. There's a tiny note, too: "Keep on truckin'."

"That's damn good advice," I say. "Wow, Donovan. Thank you."

"Don't mention it."

"I'm afraid I don't have anything for you."

"That's okay. Just write me a book with the pen. That will be fine."

"I'll get right on it. How did you know I write?"

"Word gets around. What kind of book is it going to be?"

I think about it. "Well, I do have one idea I came up with in high school. It's kind of weird."

"Let's hear it."

"It's just one scene, but I think there's a story there, somewhere. A man's lying on the ground holding a surgical scalpel, and the woman who broke his heart stands nearby. He keeps demanding she use the scalpel to cut out his broken heart. She refuses, and calls him crazy. It's supposed to be funny, but also a little sad."

Donovan touches my forearm. "If it pleases God, you'll do well."

"Do you think assisted suicide pleases God?"

"God works in mysterious ways."

A few weeks ago, I heard a rumour that Donovan regularly visits Frank's office and reads the Bible with him. When I asked, Donovan said it's true. He said Frank doesn't have many people he can discuss religion with. "He has a lot of questions. Especially about the Old Testament."

When Casey comes back, I ask if he liked Donovan's gift.

"I liked throwing it out."

"You threw out his gift?"

"Damn right. I don't want anything to do with fucking Christmas. I don't celebrate lying."

"What?"

"First, they lied to me about a fat guy who rides a flying sleigh. Found out the truth of that when Dad tried putting out the presents drunk one year. And they still expect me to believe thousands of years ago a guy was born who can turn water into booze and knows when I'm watching porn. Fuck it. Fuck Christmas."

Personally, I always liked Christmas. Mom would put on the fireplace channel, and we'd eat caramel corn.

A woman named Felicity Rogers calls the store with a list of groceries she'd like someone to put together for her. If we'll gather the items, she'll send a taxi to pick them up. I write them down, hang up, and tell Casey. He rolls his eyes.

"That bitch again. She calls all the time. Too lazy to do her own shopping." He grabs the list. "I'll get these. I need a break from Dairy anyway. It's cold in that cooler."

After the taxi collects Ms. Rogers' order, Casey asks me to take my break and walk with him to a nearby gas station, which is where he buys his coffee.

"Isn't there supposed to be Grocery personnel on the floor at all times?"

"Is work all you think about, Sheldon? It's Christmas, for Christ's sake."

We put on our coats and walk to the gas station. Casey buys an extra-large coffee and stirs in ample sugar and cream. He confides he has no idea whether the cream affects the taste. He just can't bear the thought of drinking liquid that looks like it was spooned from a bog.

When we get back, Betty tells us Felicity Rogers left a message for us to call her. Betty gives me her number, and I take it back to the warehouse.

Ms. Rogers tells me half her groceries didn't arrive. I put her on hold, and I fish the list out of the trash, where Casey threw it when he was finished. I think I know what happened. I wrote half the order on one side of the page, and half on the other. Casey probably missed the second side. I go up to the break room, and he confirms my suspicion. Shit.

"I'm sorry, Ms. Rogers, it appears my co-worker missed half your order. He didn't realize I wrote it on both sides of the paper."

She tells me she can't afford another cab.

"I'm very sorry, ma'am. I'm going to try and fix this."

Casey comes bounding down the stairs and grabs his cart from next to the cardboard compactor. He's downed his extra-large, and he's a lit light—an engine firing on all cylinders.

"She can't afford another cab," I say. "Now what?"

"Now, screw her," he says. "Now, it's her problem."

He jitters out of the warehouse.

I follow him. "The error's on our end, Casey. It's not her fault."

"You think Spend Easy will spring for a taxi? Forget it. Go back to work."

I stare at the list in my hand. Maybe I should call Ralph and ask him what to do. I don't want to bother him on Christmas Eve, though.

I walk up to Frank's office. I don't expect him to be there, but he's there anyway, bent over his desk, poring over some papers. "Merry Christmas," I say.

He looks up at the wall. He grunts.

I explain the situation, volunteering to round up the missing items. I ask if Spend Easy will pay for their transportation to Ms. Rogers' house.

"No," he says. "And I don't want you wasting company time gathering them. There's an order to finish."

"But it's our mistake, and she can't afford a cab. She may need the groceries for Christmas dinner tomorrow."

"Are there no prisons?" Frank says. "And the union workhouses—are they still in operation? I wish to be left alone, sir! That is what I wish! I don't make myself merry at Christmas, and I cannot afford to make idle people merry. I have been forced to support the establishments I have mentioned through taxation, and God knows they cost more than they're worth. Those who are badly off must go there. And if they'd rather die, then they had better do it and decrease the surplus population!"

Okay, so that's not exactly what he said. But you get the idea.

I go back to the warehouse and decide to call Ralph after all. He picks up on the fifth ring.

"Hello?"

"Hi, Ralph. Merry Christmas."

"Merry Christmas, Sheldon. Is there a problem?"

I explain the situation.

"I'm afraid we can't do anything for her," Ralph says. "Gathering Felicity Rogers' groceries is a special service. We don't have to do it, and we're certainly not responsible for her cab costs. It isn't Spend Easy's fault not all the groceries arrived.

You'll have to excuse me, Sheldon. My family and I are late for church."

I hang up, and stare at the receiver for a few seconds. Then I walk to the freezer, where Casey is loading his cart. "I'm taking my second break."

"You just had your first," he says.

"Yeah. And now I'm taking my second."

By now, I've made over $45 in tips. That covers most of the missing groceries, and I buy the rest using my credit card. My break ends just as I finish.

I call Felicity Rogers to tell her someone can come by with her groceries shortly after 10:00. She gives me the address. She lives in a different part of town from me, but our house numbers are the same.

I return to the sales floor to find Lesley-Jo chasing Casey around the frozen goods bunker, a sprig of mistletoe dangling from her fist.

"Stay back, woman!" he shouts. "I'm wise to your schemes!"

"Come back here, Casey-face!"

After my shift, I leave my bike chained in the parking lot and get in the cab with the groceries. The driver is untalkative. When we arrive, I see it's actually a pretty nice house.

I grab the bags and bring them to the front door. A woman in her thirties answers, a small girl wrapped around her leg. Somewhere behind her, a stereo plays "Have Yourself a Merry Little Christmas".

"Felicity Rogers?" I say.

"She lives downstairs. The door is around the house, to your right."

I walk around and descend six steps to the basement door. My first knock produces no results, and neither does my second. After the third I turn to go, but the knob turns, and the door opens a little.

"Yes?" The raspy voice is the same one I spoke with on the phone.

"Ms. Rogers?"

"Yes?"

"My name's Sheldon. I brought your groceries."

"Oh."

"Would you like me to bring them in?"

She shuffles backward.

I nudge the door open with my foot and carry the bags in. Felicity Rogers is an elderly woman with white wisps for hair. She leans heavily on a walker, and her eyes are rheumy. Her back is bent. Gravity has been dragging on her face and arms and legs for a long time.

I say, "Can I help you put these away?"

She moves backward again, deeper into her living room, which is also her kitchen, and her bedroom. It smells musty.

"Put them there."

I carefully lay the groceries on the floor.

"Are you sure you don't want any help?"

"Yes."

I smile, and I back away. "Merry Christmas."

She says nothing.

As I walk back to the cab, it begins to snow—big, fluffy flakes. For an instant, the driver and I make eye contact. But on the ride back to Spend Easy, we still don't talk.

"Thank you," I say once I've paid. "Merry Christmas."

"Merry Christmas."

I pedal hard to get home quick. The snow lands on my uncovered face, melting and running down my nose and cheeks in tiny rivulets. It tastes clean, and white.

And then it tastes salty.

Chapter Thirteen

The day after Boxing Day, Frank receives notice that on December 29th, the health inspector will be paying the store a 'surprise visit'. Immediately, Spend Easy becomes a beehive of activity.

Gilbert and I are working the morning Frank finds out. He calls Ralph in to work on his day off, and Ralph calls in Paul and Casey.

"Inspections are a joke," Paul says. "They don't make anything safer for anyone. Last time we were getting ready for one, I found mouse shit on a box of cranberry sauce. I showed Frank, and he said, 'It's in cans, isn't it? Wipe them off and put them out.'"

Ralph starts getting the warehouse in order, and sets Gilbert to working the overstock racks. Casey and Paul are tasked with fronting. Meanwhile, Frank double-times around the store, avoiding eye contact and barking orders. He gives me a series of undesirable chores, since he knows I'm the only one who'll do them. He gets me to lift the grates out of Dairy's bottom shelf and clean underneath—a cold stew of milk, eggs, and whatever else. Then I'm told to walk around outside, in the cold, and pick up any litter I see. After that he orders me to take a broom, go to Aisle One, lie on my stomach, and scoop out whatever shit I find underneath the shelves. This includes several rotten fruits and vegetables, a wristwatch, a dead rat, and a used condom.

And that was just Aisle One.

Gilbert, it seems, has acquitted himself admirably today. Walking downstairs from the employee washrooms, I find Ralph talking to him near the cardboard compactor. "I'm impressed with the turnaround you've made, Gilbert," he's saying. "You haven't called in sick for almost a month, and you've become one of Grocery's most valued employees. Do you think you'd be able to come back tomorrow and help us out again?"

"I'd be happy to," Gilbert says. He sees me, and winks.

I'm working the next day, too, and I'm assigned more disgusting tasks. But it seems I'm not the only one suffering. After my first break, I come downstairs to find a Meat employee mopping up a puddle that's seeped under the wall, from the Meat department into the warehouse. The puddle has been there since I started working. It's rancid, and I'm glad someone's finally cleaning it.

Hours later, he's standing there again. Eric's there too, yelling at him for slacking off: the puddle's still there.

It isn't the same puddle, though. I saw him mop it all up. There's obviously a hole in the wall, or something. It's not his fault.

He doesn't say that, though. He just stands there, shoulders hunched, eyes on the floor, while Eric towers over him and screams.

Later, I run into the guy in the warehouse—Theo's his name—and I ask him what it's like, working for Eric. He reacts to my question the same way he reacted to Eric.

"You don't have to put up with him shouting at you like that, you know," I say. "It's abuse."

"What do you care, vegan?"

I look up. Eric is standing at the top of the stairs that lead to the washrooms and the break room, staring down at us.

I don't answer him. Theo quickly leaves the warehouse, and Eric stands glaring at me until I leave, too.

*

I'm not scheduled to work the day of the inspection, and neither is Gilbert. I know this because he calls and invites me to hang out.

"Sure," I say. "I can walk to your place. Where do you live?"

"Actually," he says, "my mother's here, and I don't think I can stand her for another minute. Can we hang out at your place?"

"Sure."

When he arrives, I offer him a choice of coffee and water, which is all I have. He chooses coffee, and sits on the left side of my couch drinking it. I sit on the right—the couch is the only place to sit. Gilbert's the first guest I've ever had here.

He isn't saying anything.

I clear my throat. "Is your Mom visiting from out of town, or something?"

"Nope. She had a fight with Dad, so she's crashing at my apartment indefinitely. It's not the first time. Actually, she recently bought a bed for my spare room, for such occasions."

"Oh. Well, I hope they work it out."

He doesn't answer. He bends over to scratch Marcus Brutus, who's rubbing against his ankle. Gilbert places a hand under his belly.

"He doesn't like being picked up," I say.

He scoops Marcus Brutus into his lap, where he settles down and starts purring.

"I take it he doesn't let you do this," Gilbert said.

"I'd probably be bleeding by now."

He puts Marcus Brutus back on the floor. "I need to smoke a joint. Can I do it in your shed? You probably don't want me smoking in your apartment."

"Uh, okay. I'll get you the key."

Five minutes later, he's still out in the shed. I pour myself another coffee and bring it back to the living room, turning on the TV and flicking randomly through the channels. After 20 minutes, I put on my shoes and go out.

When I open the shed door, I find him peering out the only window.

"How was the joint?" I say.

"Fine."

"Must have been a big one. You've been out here for almost a half hour."

I join him at the window. It doesn't offer much of a view, other than Sam's deck. "What are you looking at?"

"Have you seen Frank go into the upstairs apartment lately?"

"No."

"And you're sure it was him, the first time?"

"Pretty sure."

He looks out the window again. "Well. I gotta go. I promised Mom I'd bring her dinner."

He walks out to his Hummer, leaving me alone in the shed with the smell of weed. My eyes fall on the stool in the corner.

*

On New Year's Eve, I come in for my shift to find Gilbert in the warehouse, playing with the label maker that's usually sitting on Ralph's desk. But Gilbert isn't scheduled to work tonight. I'm supposed to be working with Donovan, on the Frozen order.

"Why are you here?" I say.

"Just putting in some overtime. For the good of Spend Easy."

He presses a button, and the label maker starts printing. I walk over and read it: "HELP! I'M TRAPPED INSIDE A LABEL MAKER!"

"Pretty hilarious. Are they paying you for your services?"

"No, no. This is pro bono. Come with me."

We leave the warehouse and turn right, walking past the aisles, past Meat. We end up outside the customer restroom. Gilbert glances toward Produce. There's no one over there.

He untucks his shirt, and out drops a piece of paper, which he'd apparently been keeping next to his stomach. He takes a roll of tape from his pocket and posts the paper on the bathroom door. It reads, "THIS BATHROOM IS NO LONGER FUNCTIONING. IF I HAD THE AUTHORITY AND THE RESOURCES, IT WOULD BE FIXED IMMEDIATELY. BUT

UNLIKE MY SUPERIORS, I HAVE YOUR CONVENIENCE IN MIND—NOT YOUR MONEY."

Gilbert studies it for a moment, nods, and walks back toward the warehouse.

"Gilbert," I whisper. "What are you doing?"

"I've been thinking. So far, we've only reacted to Frank. I think it's time to be proactive."

"He'll know you did that."

"No he won't. The cameras don't point at the customer restroom. Anyone could have taped that sign there. And I'll look less suspicious than everyone else, because the recording will show me going there with Sheldon Mason—Grocery's star employee."

He turns down Aisle One, and I follow him. "What happened to taking the high road?" I say.

He shrugs. "I took a few bong rips before I came in. Does that count?"

There's an abandoned shopping cart sitting next to the drain cleaners. Gilbert grabs a bottle of Vaseline and tosses it in. Then he walks to his cart, which is waiting nearby, and takes a box from it. He dumps its contents into the shopping cart—numerous packages of condoms.

"Perhaps this cart belongs to a housewife," he says, "whose husband just got a vasectomy. Maybe her husband will see the stuff I tossed in, and ask her why she needs all these condoms. That should make for an interesting New Year's!"

I find Donovan in the walk-in freezer, loading up his cart. "Have you seen what Gilbert's doing?" I say.

"Yeah. He threw five bags of chips into some fat guy's cart while he wasn't looking, and said that should get him off the stupid diet he's probably on."

"I don't get it. He tells everyone we need to work harder, to show Frank and Jack we're better than them. And now he starts doing shit like this."

"Gilbert's been working here a long time, Sheldon."

"Gilbert has gone insane, Donovan."

I go searching for Gilbert again, and find him in Aisle Three. He's removing the price tags for the Remembering brand salad dressings and replacing them with new tags, which he's taking from his pocket.

"What are you doing now?"

"Flexing my creativity. Check this out. They rebranded salad dressings to make customers feel worldly when they buy them. Italian dressing is now 'Remembering Venice'. Instead of Ranch, it's 'Remembering Santa Barbara'. So I figure, if customers can 'remember' places they've never been, why can't they recall an event they never experienced?" He passes me a handful of his replacement tags.

"Remembering Auschwitz," one reads. "Remembering Guantanamo Bay". "Remembering Tiananmen Square".

"I printed them at home. I think they're going to be really popular."

"Gilbert, seriously. Why? When I started working here, you were the slackest person I've ever met. Then you became a workhorse. And now this."

"Let's change the subject. My girlfriend's having a New Year's party tonight. Want to come?"

"No. I want to know why you're doing this."

"If you come to the party, I'll tell you."

I hesitate. "I'll have to go home and change after work."

"Pick you up at 11, then."

Chapter Fourteen

There are only five people at the party when we get there, sitting around the living room and drinking. "Gilbert, thank God you're here," says a girl who's sitting on the floor. "We're lacking men."

There is, in fact, already a guy, straddling a footstool near the coffee table. He gets up and extends his hand. "Gilbert Ryan! God, I haven't seen you since high school! What are you doing all the time?"

Gilbert shakes his hand. "Masturbating. Vigorously."

The guy nods with his mouth open, withdraws his hand, returns to the footstool. Discreetly, he wipes his palm against the fabric.

"Who's your friend, Gilbert?" says the girl on the floor.

"This is Sheldon. He plans to be kind of a big deal."

She holds up her drink. "Hail Sheldon, future big deal."

"No autographs," I say.

A toilet flushes, and a door opens down a hallway. A girl emerges and walks up behind Gilbert, wrapping both arms around his chest. "Hey, babe." She's makeup-commercial beautiful.

"Hi, Kerrin."

She glances around the room. "We have three guys now. Let's play Spin the Bottle."

"I'm not playing Spin the Bottle," I say. "What is this, *Garden State*?"

"Well, we just ate all this fucking X," Kerrin says, "what the hell else are we supposed to do?"

"We're not playing Spin the Bottle," Gilbert says. "Give me some ecstasy."

One of the girls on the couch goes to get him some, and I steal her spot. "It's almost the new year," I say. "Are we doing a countdown?"

The head of the girl I'm sitting next to flops sideways so she can see me. "Countdowns are so 2012."

"Let's play a drinking game," Kerrin says. She looks at Gilbert.

"Whatever."

She produces a deck of cards and assigns each one a meaning. If you draw an Ace, everyone drinks. If you draw a 5, you take five sips. A 7 means you get to make up a rule.

Gilbert makes it a rule that in order to speak, you have to stand up. After that, I don't say much. I can't think of anything worth standing up for.

More people start showing up, and by 1 AM the house is full. The drinking game is over, but I'm still sitting on the couch. There are people standing over me and talking, cuddling on the couch beside me, watching TV. Maybe if I'd taken some ecstasy, time wouldn't be crawling the way it is right now.

The girl who was sitting on the floor earlier comes over. She has black hair, which she brushes back over her ear as she sits. She tucks her legs under her. "Hey there, Mr. Big Deal."

"I can't keep up a conversation for shit, so I wouldn't bother."

She raises her eyebrows, and laughs. "Come on. It's easy. Example: what do you do?"

"Stock shelves at a grocery store."

"With Gilbert?"

"Yeah."

"Do you have a girlfriend?"

"This is your idea of a conversation? Small talk?"

"That wasn't small talk." She rests a hand on my leg. "I'm genuinely interested."

I stare at her. She removes her hand.

"You didn't have any X, did you?"

"No," I say.

"Will you have some?"

"No, thanks."

She glances sideways, at the TV. "All right, then." She stands up and leaves the room.

I go to the kitchen, where Gilbert's talking to the girl who just asked if I'd taken ecstasy. When she notices me, she leaves the room.

"She thinks you're gay," Gilbert says.

"What? Why?"

"She said you just sat there while she flirted with you."

"Oh."

"What's wrong with you? She's Italian. And hot."

"She's also high."

"So?"

I take a beer from the fridge and twist the cap, producing a slow hiss. "What's her name?"

"Capriana."

Kerrin comes into the kitchen and wraps herself around Gilbert again. She kisses him until he pushes her away.

"Katie wants to buy some pot," she says.

Gilbert glances at me, and then glares at Kerrin. "How does Katie know I sell it?"

"She doesn't. I told her an anonymous friend of mine does."

"An anonymous friend who's obviously here at this party. So you've narrowed the possibilities a bit."

"Jesus, Gilbert, you're so uptight about it."

"Katie's not getting any pot."

Kerrin frowns. "Your jeans are ripped, you know."

"So are yours."

"Mine were bought this way. Yours ripped on their own, and you need a new pair." She walks away.

I clear my throat. "You sell weed?"

He lowers his voice. "I sell it to half of Spend Easy. I even sell to one of the managers. But if you tell anyone—"

"Calm down, Gilbert. I'm not going to tell anyone. Christ."

"Sheldon Mason!" a guy says as he enters the kitchen. "Long time no speak." He walks over, holding a red plastic cup. He's tall—taller than Gilbert—with straight black hair. "You remember me, right?"

I take a swig of beer. "Hi, Sean."

"This is the last place I'd expect to see you. Is that beer you're drinking?"

"Who are you?" Gilbert says.

"I'm the only friend Sheldon had in high school."

"Yeah?"

"Yep. Sheldon was always too good for everybody. He never drank, never toked, barely spoke to anyone. Wrote a lot, though. How's that going, by the way, Sheldon? Have you written the story yet where the main character's only friend steals the girl he loves? I'd read that."

"I haven't, actually. Doubt it would be very interesting."

"Well in case you do, I have a plot twist for you. I broke up with Cassandra two months after graduation—but that doesn't mean we stopped having sex. She seemed reluctant to let that part of our relationship go. We got back together later, but—"

"What's your point?"

"Come on, Sheldon. Consider the irony. For a while there, the love of your life was basically my fuck buddy."

I've never hit anyone, but Sean comes close to being my first. Before I can move, Gilbert plucks the red cup out of Sean's hand and splashes beer in his face.

Sean backs up, eyes wide, beer dripping onto his shirt. "Why'd you do that?"

"Wanted to see what would happen." Gilbert studies Sean for a few seconds. Sean glares back. Gilbert laughs. "That's what I thought." He looks at me. "Game of pool, Sheldon? Kerrin has a table downstairs."

"Sure."

As we walk away, Sean shouts, "Hey, bite me!"

Downstairs, Gilbert grabs a pool stick and rolls it on the table. He shakes his head, choosing another. After he finds two straight sticks, he chalks the tips and passes me one.

"People didn't like me much in high school," I say.

"Who gives a fuck?" He racks up the balls. "Wanna break?"

"Okay."

Gilbert takes off his ring and places it on a windowsill. I mess up the break, so he returns the cue ball to its original position, pulls his stick back, and thrusts. The balls scatter, the 14 falling into a corner pocket. "Guess I'm high," he says.

The next ball he sinks is the 13, leaving him a clear path to the 9. A tap of the cue, and it spins slowly to a side pocket, tumbling in with a gentle *thud*. Now the cue ball is trapped behind three of mine, and it seems Gilbert's turn must end. But it doesn't. He jabs downward with his stick, the white ball hopping over the 7 to push the 12 into a pocket. A couple girls leaning against the nearby bar have stopped talking to watch the game.

Silently, without looking at me or anyone else, Gilbert sinks his remaining balls, leaving only the 8. It sits at one end of the table, and the cue ball sits at the other. The path between them is clear of obstacles, but the angle seems impossible.

He looks up with a small smile and points at the 8. "That's you." He walks around the table, tracing his finger along the fabric, from the 8 to a corner pocket. "This is your life." He points down the hole. "That's your grave." He walks back to the cue ball, pulls back his stick, and drives it forward. There's a streak of white, and then a streak of black.

The girls clap.

I follow him through a door, through a storage area, and through another door, which leads to a stairwell outside. He takes a joint from his pocket, and a lighter. "My uncle lives in the apartment above yours," he says.

"Sam?"

"Sam Ryan, yeah. He came out on his deck while I was in your shed."

"You didn't know he lived there?"

"He hasn't spoken to my family in years." He holds out the joint. "Want some of this?"

I wave it away. "Tell me why you were trying to cause trouble at the store tonight."

"Not now."

"You said you'd tell me if I came here."

"I didn't say I'd tell you tonight."

"Why not?"

"Because right now, your top priority should be drinking, and talking to Capriana. By the way—there's a guest room you can crash in. Kerrin doesn't care."

I consider pressing it, but there's no point. "Thanks."

I return to the kitchen, chug two beer, grab a third, and go looking for Capriana. I find her talking to some guy wearing a beret. "Excuse me, Charles," she says, and leads me by the hand back to the couch. "Did you take some X?" she whispers, smiling. Her pupils are enormous.

"No. But you're very pretty."

Still smiling, she slowly licks her lips.

We kiss, and immediately there's tongue. It seems like a tasteful amount. I try not to let on how new this is for me.

"Kerrin has a spare room," she whispers in my ear. She takes my hand and leads me there, locking the door behind us.

We lie on the bed in our clothes for a long time, feeling the contours of each other's bodies through the fabric. I'm wearing a silk shirt, something Mom bought me years ago, and Capriana seems to enjoy running her palms along it. I want to start undressing her, but my instincts tell me to continue following cues. She smells of coconut.

I reach under her blouse to cup one of her breasts, squeezing and kneading it as I kiss her. At first she responds by moaning softly, but now she lays a hand on my elbow. "Not so hard," she whispers.

"Sorry."

Having to apologize during foreplay might not be a good omen, but she starts undoing my belt, so I don't worry about it so much. Then I'm inside her mouth, and I know we're going to have a problem.

I try to think about something else. Stocking shelves. Typing. Reading a book.

The sensation intensifies, and I don't know what Capriana expects of me right now. Is this meant to be a segue into intercourse? Does she assume I can last that long?

Think about anything else. Baseball. Rock climbing.

Getting smashed in the face with a line drive by my little league coach. Nearly freezing to death in Spend Easy's walk-in freezer.

It's too late.

Capriana is staring up at me, eyebrows raised. It's been maybe 15 seconds.

"A little warning might have been nice," she says.

"I'm sorry."

I don't know if I'm supposed to return the favour, now. I mean, that seems right, but I would have no clue what I'm doing. There have to be how-to guides for this online, and I sure wish I'd read one. I feel like I'm about to write an exam for which I had no advance notice.

But she doesn't seem to expect me to reciprocate. She comes up for a kiss instead. I'm not eager to find out what I taste like, but I feel awful, so I don't pull away. Thankfully, we're easier on the tongue this time.

Slowly, we work our way out of our clothes. Soon, I'm ready to go again. She takes a condom from her back pocket, tears it open, and gently rolls it on.

She lays back on the bed, maintaining eye contact. She's perfect—her eyes, her skin, her breasts, her stomach. I can't think of a single thing that would make her more beautiful.

Her expression isn't quite bored, but...she must think I'm pathetic.

I ease myself on top of her. She helps me enter.

It's hopeless. I ejaculate after 30 seconds.

She looks up at me. "Did you—?"

"Uh—"

She rolls her eyes. "There are more condoms in my jeans."

My face is burning, and I feel like I'm about to cry. I wish I was just about anywhere else. I wish I'd never let Gilbert talk me into coming here.

"I'm sorry," I say, struggling to keep my voice level. "Let's stop. I should—"

"If you go out there now, everyone will know what happened." She cups my chin in her hand. "This is your first time, right? I'm going to be awake all night, and there are more condoms. Let's keep trying. It will be good for you."

My eyes are on the floor, and I'm anything but turned on, now.

But she's right.

"Okay," I say.

Chapter Fifteen

The following evening, I create a Facebook account and search for Capriana. She hasn't done much with her privacy settings, and I can see everything. Apparently she travels a lot—there are many photos of her wearing bikinis on foreign beaches. Italy, Jamaica, Cuba. She's so beautiful. I can't believe we had sex.

She was so understanding, and kind. Incredibly, her relationship status is listed as single. I scroll through her profile to see who posts on it. It's mostly guys, but that probably doesn't mean anything. She just has a lot of guy friends, I guess. I wonder if I should add her as a friend. Probably not. That would make it pretty obvious I only created an account to creep her. I should wait till I have more friends.

I search Gilbert. Doesn't look like he has an account.

Who else?

I try Sam. He doesn't have one, either. I go around the house and knock on his door.

"Hey, Sheldon."

"Hey. How come you don't have a Facebook account?"

He shrugs. "Didn't seem to go with being a drug dealer."

"Oh."

"Want to come in?"

"Sure."

He goes to the kitchen to get me a beer. "Besides," he calls through the swinging doors. "Facebook's like a sugar rush when what you really want is heroin."

"How do you mean?"

He comes back and passes me the bottle. "We're all searching for something we can never have. I mean, deep down, I'm sure we all want to have sex with each other. But I think we crave a deeper connection. I think, subconsciously, we want to actually be other people. And Facebook is a very poor substitute for that."

"How would you know? You don't have an account."

"It's not hard to piece together. The people you interact with on Facebook aren't even in the same room. Why are you asking me about this?"

"It's kind of a long story. I met a girl last night."

He pauses with his beer halfway to his lips. "Where'd you meet her?"

"New Year's party. My co-worker's girlfriend hosted it."

"Was it fun?"

"Yeah, actually. Hey, so you have a nephew named Gilbert Ryan?"

He puts down his beer. "Yes, I do."

"He mentioned last night. Small world, hey?"

"It's a really big world, actually."

"You know what I mean."

"I should warn you about Gilbert. He might seem cool to you, but his confidence stems from an awareness of other people's faults. If he doesn't think poorly of someone, he isn't comfortable being around them."

"Wow, Sam. You're always telling me to go out and make friends. Now you're bashing the one friend I have made?"

He returns my gaze. "The friend count is one, now, is it Sheldon? You've made just the one friend."

"Who else?"

"How should I know? I'm taking a nap. Can you leave?"

"See ya." I put down my half-drunk beer and walk around to my apartment.

*

Sam never told the nurses I wasn't eating my meals. "Forcing you to eat would be delaying the inevitable," he said, with a sigh. "You need to come to it on your own."

At the time I nodded and didn't comment, but now I think he was wrong. As long as Fred was a patient, it was easy to donate my food, and continue giving up. I needed someone to snap me out of it.

That someone ended up being Theresa.

I was lying in bed when the lady in purple pushed the breakfast trolley down the hall. Patients were supposed to get up an hour before breakfast was served, but I found that if I lay there and didn't move or speak, no one bothered me. I hauled myself out of bed when I saw breakfast roll by, though, and trudged to the cafeteria. To maintain appearances.

Fred poked his head out of his room as I passed. He looked down the hall, at the lady pushing the trolley. "Blue Wizard needs food, badly!" he called. He came out and fell into step with me. "How are you, Sheldon?"

"Good."

"Beautiful day!"

"Sure."

"Have you been outside yet?"

"No."

He put a hand to his mouth and whispered. "You eating your breakfast?"

"Guess not."

I sat on the couches near the window. I twisted around and looked outside. It was bright.

"Excuse me. Do you have a dysmorphia?"

I turned around. It was the skinny girl. She had dark shadows under her eyes. Really pretty, though. Long brown hair and bright blue eyes. My hands started to sweat.

"Sorry?" I said.

"Have you been diagnosed with an eating disorder?"

"Um, no."

"I couldn't help noticing you never eat your meals."

"Not hungry."

"Bullshit."

"Sorry?"

"You're my age, and you're healthy, and you barely eat anything. You've lost weight. I notice these things. I have been diagnosed with an eating disorder—anorexia nervosa. I'm working hard to convince myself that I do have a healthy body, and that there's nothing wrong with eating. It's really hard to watch someone stop eating just to prove a point, or something."

"I—I'm sorry."

Across the room, Fred was returning to the table with tray number two—my tray. My new friend marched over, snatched it out of his hands, and marched back, placing it on my lap. Fred stood with his hands still curled as though holding the tray.

"Now, eat up," she said. "You're too cute to waste."

I felt my face heat up.

She took her own tray from the trolley and came back. We looked at our food.

"I'm Theresa, by the way."

"I'm Sheldon."

"The first bite is the hardest," she said.

They served scrambled eggs, Friday mornings. I spooned some up with my fork. Theresa picked up a slice of toast.

We ate.

*

Around eight, I go for a drive with Gilbert.

He's playing music from his phone over the Hummer's stereo system, and he reaches down to change the song. I eye the road nervously. "So," he says. "Did you enjoy Capriana last night?"

"She's nice."

He laughs. "That's one way of putting it. Did you get with her?"

"I don't kiss and tell."

"I'm not asking if you kissed her."

I grin. "We had sex."

"Well, you're welcome."

"What?"

"Capriana loves books. I knew she'd be at the party, so I texted her that I was bringing my writer friend. She said she'd never slept with one before."

"Wait—she had sex with me because I write?"

"Don't be hard on yourself. I'm sure it's not the only reason. The fact she thought you were gay helped, too. Gay guys drive girls wild. Plus you're not that bad looking."

"Thanks."

"Plus, she ate a lot of ecstasy. You know, it wouldn't hurt you to cultivate a little sexual ambiguity. A girl can't resist the idea she might be so hot even gays want to do her."

"Girls aren't all like that."

"Most of them are. You know, the mystery could translate into book sales too, if you ever get a novel published. People would probably buy it just to figure out if you're straight or not."

"Right."

"I'm serious. The more rumours, the more book sales. Count on it."

I look out the window and don't say anything for a while. We enter a subdivision, passing home after identical home. Gilbert pulls into one of the driveways.

"Who lives here?"

"Him."

Donovan emerges, and walks toward us.

"You didn't tell me we were picking him up."

"There's something I want to discuss with you both."

Donovan opens the door behind me and gets in. "Hey."

Gilbert pulls out and drives deeper into the subdivision. He tells Donovan to pass him a CD case. One hand on the wheel, he unzips the case with his other hand and takes out the first disc, slipping it into the player.

"They play this song at Spend Easy all the time," I say. "It's terrible."

"They do. And it is. A couple years ago I took my laptop up to the control room, and I ripped one of their CDs to my hard drive."

"Why?"

"I had a hunch. I took it to my friend, who's a DJ, and asked him to analyze it. Here's what he found."

He changes the track. A man's voice emerges from the speakers, whispering. It's Frank. "Kellogg's Froot Loops are on sale this week. Kellogg's Froot Loops are cheap and tasty. Kellogg's Froot Loops make your mornings quick and easy. Buy Kellogg's Froot Loops. Buy Kellogg's Froot Loops. Buy Kellogg's Froot Loops. Johnson's Baby Wipes are clean and moist. Make your little one happy with Johnson's Baby Wipes. Your baby's hygiene is quick and easy at Spend Easy with Johnson's Baby Wipes. Buy Johnson's Baby Wipes. Buy Johnson's Baby Wipes. Buy Johnson's—"

Gilbert switches it off. "You get the idea."

"Um," I say. "I'm having trouble processing what I just heard."

"Spend Easy's in the hole, man. Has been for years. Frank is trying everything."

"What did you do, when you found this?"

"I went to Frank's office and played it for him. Then I told him what I wanted. A raise, for one. And I told him I'd be taking my groceries out the back door from then on, free of charge. Also, that I wouldn't be doing very much work."

"And he agreed to that?"

"Sure. I'd go straight to the media, otherwise. Subliminal advertising is illegal."

I turn around and look at Donovan. "Did you know about any of this?"

He exchanges glances with Gilbert in the rearview mirror. Gilbert nods.

"I've known about it since I was hired."

"And you're okay with it? Isn't there anything about not blackmailing people in the Bible?"

He's solemn-faced. "I think God has a plan for Gilbert."

"Oh, wow." I face the front again. "Why are you telling me, then, Gilbert?"

"You asked why I was changing the tags at Spend Easy. Frank's been showing signs of trying to get rid of me. He gave his son a job in Grocery, and he installed cameras that actually work. And he told Brent he could keep his job if he offered up some dirt on me."

"So Brent took the fall for you?"

"Not really. What could he have told Frank?"

"Oh, I don't know, that you're selling weed out of the warehouse?" I glance back at Donovan. "Oops, did you know about that one?"

"Of course he knows."

"So is this why you've been working so hard lately?" I say.

"It's also why I convinced everyone else to start working hard. I wanted to give Frank a false sense of security. Now, it's time to do the opposite."

"And what does that consist of?"

"For starters, a certain local newspaper got an anonymous tip today about the new Remembering price tags. They're very interested in doing a story on them. That should give Frank an idea of what media pressure feels like."

"And what do you want from me?"

"The same thing I want from Donovan. I need more dirt on Frank. You're both uniquely situated—Donovan conducts his little Bible studies with him, and you're the hardest worker in the store. No one will expect you to spy. I also want to know immediately if Frank visits Sam again. If you help me, I'll see to it you get a raise."

"You lied to me."

"I never lied. I omitted. I wasn't sure I could trust you."

"How do you know you can, now? What's stopping me from bringing this to Frank?"

"Nothing. You're right—I don't really know I can trust you. All I have is a strong feeling. I don't think you'd rat me out, after everything we've been through."

"What are you talking about? What have I been through with you?"

Gilbert shakes his head slowly, a tiny smile on his lips. "Have you already forgotten about the night we broke into Spend Easy and ordered 500 boxes of condoms?"

Of course. Gilbert has insurance in place.

"Take me home."

"Need time to consider my offer?"

"This isn't an offer. You're trying to blackmail me like you blackmailed Frank. But I won't be coerced. You can tell whoever you want about the condoms. I'm not helping you spy."

"You don't understand, Sheldon. I'm not trying to threaten you."

"You lied to me, Gilbert. By omission. I thought we were friends."

"We are."

Donovan puts his hand on my shoulder. "Think on this, Sheldon. Pray on it."

"Take me home. Now."

"Very well," Gilbert says.

Chapter Sixteen

I decided a couple days ago I don't care if Capriana knows I only got a Facebook account to find her. I sent her a message asking if she'd like to meet up. She continued posting status updates and pictures, but she didn't reply.

Assuming my message got lost somehow, I tried again, and she still didn't answer. I don't understand. Doesn't she want to talk about what happened?

Earlier today, on her profile, she arranged to meet someone for coffee at a place near Spend Easy—the same one Gilbert and I went to a couple times. I decide to meet her there, too. I can't handle wondering what she's thinking any more.

It takes less than 10 minutes to get to the coffee shop by bike. When I arrive, I spot her sitting at a table in the middle of the store, with a guy. I sit near the door and take several deep breaths. I walk over. "Hey, Capriana."

She looks up, and so does the guy she's with. "Hi," she says.

"Can I speak with you?"

Her lips tighten. "Excuse me, Andrew," she says, and moves to another table. I sit across from her.

"Can I buy you something?" I say.

"I have a latte waiting for me."

"Did you get my Facebook messages?"

"I got them."

"Why didn't you answer?"

She shrugs. "Couldn't think of anything to say."

I can relate to that.

"Are you interested in hanging out again?" I say. "I'd like to get to know you."

"Not really."

I swallow. "Why not?"

"You're not my type."

"But we..." I lean forward, and whisper, "We had sex."

"Yes, we did. At a party, when I was on ecstasy. Did you think I was looking for a relationship?"

"I just thought having sex meant a little more than that." She seemed so into me.

"Not to everyone. And usually not with a person you just met."

"Who's he, then?" I point at the guy she's with, who's looking at his phone.

"A friend."

"Are you going to sleep with him, too?"

"That's none of your business." She stands up. "Don't send me any more messages, please. Bye."

*

I turn on my computer as soon as I get home, and I delete my Facebook account. Sam was right.

Above me, Metallica starts to boom through the ceiling. Sam's been blasting music every day for a while now. Heavy metal, mostly. So loud the light fixtures vibrate. I believe he's having a midlife crisis.

I used to think *Romeo and Juliet* was unrealistic—they meet, fall in love, and kill themselves for each other all in three days. I don't think that anymore.

Four days ago I didn't know Capriana existed, but now her rejection has removed all possibility of happiness. I feel like I laid my heart on the ground before her, and she stomped it till there was nothing left but crimson jam.

I keep a deck of playing cards on my desk to use as bookmarks, and now I shuffle them to try and distract myself. I shuffle faster and faster, until the cards start hitting against each other, some of them tumbling out of the deck. I pick these up and slam them between the others, bending a few.

Finally I throw the deck onto the floor, the cards fanning out on the laminate, all face-up except for one.

I reach down and turn it over. It's the king of hearts.

I turn back to the computer, close the internet browser, and click open a word processor. I type that in: "The King of Hearts". I centre it, and underline it.

And I start to write.

*

"Your friend's pretty promiscuous, isn't she?" I say.

It's just me and Gilbert scheduled to work tonight in Grocery, and the only reason I'm speaking to him at all is we're fronting the store together.

"Capriana?"

"Yeah."

He shrugs. "That might be why she slept with you the first night you met. But you did the same thing."

I laugh. "I'm definitely not promiscuous. I want to keep hanging out with her, for one."

"You know, before humans became farmers, we had no concept of sexual monogamy. 10,000 years ago, everyone pretty much slept with whoever they wanted. Relationships only became useful when we quit the hunter-gatherer life and started living in one spot year-round. That's where the idea of owning stuff came from. Farms are a lot of work, and they don't produce as much food, so it was important that your neighbours had a clear idea of what you owned—your land, your cattle, your wife. All valuable assets."

"Thanks for the history lesson, Gilbert. Unfortunately, I don't live 10,000 years ago—I live in the 21st century."

"You're right. Here you are, in the 21st century. You went to a party, slept with a girl on ecstasy, and you didn't get the relationship you hoped for. Would you like a nontissue for your nonissue?"

Gilbert leaves Aisle Two without saying anything, and doesn't come back for a long time. I keep glancing toward the ends of the aisle, expecting to see him again any minute. I assume he's still trying to maintain the illusion he's a hard worker, but he's doing a pretty poor job of it tonight.

I see a flicker of movement in my peripheral vision, but when I look no one's there.

It happens again.

The third time, I run toward it, as quietly as I can. I come upon a startled Ernie. "Evening, Sheldon," he says, his voice cracking. "Slow night, hey?"

He's holding a phone in his right hand.

"What are you doing, Ernie?"

"I'm just—uh—I'm here to check the schedule."

"Ralph emails us the schedule. The schedule can't be checked here anymore."

"Right. That's true, isn't it? God. I feel dumb. Well—now that I'm here, I might as well take a look around. See if I can help you guys out with anything, hey? Have you seen Gilbert?"

"Not for a while. Why?"

"Curiosity. That's all. I'm just wondering."

"Okay."

"Yep. Not too many customers, are there?"

"I'm going to continue fronting, now."

"All right. Sure. Take care, Sheldon. Good talk."

"Yeah."

*

I'm at my computer, in the middle of a scene, tapping feverishly on my keyboard, when the phone rings. I finish my sentence and answer it. "Hello?"

Breathing.

"Hello?"

"I..." Whoever it is clears his throat. "Can I speak with Sheldon Mason?"

"Speaking."

"I'm calling to tell you how badly I feel."

"Who is this?"

"This is—" He swallows. I can hear how dry his throat is. "This is Herman Barry."

The rage is like every molecule in my body sifting downward, trading places with all the heat, which rises to the roof of my skull. The hand holding the receiver to my ear begins to tremble. The muscle tissue in my throat pulses upward.

"Are you there?" he says.

"Who let you call me?"

"I joined the Alcoholics Anonymous group, here in the prison. I'm trying to deal with my problem. I've been sober for almost three—"

"That's because you can't get any alcohol."

"Every day, I think about what I did to end up here. As part of the program, we're encouraged to ask forgiveness from everyone we've wronged. I'm calling to ask if you'd consider forgiving me for what I did."

"Well, let's see," I say. "Are you delayed?"

"Sorry?"

"Are you mentally delayed?"

"No."

"So, you understand alcohol impairs driving ability?"

"Yes, I do."

"And you get that cars kill people?"

"Yes." Herman Barry is sobbing.

"You must understand, then, that when you got in your car shitfaced and started to drive, that made you a murderer. You have enough brain cells to grasp that, right?"

Big, gasping sobs.

"Of course I don't forgive you, you piece of shit. And neither does the higher power AA insists you accept. You murdered my mother, Barry. If there's a hell, you're going to rot in it. Okay?"

I slam the receiver into its cradle. I pick it up, and slam it down again.

Chapter Seventeen

After that first short story in grade three, everything I wrote was a writing exercise for one of the courses Mom enrolled me in. Write a story that's all dialogue. Write a story using third person perspective, then write the same story in first person. Write a story about a photograph. Write a story using the first words that come to your head.

I wrote that first piece, about a man who could turn stuff into food by touching it, because I was hungry. Now, I'm writing because I'm angry.

What results is a bitter humour that sprawls across the screen as I punch the keys. The main character's only name is the King, and he's even dumber than everyone around him. He's dumb for participating in the first place—a reality he masks with booze, and with frequent public executions. He's guided by his whims, and his temper.

Sometimes, I find myself whispering the words as I type. Sometimes, I find myself smiling.

I have a shift today. As I'm chaining my bicycle to the rack, Gilbert storms out of the store and spots me. He comes over.

"I just got fucking fired," he says.

"You did? For what?"

His hands are clenched, his eyes wide. "I—" He pauses. He kicks the concrete garbage receptacle. "Fuck!"

I run the chain through the front tire and snap the padlock closed. I stand.

"Someone filmed me taking a girl into the customer washroom," he says. He runs a hand through his hair and stops halfway through, clutching a clump of it. "The store cameras don't cover there—I thought I was safe."

"That was stupid."

"I know. I know that, all right?"

"I saw Ernie sneaking around the store last night with his phone—it might have been him."

Gilbert releases the patch of hair, and it sticks straight up. "You what?"

"I saw—"

He pushes me with both hands and I stagger backward a couple steps. "You saw Ernie snooping for Frank and you didn't tell me?"

"What was I supposed to do? Find you while you were having sex and let you know?" I push him back.

Gilbert grabs the front of my coat, shoving me back over the bike rack and against the wall, the bar hard against my spine. "You could have called me. Texted. You let that fat piece of shit ruin everything."

"Screw you, Gilbert."

With a wet, sucking sound, Gilbert draws phlegm into his mouth and spits in my face. He releases me, and I nearly fall backward over the rack. I catch myself, stand up, and watch him walk to his Hummer.

I go inside the store, walk to the customer restroom as fast as I can, shut the door, and wash the spit and snot from my nose and eyes.

It smells strongly of disinfectant in here.

Later, Paul asks if I've done any writing lately, and I tell him I've started a novel. He congratulates me, and tells me he's finished his first draft, and is now in the process of editing. Good for him, I say.

Later than that, after my shift, I take a glass of water into my bedroom and pick up the bottle of Zoloft from my desk, pop off the cap, and pour all the pills into my hand.

I sit on the bed. I stare at them for a long time. I count them. There are 37 left. Of course there are.

To cram all these into my mouth, washing them down with the water—it would be the easiest thing in the world.

Fuck it.

I take them to the bathroom, drop them in the toilet, and flush.

*

We all made a pact, instigated by Gilbert, that we would all quit if one of us got fired. When Frank fires Gilbert, though, nobody quits. No one even mentions it.

Ernie gets promoted to Back Door Receiver, and he shows everyone the video of Gilbert entering the restroom with the girl. Judging by the angle of the footage, Ernie must have been standing in Aisle One. He skips ahead 10 minutes or so, and the girl comes out, looks around, and taps on the door. Gilbert emerges too, and then the camera jerks away, swinging back and forth as Ernie scampers toward the front of the store.

The girl in the video isn't Gilbert's girlfriend, Kerrin. It's one of her friends, who I also met at the party.

What an idiot.

Having sex in a public place is illegal, Ernie tells us, and can incur a fine of up to $2000, six months in prison, or both. Frank, Ernie tells us, has generously decided not to press charges.

Ernie probably doesn't know Frank's not pressing charges so Gilbert doesn't go to the press about the subliminal advertising.

With Gilbert gone, everyone in Grocery continues working hard. The security cameras' effectiveness was established by Brent's termination, and now we know the blind spots are filled with Frank's spies. Ernie becomes an even bigger pariah than before, but he doesn't seem to mind. He struts around the store, checking our work, nodding approval. Sometimes he pats us on the back, and we all put up with it, resisting the urge to punch him in the teeth. Ernie does less work than anyone, now.

Sam continues to blast heavy metal in his apartment, pretty much daily now. Ironically, since Gilbert was fired, I've seen Frank go into Sam's apartment twice.

I don't understand how catching Frank at Sam's would have helped Gilbert, though. Even if he managed to get a picture of Frank smoking, how could he prove it was weed? Doesn't seem like effective black mail fodder to me.

Anyway, Frank's clearly prepared to risk exposure for planting subliminal messages. I doubt he'd feel much more threatened by a pot habit.

*

I bring Bernice a thank you card, for helping me. "I've made breakthroughs," I say. "Because of CBT, and because of talking things through here. I truly appreciate it."

"You're supposed to continue seeing me for three years, Sheldon."

"I know. But I feel like I've gotten all I'm going to from therapy—no offense. I'm more confident. I'm writing again. Sure, things are messed up, but I'm certain I don't want to kill myself. I want to see where life takes me."

"I'm glad to hear that. But I have to recommend against stopping therapy now. You've only been coming here a few months. It would be much better to continue, to make sure you carry on doing well."

"Thanks. But I think I'm good."

"I should also remind you that even though everything you've said to me is confidential, my notes are still open to subpoena by a court. If you ever get into legal trouble, they'll see you didn't finish your therapy."

"Understood. Thank you. For everything."

Chapter Eighteen

I do my best writing late at night, and this past week, more than once, I've watched dawn's light creep across my typing fingers. Finally, two days before Tommy's apocalypse, I finish "The King of Hearts". It isn't long enough to be called a novel—I'm not sure I'd even call it a novella. But it's the first thing I've written in two years, and though the writing drained me, I'm not angry anymore. I feel good about things.

I've been sleeping in a lot, and a couple times I've been almost late for a shift. Today I'm scheduled for noon, and I actually am late—for the first time since I got the job. It's 12:04 when I punch in.

Ernie's leaning against Ralph's desk. "Good afternoon," he says.

"Hi."

"Not good morning," he says. "Good afternoon."

"I'm aware I'm late."

Tonight's an order night, and Donovan is also working. He says Spend Easy isn't the same anymore, with Gilbert gone. "Yeah," I say. "I guess God's plan entailed him getting sacked."

"I wouldn't worry too much about that," Donovan says. "Gilbert's time here will likely prove an insignificant chapter in his life. He'll go on to do great things."

"Think so? Gilbert?"

"I'm sure of it." He places a bottle of beets on the shelf. "So. Paul tells me you've started writing your book. Are you using the pen I gave you?"

"No. Sorry. It does sit on my desk while I write." That's true, but it's not intentional.

He nods. "What's your novel called?"

"It didn't end up being a novel. It's more a short story. I titled it 'The King of Hearts'."

"Ah. The suicide king."

"Sorry?"

"The king of hearts is sometimes called the suicide king. In a lot of decks, he's pictured driving a knife through his own head."

The next morning I'm off, and I walk to the graveyard where my mother's buried, for the first time since she died. I stand over her plot for a while. I don't say anything, and I don't pray—either would be pointless. I just stand there.

Someone was here, recently. There are footprints, and a bouquet of black roses atop the snow.

After a while, I leave.

*

The last movie Mom and I ever watched together was *The Sound of Music*. But it wasn't the first time we saw it. *The Sound of Music* was her all-time favourite film.

I made fun of her so much for that. I watched it with her whenever she wanted, but I reserved the right to bash it mercilessly.

The music is terrible. It's nearly three hours long. And the von Trapps escape the Nazis in Salzburg by hiking over the mountains to Switzerland—but Switzerland doesn't even border Salzburg!

When I get home from the graveyard, I put it on again. I sit, rapt, as Liesl wonders at her approaching adulthood. I don't miss a lyric as Julie Andrews sings about her favourite things. And when the von Trapps magically travel a hundred miles by walking over a few mountains, I start to cry.

*

"Hi, Sheldon," Gilbert says, standing on the concrete step outside my door.

"What do you want?"

"Can I come in?"

"No."

"I want to talk to you."

"You can't come in."

"I came to apologize. Please."

I step back, and he enters, sitting on the couch. I remain standing, hands on hips.

"I'm sorry I pushed you."

"You spit on me, too."

"I'm sorry," he says, his eyes on the floor. He does look ashamed. "You didn't get me fired—it was my stupid fault. I was so used to getting away with whatever I want, at Spend Easy.

The cameras don't point at that washroom, and I didn't expect Ernie to be there. I did it for the thrill. And it was stupid."

"That's for sure."

"I don't want you to think I was just using you to cover my ass." He swallows, rubbing his nose. "I like you, Sheldon. You may not believe it, but I really wanted to help you. You know, I think you let people take advantage."

I sit down. Loud music starts blaring through the ceiling. It sounds like Rage Against the Machine.

"I brought you something." Gilbert takes out a long box and passes it to me. I open it to find a pen resting in velvet. I don't tell him Donovan already gave me a pen—a nicer pen. That I don't even use.

"Thanks," I say.

"You're welcome. I want to keep our friendship. Life's too short."

"Yeah."

"How's the writing going, anyway?"

A drop of water falls from the ceiling and lands in a glass sitting on the coffee table. "God damn it."

"What was that?"

I sigh. "The landlord was supposed to replace Sam's toilet months ago. Sam must have flushed and forgot to check it." I stand. "I'll have to go up there."

I put on my sneakers and run around the house. Gilbert puts on his, too, and follows close behind.

Sam's door is locked. I knock as hard as I can, but no one answers—the music's too loud, I guess. I walk down the steps and drag out the flower pot, sifting through the rocks till I find the fake one with the key inside. I stick it in the lock and turn.

As I enter the porch, I hear a moan. Gilbert pushes past, and I follow.

Frank is bent over, gripping the armrest, with no clothes on. Sam is standing with one leg on the floor and the other bent on the couch, pressed against Frank from behind, thrusting. Sam sees us first, his eyes widening. He starts to pull away.

But Gilbert already has his phone out, holding it in the air. It makes a faux camera-shutter sound. Sam and Frank separate, attempting to cover themselves. Gilbert's phone makes one more shutter sound, and he smiles, turns, goes to his Hummer, and drives away.

Chapter Nineteen

It's Saturday, and I'm working 9-5 with Tommy, who's freaking out. We're in the warehouse, piling boxes from the overstock racks onto our carts.

He fumbles a case of granola bars, dropping it, and sits on his cart. He puts his head in his hands and starts to cry.

"Hey, Tommy, it's okay, you know." I pat him twice on the back. "The sun's not going to explode. It really isn't. There's no science to support that. Okay?"

He takes a Kleenex from his pocket and blows his nose.

I say, "Why are you here today, anyway? If you really think the world's ending, why didn't you just skip work?"

"My parents made me come. They don't believe me—they say I just have too much free time." He shakes his head. "No one believes. We're all going to die at any moment, and I feel like I'm the only one who knows."

"Get up, Tommy. Come on. Focus on the overstock."

He gets up and kicks the box of granola bars under the racks. "What's the point in putting food on the shelves that no one's going to eat? I need to use the washroom." He turns and runs up the stairs.

Donovan doesn't think Tommy will be a Christian for much longer. He figures once the world fails to end, Tommy will abandon the faith to search for another belief system from which to extract self-worth. "Right now he thinks he's some kind of prophet," Donovan said. "When he finds out he's not, he'll find another religion—my money's on Buddhism."

I take out a couple more cartloads of overstock. After the second one, I pause at Ralph's desk to jot down an idea for a short story. Gilbert falls from above, landing nearby and scaring the shit out of me. I shout.

"Hey," he says.

I look up. "Did you just jump from the top step?"

"Yeah."

"Um, did you break any bones?"

"Nah."

"Why did you do that?"

"Practice."

"For what?"

"Landing—life's most important skill. Wanna take a break?"

I punch out, and we go outside to lean against the bike rack. Gilbert takes out a joint and a lighter. I ask him not to smoke it here, since I'd rather not smell like weed for the rest of my shift.

"Chill. Neither of us has to worry about getting fired anymore." He flicks the lighter and inhales.

"You mean you don't have to worry."

"Neither of us. We both saw Frank with Sam."

"You're the one blackmailing him, Gilbert. Not me."

Gilbert told me that when he visited Frank the morning after, it wasn't necessary to mention what we witnessed. He merely said he wanted back on the schedule—along with another raise.

"You're the store's hardest worker, Sheldon," Gilbert says. "You're telling me if Frank tried to fire you right now, you wouldn't bring up what we saw?"

"That's what I'm telling you. I wouldn't do that. What we saw is Frank's personal business. It has nothing to do with Spend Easy."

"What if you had three kids and a wife to support, in a tight job market? Would you let him fire you, then?"

"What are you getting at?"

"Just answer the question. Would you let him fire you if it meant your kids might go hungry?"

"God, I don't know. Why are you asking that?"

"I just think it's important for you to realize something. If you don't believe in God, then morality is about one thing: consequences. That's it. If you can shed your morality and escape the consequences, you win. But if you constantly obsess over doing the right thing, your options are restricted, and you'll get left behind. As for me, I'm running a business."

"What business?"

"Selling dope, duh. I'm thinking about expanding."

"What time is it?"

He checks his cell phone. "12:06."

"Shit. My break ended four minutes ago."

Gilbert chuckles. "Eventually you'll learn to relax."

*

My living room ceiling needs to be repaired, if not replaced. There's a huge bulge near the light fixture. I told my landlord, and he said he'd fix it soon. But that's what he told Sam about the toilet.

After Gilbert ran off with his blackmail pictures, I didn't stick around to chat. I went back to my apartment right away, and put buckets under the leaks. I haven't spoken to Sam since.

I did see him once, as I was arriving home from a shift— silhouetted behind the curtains in his living room.

The book he gave me, *Crow*, was lying on the coffee table when the leak started. A couple inches of water accumulated in one of the buckets, and I accidentally knocked *Crow* right into it.

The last poem I'd read was "A Horrible Religious Error", on page 37.

I left it to dry on the kitchen counter, but Marcus Brutus leaped up and tore it to shreds.

I have no problem with Sam's sexual preference. That's his business. But I don't like that he didn't tell me.

Gilbert told me Sam's sexuality is the reason he doesn't talk to anyone in the family. He came out of the closet a few years ago, and when he did, everyone shunned him. The Ryans are mostly Catholics, Gilbert says, and now the only one who'll talk to Sam is his cousin, the marijuana farmer.

I asked Gilbert if the cousin's outcast too, for growing weed, and he told me no—he still gets invited to family dinners.

*

Gilbert calls, and tells me to put my jacket on because he's hiking to the top of Foresail Bluff with Paul and Donovan, and I'm invited.

"That's your plan for Saturday night?" I say. "Trudge through the snow and freeze your ass off on a cliff? Isn't it, like, a two-hour hike?"

"10 minutes, the way we go."

"All right. I'm in, I guess."

The only trail I know of leading to the top starts at the beach below, and winds back and forth up the steep slopes. But Gilbert drives us through a subdivision, Eminem booming out the open windows, and stops at a dead-end in front of a huge pile of rocks. Donovan takes out a bag of weed and starts rolling a joint on top of a CD case.

"Do you smoke?" I ask Paul.

"Every now and then. You?"

I shake my head.

We wade in through the snow, which is knee-deep in parts. My jeans are soon soaked. It's a cloudless January night, and the stars are brighter here, without streetlamps. They provide enough light to walk by.

"I guess it's safe to say the sun isn't going to explode," I say.

"It's only 11," Gilbert says. "There's still time."

We reach the cliff. The view is nice: a sea of lights on the left, a sea of water on the right. Donovan takes out the joint, holds it up, and says, "To Gilbert's restoration to Spend Easy." He lights it, takes a couple puffs, and passes it to Gilbert, who does the same.

Gilbert holds it out to me.

I take it, and hold it in front of my eyes. Donovan rolled it well—his joint looks almost factory-produced, like a cigarette. I notice my hand is shaking a little.

"Don't suck from it," Gilbert says. "Breathe it in. And hold the smoke in your lungs."

I inhale, breathing deep, and hold my breath for five seconds. I exhale.

I inhale again, holding it for 10 this time, and exhale.

I inhale—

"Sheldon?"

"Yeah?" I croak.

"You're bogarting the joint, dude."

"Sorry." I pass it to Paul.

I look out over the water. There's a ship passing in front of Chime Island. It seems so small and fragile, from up here. One rip in its hull—that's all it would take to bring it down.

"Hey," I say. "If you could choose how the world ended, what would it be?"

"Judgment Day," Donovan says. "Obviously."

"Giant meteor," Paul says. "Same way the dinosaurs went. Coming down right here in front of us, into the water." He gestures. "Quick and easy. And we'd have a great view."

"What about you, Gilbert?"

"Natural causes."

"That's not very specific."

"I know. What about you? What would you pick?"

"Stoned to death."

That didn't make any sense. But we all laugh.

Paul takes out a hacky sack. We play Killer, in which you have to kick the sack into the air once, and then, as it falls back down, kick it at someone. If you hit your target, and he fails to kick it again before it hits the ground, he's dead.

Our eyes have adjusted to the darkness. There's just enough light.

I haven't played much hacky sack, but I'm better than I expected. We're all doing well. We barely speak. Paul handles the ball best, but doesn't go for many kills. Gilbert dodges well. And I save myself several times—sometimes in spectacular fashion, like when Gilbert tries to kill me and the hacky sack grazes off my shoulder, ricocheting into the air. I turn, follow it with my eyes, and intercept with my foot, sending it back to Donovan, who kicks it at Paul. I had no idea my reflexes were that good.

Gilbert kills Donovan, and a couple minutes later, the game ends when Paul sends the sack speeding toward Gilbert. He dodges, and the hacky sack sails over the cliff.

"That was awesome," Donovan says. "The whole thing."

"We'll never recreate it," Paul says.

We return to the Hummer. I check the time—we were only gone for 30 minutes, but it felt like hours.

Gilbert puts the car in drive.

"Wait," I say. "What are you doing?"

He glances at me in the rearview mirror. "Driving." The Hummer moves forward.

"You can't—you're stoned."

"I can, actually."

"Stop the car."

He brakes suddenly, and we're all jerked forward. "What?" he says.

"You're stoned, Gilbert. You're impaired. You can't drive."

"Six years of driving stoned say different. You need to calm down, now, Sheldon. The weed is making you paranoid."

"I'm not being paranoid. You could kill someone."

"Jesus, Sheldon. What did you expect? Did you think we'd sit in the car and wait to be sober?"

"Can't we just listen to music for a while?"

"We could. But we're not going to."

"Well, I'm walking, then."

"Bye."

"You're going to make me walk to my apartment? From here?"

"I'm not making you do anything."

I hesitate. "Fine," I say. "Bye." I open my door.

"See ya, Sheldon," Donovan says.

I get out. It feels even colder than before. The Hummer drives away, and I stand there, watching it go.

I start walking.

Chapter Twenty

Theresa and I were the only patients in the ward with any interest in spending time in the small garden outside. We went out there whenever we could. The nurses wouldn't always unlock the door for us—I didn't know what set of rules governed these decisions, and neither of us asked. Despite how strong she seemed, I think Theresa generally felt as defeated as I did. I got the impression that it helped her to help me, but I never said that, out of fear she would stop.

We sat out there when allowed, side by side on the concrete bench. Through the chain-link fence we could see a busy road, and beyond that was the university.

"That's where I'm headed," she said. "When I get out."

"You're starting a degree?"

"Finishing one. Linguistics. I have a year and a half left, anyway. Being in here set me behind—I was in the middle of a summer semester when everything fell apart." She sighed. "I won't graduate with my best friend, now."

During that first meal together, I told Theresa why I was in the psych ward. It seemed fair—she'd told me her reason.

She asked why I wanted to kill myself. I told her I had no money, and no friends.

"Tell me the real reason," she said.

But I wasn't ready.

"Sam says I'm looking healthier," I said now, in the garden. "I told him I have you to thank."

"Don't tell people that," she said.

I looked in her eyes. I always had so many words for her, but most of them went unsaid.

"God, Sheldon. You want to kiss me, don't you?"

I opened my mouth.

She took my hand. "I like you, Sheldon. A lot. But when I leave this place I don't want anything connecting me to it. I don't want to talk to anyone I met here, and I don't want you telling people you owe me anything. I don't want you ever to mention my name. Okay?"

"Okay," I said. And I sat there, silent, barely breathing, dreading the moment she would release my hand.

Eventually, she did.

*

Gilbert and I get off work at 10, drive to my apartment, and smoke a joint in the shed, like we have the last four nights. Then we go inside and watch videos on his phone. We're in the middle of watching a talking dog question his owner about the contents of the fridge when Gilbert gets a text message from Kerrin: "hey babe where r u". We finish watching the video, then he texts her back.

"How are things going with you guys?" I say.

He puts down the phone. "Pretty shitty."

"Really?"

"Yeah, I just broke up with her."

"Why is she calling you 'babe', then?"

"Because I just broke up with her. In my reply to her text."
He gets another message.

"What's she saying?"

"'OMG babe why? What's wrong?'" He starts texting again.

"What are you saying?"

"That I cheated on her." He turns off the phone.

"Why are you breaking up with her?"

"The sex no longer compensates for how annoying she is.
Anyway. Donovan tells me you wrote a novel. Can I read it?"

"Sure. It's not a novel, though. It's only 50 pages."

"Go get it."

"Right now? It's on my computer."

"I'll read it off the screen, then."

We go into my bedroom, and I open "The King of Hearts".
Gilbert puts it on autoscroll and leans back in the chair, hands
behind his head.

"Can you read that fast?"

"I can if you shut up."

I lie back on my bed and watch him. On the second page, he
chuckles.

"What'd you just read?"

"Shut up."

It takes him 15 minutes, during which he laughs, grunts,
points out grammatical errors, and yawns. When he's finished,
he closes the document. "Have you let anyone else read this?"

"No. Why? Do you like it?"

"Some parts are pretty funny. But I'm pretty sure you're supposed to try harder to hide your source of inspiration."

"What do you mean?"

"Come on, Sheldon. It's pretty obvious the girl in the story is Capriana."

"No she's not."

"It's fine, Sheldon. I think fiction writing is a great way to work out all your angsty emotions. You get to drag her name through the dirt, and she has no avenue for rebuttal. You make her look like a complete slut."

"First of all, Gilbert, Capriana is a slut. Second of all, the story isn't about her, so shut up."

"You don't have enough data to call her that."

"Whatever."

"One piece of advice: I wouldn't let anyone else read this. It would be social suicide."

*

Since his coup, Gilbert has made the break room his domain. I'm sitting up there with him, taking the first break of my shift, when Ernie comes up holding two coffees. "I bought you one, Gilbert," he says, his eyes on the table, a tremulous smile on his lips.

"Thanks," Gilbert says, and starts slurping from it.

"Where's mine?" I say.

Ernie laughs a single syllable and sits down, as far away from us as he can get. He smiles again at Gilbert. "So, you're such a good worker that Frank hired you again. Wow."

Now that he's back, Gilbert answers the occasional page, and puts out the occasional cartload, to maintain appearances. Other than that, he gets high and sits in the break room, playing video games on his phone.

"Appears that way," he says. "You seem nervous, Ernest."

"I'm just a little tired. I went for a 10 kilometre bike ride before I came in."

"In January?"

"Yeah. Um, on my exercise bike."

"Right. Are you sure you're not hiding something?"

"Oh, yes, I'm sure. I have nothing to hide, because I don't care what anyone thinks."

"Really? No one? Not even Frank?"

"That's right, no one."

"Well, why don't you take off your pants?"

"What?"

"If you don't care what anyone thinks, why are you wearing pants? It's nice and warm in the break room, and your pants look like they're pretty tight. Why not take them off? At least till the end of your break."

Ernie gives a high-pitched chuckle. "You're so crazy, Gilbert."

"Not really. If you don't care what people think, then there's no reason to be wearing pants right now. See, I'll take mine off." Gilbert stands up, unfastens his belt, and drops his pants, stepping out of them. He leans his chair back against the wall. "This is great. Won't you join me, Ernest? Who gives a shit, right?"

Without moving back from the table, Ernie slowly unzips his fly and slips off his pants, leaving them bunched around his ankles. His face is red.

"They aren't off yet."

Ernie kicks them off his ankles.

Gilbert laughs and puts his back on. "You do care what people think. So much you just pantsed yourself to prove a point." He stands up, bends over, and grabs Ernie's pants from under the table, reaching into a pocket and pulling out a phone.

"Hey!" Ernie says. He stays sitting.

Gilbert taps on the screen a few times. "There's the video you used to get me fired, Ernest. Delete." He taps a few more times. "Looks like you sent the video to Frank right from your phone, meaning you probably didn't upload it to your computer. Meaning this email likely contains your last copy of it. Delete." He tosses the phone on the table in front of Ernie. "I wouldn't recommend trying that again." He drops Ernie's pants into the garbage, picks up his coffee, and leaves the room.

*

Weed gives me weird dreams.

Tonight, I dream Frank and Eric are conducting demented experiments in a laboratory hidden deep inside Spend Easy. They've come up with a method of crossbreeding animals with vegetables. And then their creations escape into the aisles.

I'm fronting Aisle Two when a cross between a cat and a tomato scurries under my feet. I step back, disgusted. It turns around, looks at me, and opens its mouth to meow. But no meow comes out. It makes a growing sound, instead. I've never heard anything grow before.

The cat has shiny red tomato-skin, and green stalks for ears. When it moves, its joints crackle.

"Brute?" I say.

I turn around, and Frank and Eric are walking toward me. Behind them, Aisle Two stretches into eternity.

"Do you like him?" Eric says. "We've been working on these for some time. Soon, every household will have one."

"It's perfect," someone says behind me. I turn again, and there's Gilbert, the tomato cat rubbing against his leg. He picks it up, and the growing sound gets louder. He brings it to his face, as if to nuzzle it with his nose.

He bites into the torso.

The creature writhes in his grasp, trying desperately to escape. Gilbert takes another bite. The juices run down his chin. The cat's vegetable flesh glistens wetly.

Gilbert smiles.

Chapter Twenty-One

I never want to be high at Spend Easy, so I don't smoke if I'm working later. I'm tired from being out late with Gilbert and Donovan almost every night, though, and I have to push myself to hit my usual case count numbers. It doesn't help that Ralph's relying on me more than ever, now that Gilbert's renewed his commitment to slacking off, Donovan's working a lot less, and Tommy quit.

Tommy gave Ralph two weeks' notice soon after the sun failed to explode. Apparently, Ralph told him he could have his job back any time—probably because Grocery's so understaffed. During his final shifts, Tommy leans against his cart a lot, staring into space and sighing. You'd think not dying would cheer him up.

I ask Paul why he hasn't been out with us again. He says he smokes pot pretty rarely—every few months or so.

"Cassandra's sure surprised you started smoking," he says.

"Cassandra? You talk to her?"

"Yeah, a bit. She's been reading my book."

"You know she has a boyfriend, right?" I don't like the idea of her and Paul talking.

"I do. We're just hanging out."

"Be careful, Paul."

He shakes his head. "I think you have a chip on your shoulder when it comes to her. She told me you guys have a history. Cassandra's had a rough life, you know. Her mother walked out on her and her Dad when she was young. Never came back."

"I'm aware."

My Mom's dead, and I never knew my father. But I'm not about to try and convince Paul my life is sadder than Cassandra's. I drop it.

*

Gilbert proposes we go to a Chinese buffet, to celebrate his renewed dominance at Spend Easy. Days off are getting pretty scarce for me. Last week Eric poached Matt to work in Meat, leaving Ralph even more understaffed. I've been putting in 50-hour weeks.

Matt seemed pretty bewildered at the transfer. "Why does he want a slacker like me working for him?" he asked me, but I assumed it was a rhetorical question.

It does seem like Matt would fit in well with the other Meat employees. He's quiet, and, like them, doesn't seem to have much confidence. Although, compared with a couple of Eric's workers, Matt's downright chatty.

On the way to the Chinese restaurant, Gilbert suggests we smoke a joint before eating. "The food will taste way better."

"We'll only be in there an hour. You'll be too stoned to drive."

"Not after an all-you-can-eat buffet, man. Eating kills your high. And I'm gonna eat a lot."

"All right."

So Gilbert rolls a joint after we park. It's a big one—he uses two cigarette papers. It takes us over 10 minutes to smoke, and on my way across the parking lot I decide the universe is exactly the way it needs to be.

The restaurant's only half full, and the hostess tells us to sit wherever we want. We take a table close to the food. I pile my first plate with egg rolls, chicken chow mein, spring rolls, and wonton chips. And that's just to start.

Gilbert gets a plate of fried chicken wings. He sticks one in his mouth, and when he removes it, the meat is gone. "Being tasty is a poor evolutionary strategy," he says.

"I'm really stoned," I manage to say through a masticated egg roll.

"That's perfectly consistent with what we know of body chemistry."

"Yeah? They teach you that in university?"

"Most philosophy students are acquainted with marijuana's effects." He picks up another wing.

"Why don't you finish your degree?"

He shrugs. "University isn't the only path to success, despite what we're led to believe. For a lot of people, it's the path to a fast food career." His phone rings. He takes it out, looks at the screen, and answers it. "Hello? Hello? Donovan? Hello? God damn." He hangs up. "Anyway. Universities are no longer these exclusive bastions of academic merit—they're just businesses. Nobody fails out of university anymore, because a failed student isn't worth any money. It's become a culture of lenience."

"Really?"

He nods. "It's the way of the world. Slackers prosper." We eat five plates each. I take a lot on my last one, and I struggle to get it down—they charge you extra here if you leave food on your plate. Gilbert pays for both of us, and we go out to the Hummer.

"I booked a hotel room for tonight," he says, "A bunch of us are partying there and going downtown after. You in?"

"Yeah." I'm not working till 2:00 tomorrow—the hangover should subside by then. "Will they mind us all drinking in the room?"

"Probably. The best part of partying in a hotel is seeing how drunk you can get before they kick you out."

Chapter Twenty-Two

When I enter the lobby, Gilbert's waiting at the front desk for an extra room key, so people can get back in if they leave. I lean against the desk next to him. The receptionist isn't in sight.

There's a sign on the desk that reads, "We are ladies and gentlemen serving ladies and gentlemen."

"We'll soon cure them of that delusion," Gilbert says.

The receptionist comes out with the extra key. "Who's this?" he says, meaning me.

"My friend. He just got off the plane from Bangkok. He's staying in my room, and I'm driving him home in the morning."

"Will you be drinking alcohol?"

"Excuse me," Gilbert says, "I find your questions invasive. This is my second stay at your establishment, and I may become a regular customer. Is this how you treat all your potential regulars?"

"My apologies." He passes Gilbert the key.

"Thank you. Have a pleasant evening."

"You as well."

Gilbert leads me to the third floor and unlocks room 370. Inside, Donovan is crouched on the desk, staring straight ahead, the backs of his hands resting on his hips.

I walk over to him. He shows no sign of registering my presence. "Hey, Donovan."

"I'm a gargoyle," he says in a low croak.

Gilbert shakes his head. "Man, he's messed up. He's taken, like, four different drugs since he got here. You wanna smoke a joint?"

"Is this a smoking room?"

"Doesn't matter. We're not supposed to smoke pot either way. It's non-smoking, if you really want to know."

We sit on one of the beds and light up. Gilbert passes me the joint, and as I'm inhaling, Donovan starts making bird noises. I pass it back to Gilbert.

Gilbert inhales, and speaks with the smoke still in his lungs, sounding a little like a gargoyle himself. "You want some, Donovan?"

Donovan coos.

"Come get it."

Donovan croaks his displeasure.

Gilbert sighs, gets up, and holds the joint to Donovan's lips. He inhales until Gilbert withdraws it, which is quite a while. After that, he's silent.

Gilbert gets a text from someone in the lobby, complaining the receptionist won't let them go up to the room. We go back down to find a guy and a girl, both unknown to me, each holding bags from the liquor store.

"What appears to be the problem?" Gilbert says.

"I wasn't born yesterday," the receptionist says. "You're clearly hosting some sort of gathering."

"Impressive," Gilbert says. "Not only were you born before yesterday, but you've apparently developed some dynamic powers of perception since. You're correct. We are indeed gathering."

"And you're drinking alcohol."

"That's right. Is that against hotel policy? I was under the impression policy endorsed it, given the mini fridge bristles with booze."

"You're allowed to drink. You're not allowed to have a party."

"I haven't said anything about a party."

"What are you doing, then?"

"I find your constant inquiries into our personal affairs distressing, and I'm considering relaying them to your manager. But if you must know, we're holding a meeting about starting a YouTube collective, in hopes of generating advertising revenue with which to supplement our incomes. During this meeting, we will determine the type of content we want to produce. Will that be enough private information?"

"I was asking in a professional capacity."

"I should certainly hope so. Come, lady and gentlemen."

The hotel room fills up quickly. Someone brings a CD player, and turns it up really loud. A minute into "Paper Thin Walls" by Modest Mouse, a guest from one of the neighbouring rooms comes over and complains about the volume. Gilbert puts an arm around his shoulder, offering him a beer and a joint simultaneously. He stops complaining.

There are over 20 people here, which is a lot for a small room with two twin-sized beds and a desk. Donovan remains perched, motionless, which was weird at first but now seems like a valuable civic service. He's conserving land.

With Donovan in gargoyle mode and Gilbert focusing mostly on the female population, I have no one to talk to. I focus on drinking, with the hope it will give me something to say. No luck so far.

Eventually Donovan comes down off the desk and starts arranging lines of coke on the bedside table. He takes out a 100 dollar bill, snorts a line, and hands the bill to the guy next to him.

Gilbert calls across the room. "Donovan! Delete my number from your phone!"

Donovan looks hurt. "But we're friends. We should be in each other's Contacts."

"Our friendship is being taxed by the fact that your phone keeps pocket dialing mine. If it happens again, I'm throwing it in a lake. Yours, I mean."

Donovan sees me, and seizes my shoulder. He peers into my eyes as though he lost something in there. "I have a rule," he says. "Never snort coke unless you have a 100 dollar bill to do it with."

"Why?" I say.

"So you have enough money to buy more. Duh."

I go to the washroom, where people are giggling behind the drawn shower curtain. "I need to piss," I say.

"Thanks for notifying us," someone says, and there's more giggling.

"Can you leave?"

"No. But we won't look."

"Fine."

I unzip my fly and glance behind me. Two people are peering around the curtain. They see me and withdraw from view, giggling.

As I wash my hands, I hear someone flick a lighter, and then I smell pot. "Hey," I say. "Can I get in?"

"Sure. But I get to sit on you." A hand pulls the shower curtain across, revealing a girl sitting on a guy at one end of the tub, and Cassandra sitting at the other end. She's the one who spoke.

"You smoke?" I say.

"Yep."

"Since when?"

"Grade 10."

"You smoked pot in grade 10 and I didn't know?"

"Yeah." She shrugs. "I didn't want to tell you. You were so innocent."

"Were you ever high around me?"

"I've been high pretty much constantly since I started." The other two laugh. One of them passes Cassandra the joint.

"I don't think I'll be able to process this until I'm also high," I say.

She stands up. "Sit down. Under me."

I do, and she hands me the joint.

"So," the guy says. "How do you two know each other?"

"School," Cassandra says. "But we work together, too."

"Where?"

"In a grocery store."

"What's that like?"

I adopt a British accent. "The grocery store is fascinating on every level. It even has its own unique vernacular. To describe a fellow employee as 'sick' is to suggest his work ethic is such that it may be indicative of a mental illness. To praise another's work as 'best kind' is to say that either the task is superbly done, or the task matters so little that whether it is done well makes no difference whatsoever."

Cassandra laughs. "What the hell, Sheldon? You're so weird."

Gilbert enters the washroom. "The time of our exodus is come. Hotel management has been contacted, and police involvement has been threatened. We're going downtown." He points at me. "You're baked out of your tree. How do you expect to dance with these fine ladies in this state? You need to drink more."

"I don't dance."

"Don't worry," Cassandra says. "He'll dance."

"Good girl. Now. Out of that tub."

*

I don't get home till 4 AM, and I wake up 10 minutes before my shift begins, hungover. I spent the night dancing and doing shots with Cassandra. She's much better than me at both those things. At the end of the night we smoked another joint in an alley, and I vomited.

A new hire is waiting for me by the punch clock. "Ralph told me to wait till you got in. He wants you to train me. He told me you're the hardest worker."

"Oh. Sorry I'm late."

I show him how to front, and then I start on the overstock. Working hungover actually isn't that bad. I feel kind of fantastic, actually. Sure, my stomach seems likely to empty itself with-

out warning—possibly on a customer—and my head feels like
it's gone a round in the cardboard compactor. But these symp-
toms are accompanied by an unbridled optimism I haven't felt
since I first decided I want to be a writer.

I keep remembering how it felt to put my hands on Cassandra's waist.

Gilbert starts at 5:00, and so does Tommy, who's working his
last shift. This prospect hasn't lightened his mood any.

"I used to feel important," he says to us. "Like it was my role
to warn people. For over a year, I tried to convince everyone
they needed to stop putting off the important stuff. Now,
though—now I just feel dumb." He sighs. "My parents are sending me to see a counsellor."

Gilbert places a hand on Tommy's shoulder. "You need a new
apocalypse."

Tommy takes his eyes off the floor. "Huh?"

"Come up to the break room with me."

Not wanting to miss this, I decide to take my first break, too.

"The sun won't explode for billions of years," Gilbert says
once we're all seated. "But the world will end, and likely a lot
sooner than later. As in, really soon."

Tommy's barely daring to breathe. "Really?"

"Sure. There are plenty of doomsday scenarios to choose
from. You have the mundane ones, like oil depletion. You
know—all the conventional sources are exploited, we're scram-
bling to meet demand, alternate energy sources aren't even close
to replacing it, yada yada yada. Then you have the slightly more
exciting apocalypses, like globetrotting antibiotic-resistant vi-
ruses, hitching airplanes everywhere and killing billions of peo-

ple. But I think you need something you can really sink your teeth into."

Tommy's rapt. I kind of wish I'd brought something to snack on.

"Check this out," Gilbert says. "Total. Machine. Takeover. Within no more than a few decades. All right? Some futurists predict we'll have AIs as smart as us by 2035. Computing power doubles every two years, so it's only a matter of time. But it's not just about artificial intelligence. This takeover started thousands of years ago."

"What do you mean?" Tommy says.

"As technology advances, humans get less advanced. It's the way it's always been. We've been slowly handing over our talents to machines for a long time. It started with the invention of writing, which saved us the trouble of remembering things. As the use of text became widespread, our memories got worse.

"We invented calculators—very useful, but we're not as good at math as we were. Now we have Google, and we're working on cars that will drive themselves. Soon we'll have apps that tell us how to behave in order to attain a preselected personality type. By the time smart machines arrive, humanity will be a shade of what it was, with only a fraction of the capability it started with. It will be laughably easy for AIs to take control. Nature gave us intelligence, but we didn't know what to do with it. So, we're giving it to machines."

"Will they destroy us?"

"Maybe. It's impossible to tell. We can't predict what will happen in a world with beings smarter than we are."

Tommy stands up. He's smiling. "Thank you, Gilbert."

"I haven't told you everything. And the only way you'll learn the rest is if you continue working here."

After that, Tommy's mood improves dramatically. He attacks the overstock racks with gusto, and I actually hear him whistling as he pushes his first cartload onto the sales floor. As for why Gilbert bothered, my guess is he's consolidating power—ensuring Frank can never threaten his dominance again.

By eight, I've run out of positive thoughts about my hangover. I feel dragged out, kind of depressed, and worried I'll fall over if I don't take my second break right now. I grab a bag of chips and trudge up to the break room.

I open the door to find Cassandra and Theresa sitting side-by-side at the table.

"Hey Sheldon," Cassandra says. "Have you met our new cashier, Theresa? She's officially awesome."

Theresa looks at me, stricken, and I expect my expression's similar. Cassandra's smile fades a little, and her gaze drifts from my face to Theresa's.

I walk over, hand extended. "Nice to meet you."

"Nice to meet you," Theresa says, her voice little more than a whisper.

Chapter Twenty-Three

Cassandra visits my apartment, and the first thing she does is stand in the living room, hands on her hips, and ask me the last time I cleaned it.

"Um, it's been a while, I guess."

"We're cleaning it. Right now."

"Can we get high first?"

We go out to the shed. Cassandra sits on the stool near the window and takes out a joint. "This always puts me in the mood for cleaning," she says, lighting it. "Makes it feel like an accomplishment."

I shake my head. "I still can't believe you smoke pot."

"Could say the same about you." She shrugs. "I have fun, being high. It makes pretty much anything fun."

She holds out the joint, and I take it.

"Remember how down on myself I used to get?" she says. "In junior high?"

"Kind of."

"Well, when I'm stoned, I criticize myself less. It's nice." She takes the joint back. "You and Theresa sure had a moment in the break room, the other day. What was that about?"

"I don't know. We had a moment?"

"You think she's pretty, don't you?"

I don't say anything. Every answer seems like the wrong one.

We go back inside, and Cassandra pours some Mr. Clean in a bucket and fills it with hot water. Then she starts wiping down every surface in the house. She directs me to clean out my fridge, and throw away the stuff that's gone bad.

When we finish that, she puts the bucket of water on the coffee table, and we sit on the couch. "This is a bigger job than I thought," she says.

Marcus Brutus jumps up and puts his head in the bucket. He thinks better of drinking from it, though, and jumps back down.

Cassandra leans forward and picks up *Cat's Cradle*, which is sitting next to the bucket. She opens to the last page and begins reading out loud.

"God, Cassandra. Not this. You still do this?"

"Can't help it." She giggles. "Get ready for spoilers."

I put my hands over my ears, but she pulls them away, holding the book open on the coffee table with her foot and shouting the ending.

"Thanks for that," I say when it's over.

"Any time."

"Not much point finishing that book, now."

"Maybe I wasn't really reading it—maybe I made that up." She looks at me. She has these huge brown eyes—they're what I've always found most attractive about her. "It could be worse. I could have told you that Frodo really does end up destroying the One Ring."

"I didn't know you read *Lord of the Rings*."

"Of course I have."

I narrow my eyes. "I'm learning a lot about you, lately."

That's when I kiss her, and she kisses me back. And we kiss for a long time.

*

I make vegetarian lasagna for the express purpose of wrapping a healthy portion in cellophane and bringing it up to Sam. We haven't spoken since Gilbert and I walked in on him having sex with Frank, so I'm expecting this to be at least a little awkward. When he opens the door, he doesn't look very different. He's fully clothed, instead of wearing just pajamas. I guess that's new.

"Hey," I say.

"Hi."

"I brought lasagna."

"I see. Tell me, what am I supposed to think, when you find out I'm gay and then don't visit for weeks?"

"You didn't visit me, either."

"I'm pissed off. You let my demonic nephew into my home."

"He followed me, Sam. The ceiling was leaking! I didn't know you'd be—you know—"

"Having sex with your boss?"

"Um—"

"Do you know how thoroughly that asshole has destroyed Frank? He lies in my arms and cries, out of fear that Gilbert will tell his family the truth. Of course, it's pointless telling you that—I doubt a man crying earns much sympathy from you."

"Jesus Christ, I don't care that you're gay, Sam."

"I'm not convinced." He closes the door.

I stare at it for a while. Then I go back to my apartment.

I want to smash something. I want to write something scathing.

I don't, though. I unwrap the lasagna and put it in the oven.

Chapter Twenty-Four

The Professor was a patient the day I arrived at the psych ward, and he was a patient the day I left. In between, I didn't detect much of a change in him. I wasn't the keenest observer at the time, preoccupied with my own imbalances as I was. But going over my memories now, I think I'm right.

One day he emerged from the TV room and walked over to where Sam and I sat at one of the cafeteria tables. "Infomercials," he said to us, still standing. "What an excellent guide to what Western society is really about: playing house while the world burns."

Sam and I looked at each other.

"Some people here are trying to maintain a positive attitude," Sam said. "Do you think maybe you should keep those thoughts to yourself?"

The Professor nodded. "Positive thinking is an excellent way to overlook the atrocities of our age." He turned and walked toward the rooms.

"That guy starts to grate on you after a while," Sam said.

The Professor stopped—I think he overheard Sam. He shouted: "Did you know mental illness affects one in four people? Huh? Did you know that, asshole?"

His chin was trembling slightly. Sam had no reply, and neither did I.

The Professor turned and walked away.

*

"Do not kill insects," Tommy says to me 10 minutes into one shift. "There may be hope for you if you spare insects."

"What are you talking about?"

"We will be as bugs to our computer overlords. How can we beg their mercy if we are not ourselves merciful?"

"You know, Tommy, it'll be pretty easy to prevent AIs from taking over. We just won't give them appendages."

"What?"

"Appendages. We won't give them arms, or legs."

Tommy scratches his head. "I need to talk to Gilbert."

It's Sunday, and I'm working on changing the displays with Casey, who's darting around even faster than usual. Today is his 20th birthday, but he isn't relaxing. He's exasperated by Grocery's return to slackness. Tommy's actually working pretty hard since Gilbert told him about our future robot overlords, but Gilbert and Donovan are even worse than before.

Right now Casey is barreling past Aisle Three, pushing a cart laden with sacks of flour from one of last week's displays. I'm standing just outside the warehouse doors with my cart, and Casey's waving at me with his left hand as he pushes with his right. "Move, Sheldon! I'm coming through!"

There's an elderly woman walking slowly out of Aisle Five, staring at a bottle of Pepsi in one hand and a bottle of Diet Pepsi in the other. Comparing their nutritional information.

"Casey, watch out!"

He stares at me, his face screwed up. "What?"

I start around my cart—to deflect Casey's, or to push her out of the way, I don't know which—but I'm too late. Casey hits her waist-level, knocking her into her shopping cart, which spins around and rolls toward Dairy. She falls to the floor, and I hear something inside her break. Five bags of flour tumble from Casey's cart. Two of them land on her, and one of them splits open, spilling flour onto her blouse.

I'm standing, frozen, with my hands outstretched and my mouth open. Slowly, I close it.

Casey's still clutching the handle of his cart, his eyes wide, his face as white as the flour coating the fallen customer.

She lies there, motionless.

Chapter Twenty-Five

Cassandra and I see a movie at the theatre in the mall, but it's kind of disappointing. "It seemed way better when I watched the trailer," she says as we leave.

I didn't eat half my popcorn—I put way too much artificial butter on it. I offer it to her, but she doesn't want it either, so I toss it.

We re-enter the mall to find Sean sitting on a bench, his arms spread across its back. When he sees us, he points. "How was the movie, kids?"

I hear Cassandra's breath catch, but she tries to act natural. "Not so great," she says.

"And how've you been, Sheldon? Haven't seen you since the New Year."

"I've missed you."

"I'll bet. Tell me—do you think you actually have a chance with her?"

I don't answer.

"Sean—" Cassandra says.

"Don't get me wrong," Sean says. "She likes you. Loves you, even. Always has. Back in high school, she never shut up about you. Even since we've been together, I've sometimes wondered if she loves you even more than she loves me."

"That's not true," Cassandra says.

"So you gotta be asking yourself. If she feels that way about you, why didn't you end up together? I mean, you met Cassandra long before I did. Why didn't she give you a shot, instead of jerking you around for years like she did?"

I glance at Cassandra. "Give it up, Sean," she says.

"The reason Cassandra wasn't willing to even consider a relationship with you, Sheldon, was your complete lack of social status. She didn't use those words, of course. But I can tell you some words she did use. When I brought up how often she talked about you, and how she seemed to have feelings for you, know what she said? She said she'd never go out with you, because all her friends thought you were a loser." Sean smiles. "Now you know how much the 'love' between you means to her."

I look again at Cassandra, who won't meet my gaze.

"Come on, sweetheart," Sean says. "My car's outside. Let's get out of here before you make an even bigger fool of yourself. Sheldon can bus it back, the same way he got here."

They leave.

*

"How was your date?" Gilbert says.

"Gross—I keep getting bong water in my mouth."

"Don't inhale so hard."

I try again, and pass it to him. "It wasn't a date. She has a boyfriend." I don't feel like relating the particulars. How Sean showed up, and how, without Gilbert there to throw beer in his face, he made me look and feel like a piece of shit. I don't want to talk about that at all. I just want to get really stoned.

"Boyfriends are inconvenient," Gilbert says. "So, who paid for the movie?"

"Me."

"It wasn't a date, but you paid?"

"She offered to pay for herself, but I insisted."

"You're an idiot." He passes back the bong.

"I was being nice. I know it's old fashioned for the guy to get the tickets."

"It's not just that. You want to sleep with her, right? You want to have sex with Cassandra."

"Um—"

"Because if you buy her stuff all the time, it's kind of like paying installments on an expensive prostitute you might not even get to sleep with."

I lower the bong and look at him. "You live off screwing Frank. What does that make you?"

*

Frank's son, Randy, has been causing trouble for Gilbert.

He tells everyone at Spend Easy who'll listen that his Dad used to talk about firing Gilbert, but never mentions it anymore. It's odd to see Randy being so brazen about it—directly questioning Gilbert on why he's back to slacking off all the time, and openly asking the other employees what they know. No one stands up to Gilbert like this.

Obviously, Randy doesn't know what a stranglehold Gilbert has on this place. And I can understand why he's upset. According to Sam, Frank's been severely depressed. Randy must see that at home.

He asks Ernie what happened to the video showing Gilbert exiting the customer restroom with a girl, but Ernie lies to him, saying his phone crashed, and he lost it. The pants incident cowed Ernie pretty thoroughly. It doesn't take much.

"I know something's going on," Randy says to Gilbert in the warehouse, one day. "I plan to find out what."

Gilbert just nods.

Theresa seems to have meant what she said in the psych ward. She avoids all contact with me. I answered a couple of her pages, but when I did she treated me like a total stranger—not a glimmer of recognition. I've decided not to answer any more of them.

In Grocery, the same ritual unfolds that does whenever an attractive cashier is hired. "Damn," Gilbert says to me and Donovan in Aisle Two. "That body!" He makes a squeezing motion with his hands, and nudges Donovan. "You wanna do some premarital stuff to that, right?"

Casey tells me the woman he struck is in critical condition with a broken hip. The doctors are saying she's lucky to have survived, at her age. She must be a really sweet lady, because apparently during a moment of lucidity from the morphine she said she doesn't want to press charges.

"She was leaving the next day," Casey says. "To visit her sister. She was here buying groceries for the girl who was going to housesit for her." Casey sounds like he's on the verge of tears. "Her sister's sick with leukemia, Sheldon. And now she can't visit her, because she's in the hospital herself."

After he hit her, everyone in Grocery was required to watch a new safety video. There have been some catty comments made in the break room too, with Casey present.

"Why was I going so fast, Sheldon? Why do you and I kill ourselves out there, for minimum fucking wage? The customers eat either way, don't they?"

"Yeah," I say, "but that's not the point. It's about earning your salary. It's about doing a job because someone's paying you. That's all you were doing, Casey." It feels weak, but it's all I have.

"I guess so." He takes a deep breath. "I quit drinking coffee."

I've run into Matt in the break room twice since he started in Meat. The first time, I asked how he likes working for Eric. He just shrugged. There are dark spots under his eyes. I don't think he's been sleeping very well.

"I wouldn't want to work for him," I said. "I don't trust him, if you want to know the truth."

No reply.

The second time, I found Matt with a TV dinner in front of him. He was poking at it with his fork.

I tried to get him talking. He used to get pretty riled up whenever he thought anyone was gossiping about him, so I made something up. "I overheard one of the cashiers saying you have pretty bad body odour. She said you stink."

Matt nodded. "My break is over. I have to get back to work."

He stood, leaving most of the TV dinner.

*

Donovan calls, and invites me for a joint and a drive.

"Impaired driving, Donovan," I say. "Not a thing I endorse."

"Right. Well, let's get high and ride the bus around, then. We can get off periodically for buzz maintenance."

I have nothing better to do. We sit in the back of the bus with an earbud apiece, listening to music and not saying much. After an hour or so, at a seemingly random stop, Donovan takes back the earbud and puts away his phone. "Come on." He stands up.

"You wanna smoke some more?" I ask as we step off onto the sidewalk.

"Well, yeah," he says. "But also—that." He points across a nearby parking lot.

"A grocery store?"

"A superstore, man. Way bigger than Spend Easy. More than five aisles—like, 10, probably."

"And?"

"Must be different. You'd probably be just a number, working there. Just another cog. We could go in, ask them what it's like."

"If you want."

We smoke a bowl, and enter the store. This seems weird. I'm definitely letting him do the talking. When Donovan starts asking employees what it's like to have 10 aisles to stock, we're bound to look like huge stoners. I wonder if they'll throw us out.

"Hey," Donovan says when he finds an employee, in housewares.

"Hey, Donovan. You got more for us? We haven't even sold the last pound, yet."

"If I had more for you, do you think I'd come talk to you about it in the middle of the store? You dumbass."

The guy frowns. "Geez. Sorry."

"Did you know Randy Crawford when he worked here?"

The guy starts cutting open a box sitting on a nearby cart. "You're talking about Crohner, right?"

"Crohner? What does that mean?"

"Oh, he used to stay in the washroom for like a half hour at a time. We asked him why, and he told us he has Crohn's disease. After that, we called him Crohner. He was a weird guy, anyway."

"How did he react?" Donovan says.

"Some of the guys think he quit because of it."

"Wow. That's a stroke of luck, then."

He gives Donovan a strange look. "I guess so, man."

"Come on, Sheldon." We walk back through the store.

I'm trying to piece together what just happened. "How did you know Randy used to work here?"

"Gilbert found his résumé on file in Frank's office."

I stop walking.

Donovan returns my gaze, expressionless. "Gilbert wanted me to come here and dig up some compromising info on Randy. He told me to bring you."

"Why?"

"He wants you to see how we're doing things, now."

"We?"

"You know."

"So, you work for Gilbert now, or something?"

"I work for Frank. Frank works for Gilbert."

"What was that guy talking about, asking if you had more for him?"

He waits until we're outside to answer, and when he does, his voice is low.

"Gilbert has started distributing dope to stores all over the city."

"Why didn't he tell me?"

"Do you wanna help, or something? Wanna do what I'm doing—legwork?"

"No."

"Well, don't worry about it. Anyway, you've helped him in your own way."

"What are you talking about?"

"Without you, Gilbert never would have gotten proof Frank is gay. And when you started smoking his weed, he saw a healthy bump in sales. Did you know that? People think you're a good guy, Sheldon. When people hear you're smoking his product, they want to smoke it, too."

"You're full of shit."

"I'm really not." Donovan smiles. "Your endorsement meant money to him. You should embrace it. He got me a raise, and now he's giving me a cut of his profits. I bet he could make your life a little easier, too."

Chapter Twenty-Six

Gossip about Randy's disease spreads through Spend Easy in short order, along with his old nickname: Crohner. Nobody uses it to his face, as far as I know, but it's used whenever he's talked about, which is a lot. His quest for romance among the cashiers becomes a popular topic. Along with his frequent washroom breaks.

On a couple occasions, I witness the break room go silent when Randy enters. A lot of cashiers avoid him now. Before this, he was quirky. Now he's weird. It reminds me of high school.

There was already a lot of resentment toward Frank, and it required only a light nudge for some of that to trickle down to Randy. He would have had to be a politician to avoid it.

"Sheldon!"

I'm walking toward Spend Easy to work an evening shift when Cassandra calls out to me from the corner of the building. It's the corner where I found Brent smoking pot, so many months ago. When I walk over, Cassandra's doing the same.

"Aren't you worried you'll get caught?" I say.

"I've been smoking here before work for years."

I slide my hands into my pockets, glancing across the parking lot.

"Sorry about the other night," she says.

"It's fine, Cassandra. I wasn't cool enough to be with you. I get it."

"It was years ago, Sheldon. I was a stupid high school girl."

I nod. "And I was a stupid guy. Still am."

"No, you're not. You want a puff?"

"I'm working."

"Me too. Scared you won't be Ralph's favourite stock boy anymore?"

She holds the joint to my lips, and I inhale.

"Did Sean know we were hanging out?" I say. "Before he saw us together?"

"He knows now."

"What does he think?"

"He doesn't like it."

"Does he know we kissed?"

"I didn't tell him. It was only one time."

She's fingering the front of my jacket.

"Is he right, Cassandra?"

"About what?"

"He said you talked about me a lot. He said he thought—"

She presses her mouth against mine. She bites my lip. I place my hands on her hips and press against her, pushing with my tongue until it meets hers.

Someone coughs, and we both look. It's Theresa, walking past us, eyebrows raised.

"Can we help you?" Cassandra says.

She continues toward the sliding doors, not answering.

Scott Bartlett

"What a creep."

My hands are still on Cassandra's hips. "I thought she was officially awesome," I say.

"Having worked with her a few times, I'm thinking that was a misdiagnosis."

I look at her for a moment without speaking. Then I remove my hands. "I'd better go in."

When I enter the warehouse, Theresa's standing by the punch clock, arms crossed. I search for my punch card, ignoring her. I ignore her, she ignores me—we never talk. Ever.

"That girl has a boyfriend," she says.

I stop searching the punch cards. I turn toward her.

"Wait. You're talking to me."

"I'm talking to you about what a dick move you just made."

"You're finally talking to me, Theresa. You're talking to me about how I just kissed Cassandra."

"That's what's happening, yeah."

I tilt my head to the side. "Are you jealous?"

She rolls her eyes. "Your punch card's right there, Sheldon. At the very bottom." And she leaves through the red swinging doors.

*

Gilbert says the reason I like Cassandra so much is she's excellent at playing hard to get—a classic strategy, effective since it creates the illusion of value. Because Cassandra makes me work to get her attention, with the possibility of having her always slightly out of reach, I'm tricked into overestimating her worth.

"I don't think she's playing hard to get anymore, Gilbert. I mean, we've kissed twice, and the last time, she kissed me. I think she might be ready to try something."

He shakes his head, chuckling. "Of course she's still playing hard to get. She's just raising the stakes, to keep things interesting. She loves being chased too much. She never wants the chasing to end."

"Well, Sean won't put up with it much longer."

"There's probably nothing I can say to save you from being a sucker. Love is basically a drug addiction. They actually compared brain scans of recently dumped people with scans from cocaine addicts—they were almost identical."

"Pretty sure pop stars already knew that."

I'm sure I'm fooling Gilbert about as much as I'm fooling myself. Which is to say, not at all. I know he's likely right—I just don't want to tell him that. Cassandra may never break up with Sean, and even if she does, I'm sure she'll leave me hanging, like she has every other time. I think she has this ideal for what love is supposed to be, and so she never fully commits, out of fear the ideal will prove false.

But there's something else I keep going back to, and I won't tell Gilbert that either, because I can't.

Theresa finally talked to me.

*

The next time I'm working the same shift as Theresa, I volunteer to go fronting. She's working a 5-10, so I figure she'll probably take her break around eight o'clock. While I'm fronting Aisle Three, I have a clear view of her in Checkout Lane

Four. I take my time in Aisle Three. Just as I'm finishing it, I see her leaving the front. Bingo.

I head for the warehouse, and end up at the punch clock just as she's punching out.

"Taking your break?" I say, pulling my punch card from its slot and holding it up. "What a coincidence. For I, too, am taking a break."

She stares. "I'm not taking a break with you," she whispers.

"And I'm not taking a break with you. We just happen to be taking breaks simultaneously. Unless you want to have a loud argument about it right here in the middle of the warehouse." I raise my eyebrows.

After a little more glaring, she turns and marches toward the stairs. I start to whistle. When we arrive at the break room, it's empty.

She whirls to face me. "You're lucky there's no one here."

"Why?"

"Because, that would be awkward."

"Don't you think it's already about as awkward as it's going to get between us?"

I take a seat, and she sits, too.

"Look, Theresa, I know you don't want anything connecting you to...the place we met. I get that, because I try to avoid thinking about that place, too. You probably hate seeing me. But the fact is, you're going to see me. A lot. We work together."

"Have you told anyone?" she says.

"No. And that's what I'm saying—we don't have to tell anyone. We can pretend we met at Spend Easy, and just talk to each other like we would anyway."

She's looking down at the table. "I—"

The door opens, and Tommy comes in, tossing a chocolate bar in front of an empty chair. "Hey," he says, sitting.

"Hi," I say.

Silence.

Then, Theresa makes eye contact. "So, Sheldon. Are you in school?"

I smile.

We spend the rest of the break catching up by pretending to be making small talk. I even make her laugh a couple times, which I don't think I accomplished once in the psych ward.

"We should take breaks together more often," she says as we're leaving the break room, resting a hand on my arm. Before I exit, Tommy flashes me a thumbs-up.

We're almost to the bottom of the stairs when we hear a crash coming from the Meat room. A couple seconds later there's a *smack*, and someone cries out.

Matt stumbles through the door. A large area around his left eye is reddened—it looks like it's going to swell up pretty bad. He glances up at us, blinking.

"What happened?" Theresa says.

"I—" he says, and brings a hand to his face, prodding it gently. "It's my fault. I tripped."

"What happened, Matt?" I say. "Did Eric hit you?"

Eric comes through the door, teeth bared, and looks up at me. "He tripped, vegan. Now move along."

Chapter Twenty-Seven

Eric clearly has something to hide. That's why he locked me in the freezer. He sensed I'd begun to suspect something, and he wanted to scare me. Maybe even get rid of me. It depends on how bad the thing is he's trying to cover up.

I asked Matt again to tell me the truth of what happened. He wouldn't give me any details, though—he just kept saying it was his own fault.

I need to be careful, now. I look over my shoulder frequently when I'm in the parking lot at night. I always make sure someone knows when I'm going into the freezer to get product. And I try to take all my breaks with other people. There aren't any cameras in the break room, and I'd hate to be caught up there alone with Eric.

One shift, restocking Dairy, I notice Eric speaking with some guy I've never seen before, in front of the Meat department. They talk for at least 20 minutes, laughing, and nudging each other. Then Eric hugs him, and he leaves.

I decide now would be a good time to bring the shopping carts in.

Just as he's about to get into his car, I intercept him. He's tall and skinny, with curly brown hair.

"Hey," I say. "How do you know Eric?"

"Oh, I used to work for him. In Meat."

"What was that like?"

"Great. He taught me meat cutting. Now I work in one of the fanciest restaurants in town."

"Awesome. Um, listen, did he ever...do anything to you?"

"Like what?"

It feels strange, to say it out loud. "Like, hit you."

He gives me a strange look. "No, man. Eric wouldn't do that. The guy's like a Dad to me. If he hadn't hired me, I don't know where I would have ended up."

"Well, a guy I used to work with in Grocery works in Meat now, and the other night his face was swelling up. He said he tripped, but—"

"Then I guess he tripped," he says, his brow furrowed. "You know Eric's been on the news, right?"

"Yeah. Anyway. It was nice talking to you."

"Sure." He gets in his car and drives away.

*

As soon as the lawn needs mowing, Sam mows it. I wake up one morning to the motor, and I look out my window to see him pushing it across the grass. It makes me feel guilty—partly because of what happened with Gilbert, and partly because I've never mowed, even once. But it also makes me feel calm. Whatever else goes wrong in my life, I know Sam's got the lawn situation covered.

The phone rings as I'm making coffee in the kitchen, and I pick it up.

"Sheldon."

"Hey, Cassandra, what's—"

"I'm pregnant."

I pause. "Just let me grind these beans." I press the button on the coffee grinder and it whirs loudly, making conversation impossible.

I release the button. "Can you give me that one more time?"

"You heard me, Sheldon. I'm pregnant."

"Did you use protection?"

"Mostly."

"Mostly?"

"Well, a couple times we—"

"All right. I don't want details. How's Sean taking it?"

"He broke up with me."

"What?"

"I told him we kissed."

"Before or after you told him you were pregnant?"

"Before. But he thinks we did more than kiss."

I clutch the phone, and I don't speak.

"Sheldon?"

"I'll call him."

"What? What would you say?"

"I'll tell him the truth."

"I already tried that."

"Maybe, coming from me..." I take a long, shaky breath. I'm getting a headache.

"Okay," she says. "Thank you."

"What's his number?"

She tells me, and I hang up, and I dial it.

"Hello?"

"Sean. This is Sheldon."

"What do you want?"

"Listen. You're overreacting about Cassandra. I'm the one who kissed her—it was my fault."

"Bad luck for her, then."

"She's pregnant, Sean. She's having your kid."

"How do I know it's mine?"

"Because it couldn't possibly belong to anyone else."

"I don't believe you. And I don't care, either way. You can have her. Okay? If she'll let you. If you're 'cool' enough to raise Cassandra's kid."

"Don't do this, Sean. I know you're angry. But you don't want to burn this bridge. This is your baby, and if you abandon it now, it's going to write you off when it grows up. Trust me. Don't blow this."

"I'm not affected by this, Sheldon. This is easy for me. Cassandra kissed you, or fucked you, or whatever it was—and now I'm done. Simple."

"Listen to me."

"Been listening. Fuck off, Sheldon." He hangs up.

I drop into a chair. Now what? I want to go be with Cassandra, but she doesn't want that, and she doesn't need it, either. She needs her baby's father. I certainly couldn't raise a kid, even if I tried. I can barely take care of myself.

I walk to my room, turn on my computer, and click open the word processor. I centre the cursor, and type "The King of Diamonds".

For a moment, I stare at the blank screen.

I type all night.

Chapter Twenty-Eight

After a few weeks of barely concealed ridicule, Randy quits Spend Easy, and I ask Donovan if he's pleased with this outcome.

"Well, it's too bad he felt the need to quit. But lots of people suffer, you know. He should count himself lucky, if a little gossip is the worst he ever has to deal with."

I wonder if Frank knows his son quit for the same reason he quit his last job. Maybe he even senses Gilbert's role in it. There's nothing he can do, of course. He has to tread softly, since pissing off Gilbert could mean everything he knows falling apart. He built his family on an illusion, and it's his bad luck that Gilbert possesses the means to shatter it.

I feel bad for Randy, but there's nothing I can do either. To tell a secret once is to tell it a hundred times. You can't stuff it back in the box.

Tonight, Gilbert and I are driving around town in the Hummer. It's raining heavily, which suits me. "I hear you managed to break up Sean and Cassandra," he says.

I stare out the window.

"So, is this your opportunity?" he says. "Is this Sheldon Mason's big chance to make it with her?"

I shake my head. "You were right—she's not interested in me."

"Well, it's probably for the best. How do you feel?"

"Pretty shitty, actually."

"Wanna smoke a joint?"

The rain is beating against the windshield. I sigh. "Fuck it. Break it out."

"That's the spirit!" He fishes it out of a cup holder, puts it in his mouth, lights it. "You're not writing about this, are you?"

"About what?"

"This whole thing with Cassandra."

"No."

"Are you writing anything right now?"

"Just another short story."

"What's it about?"

"It's a sequel to the last one. The King—"

"Jesus Christ. You got a real knack for turning a good thing into a bad, you know that?"

"What do you mean?"

"Do you plan to let anyone read it?"

"I don't know. I'll probably submit it somewhere."

"I'm telling you. Stop writing."

We pull onto the highway. A red car speeds past us, and Gilbert steps on the gas, laughing. "I love it when Toyota Tercels think they can outstrip a Hummer."

He drifts into the passing lane, a sheet of water spraying up from the Hummer's tires.

The speedometer climbs, and Gilbert soon closes the gap. Once he passes, he changes lanes again and starts slowing down. The driver of the Tercel beeps.

"His horn is pathetic," I say.

Gilbert blasts his.

The Tercel switches lanes, passes, and switches back. Gilbert does the same. The driver glares as we overtake him. Gilbert flips him off. When the Tercel tries to pass again we stay abreast of it, and Gilbert continues to look over with his finger up. "He's maxed out, for sure," he says.

The driver takes the next exit, and Gilbert follows him. It's late, and there aren't many cars on the roads. The Tercel continues to go almost as fast as it did on the highway. Gilbert continues harassing him.

Finally we see his left flicker go on, and Gilbert turns his on, too. We turn into a parking lot.

"Shit," I say. "This is a hospital. I don't think he was trying to race us."

The other car parks near the front doors. Gilbert keeps his distance. We watch the driver get out and help a woman out of the passenger seat. She's holding her belly, which is big and round.

"They weren't joyriding," I say.

"No," Gilbert says. "They weren't."

"What if we—"

"She's fine, Sheldon. Okay? Nothing happened."

*

Wednesday night I'm on with Tommy, and since there's no other work that needs doing, we front.

I sigh, and he glances at me. "Everything all right, Sheldon? You seem bummed tonight."

"I'm fine. My heart's a bit freezer burnt. That's all."

"Pop it in the microwave on defrost for 30 seconds."

"Yeah. Um, do you know if Ralph's emailed the schedule yet?"

"He hadn't, last time I checked."

I go to the warehouse and call him.

"Bit late with it this week," Ralph says. "Putting it together now, actually. I have your hours, though—got a pen?"

"I'll remember."

"Okay. Hold on." He pauses. "Oh, boy. You're not going to like me."

"All right."

"You're working Friday, Saturday, and Sunday."

He was right. I abhor him. I hope he chokes on his own vomit.

"That sounds fine," I say.

"Great. Knew I could count on you."

I hang up and call Gilbert. "Ralph just scheduled me for every day this weekend."

"That's what you get for being Spend Easy's finest. Guess you won't be coming downtown with us Friday, then."

"Who's going?"

"Bunch of us. We're drinking at Donovan's first."

"Screw it. I'm coming."

On Friday I bring a change of clothes to work, and after I go straight to Donovan's. It takes me almost an hour to walk, and I buy a half-case of beer on the way.

Hardly anyone's at the party when I get there—just Donovan, Lesley-Jo, a couple people I don't know, and a new Grocery hire named Trent. They're watching *Jeopardy!*

Donovan gets up and walks over. "Hey Sheldon. What did you get me?"

"Get you?"

"It's my birthday, man."

"I didn't know."

"So, you didn't get me anything. Wow. Now I don't feel bad about inviting Cassandra for the sole purpose of watching you be awkward."

"Is she coming?"

"Nah. Too preggers, I guess. When's your birthday? So I can remember it, and make you feel bad about missing mine."

"It's pretty soon. June 18th."

"Man, there it is again. That number."

"What number?"

"18. I see it everywhere."

"Oh. I see 37, a lot."

"Really? 37? Did you know there are 37 miracles in the Bible?"

"No, I didn't." I'm actually feeling pretty dumb about the whole thing, right now. The idea that Donovan has a similar number thing going doesn't sit too well.

"This calls for a birthday joint." He takes a case from his pocket, and opens it. "Behold."

"That's a big one."

"Duh. It's a birthday joint."

The front door opens behind me, and Casey comes in, with a guy I don't know. Lesley-Jo gets up and kisses Casey. "Hey, babe," he says.

"Um," I say, and they both look at me. "Are you guys...?"

"Together?" he says. "Yeah, for a couple weeks now. Is there enough for me, there, Donovan?"

"It's a birthday joint. There's enough for everyone." He passes it to Casey.

"You smoke weed now, too?"

Casey nods. "Gilbert suggested it. He figured it would help me relax. He was right." He grins, holding up the joint. "Much better than coffee. Haven't knocked over any old ladies in a month."

Donovan turns on Street Fighter, and Casey goes over and challenges him to a match. I didn't know he was a gamer.

More people show up during the next hour. A couple people ask when Gilbert's coming, but no one knows. "The clubs all close at three, don't they?" I say. "If we're going, we should go soon."

Donovan starts counting people, to figure out how many cabs we need. Trent, the new Grocery hire, speaks up. He says he's never had a drink in his life, so he's available to drive a vanload down. I'm out of beer, and while rides are being figured out I hunt in Donovan's kitchen for something else to drink. Casey's there, with the guy he came in with. "Hey, Sheldon, have you met Francis? He's my roommate."

"Hey, dude," Francis says.

This must be the guy who refused to drive Casey to the hospital.

"Francis is a douchebag name," I say.

Taxis start arriving, and Gilbert pulls up in his Hummer as the last one is driving away. I'm getting into Trent's van along with Donovan, Casey, and Lesley-Jo. Gilbert gets out and walks toward us, carrying a brown bag. "Shit—are you guys going downtown already?"

"It's almost one o'clock," Donovan says.

"Damn it." Gilbert takes a twenty-sixer of Jack Daniel's out of the bag, unscrews the top, and chugs half of it. He screws the top back on and tosses the rest back in the Hummer.

Donovan takes shotgun, and Casey and Lesley-Jo sit behind him, in the middle. Gilbert and I sit in back.

"So, Sheldon," Donovan says. "I hear you're writing something new."

"You hear true."

"Can I read it, when you're done?"

"Sure, man."

"Nobody reads it before I do," Gilbert says. "After that, we'll decide whether we want to release to the general public."

"What are you, his agent?" Donovan says.

"More like life coach wannabe," I say.

We arrive downtown, and everyone who isn't Trent piles out of the van.

"Where did everyone say they were going?" Lesley-Jo says once we're gathered on the sidewalk.

"Who cares?" Gilbert says. "I need drinks."

We all head for the nearest bar and order shots of whatever. While we're waiting, Brent appears next to us—Brent, of Spend Easy ancient history. A casualty of the new cameras.

"Hey," he says.

"Buy me this shot," Gilbert says.

Brent nods. He seems pretty drunk. "Okay. Sure, Gilbert. What have you been up to lately, anyway, bro?"

"Nothing."

"I hear you're still running Frank over at Spend Easy. I was talking to Claude the other day. Nicely done, man."

"Thanks."

The bartender brings us the shots. Gilbert downs his and walks away without saying anything. Brent takes a 20 out of his wallet, watching him go. "Me and Gilbert, man," he says to me. "We used to be tight. We got high together so many times."

"Yeah," I say, "because friendships are measured in joints, right?"

I turn to follow Gilbert.

"Hey," Brent says, grabbing my arm. "How many times have you smoked him up? You fucking pansy."

I pull away. "Piss off, man. You're acting like his ex-girlfriend."

I see his fist go back, but I guess I'm skeptical, because I just stand there. He hits me in the eye. I stagger back, covering it with my right hand. A few people standing nearby make pro-tracted vowel sounds. Brent steps forward, the intention of fur-ther violence written across his face. I put up my left hand. The space around us is clearing.

Gilbert steps up, catches Brent's hand midflight, and pulls it forward, tripping him with his foot. Brent goes sprawling onto the floor. Bouncers come over, pick him up, and drag him to the exit.

"Thank you," I say.

"Don't mention it."

"Where'd you learn to do that?"

"I have a brown belt in karate. I'd have my black, but that comes with legal complications."

We rejoin Donovan and the rest at a couple of stand-up tables on the other side of the bar. "You guys see that?" I say.

"See what?" Casey says.

"Never mind," Gilbert says. "Hey, Sheldon. Check out that blonde on the dance floor. Red skirt."

I look over. "She's hot."

Lesley-Jo rolls her eyes. "Must you constantly objectify women, Gilbert?"

"I'm not objectifying her. I recognize she's a unique, beautifully complex individual who's constantly blossoming into someone new. All I'm saying is she's hot, and I wanna bang her."

He approaches, and within short order they're groping each other on the dance floor. I glance at Donovan. "He moves fast."

"He's a charmer, all right." He holds up his glass, which is empty, and clicks it against mine—also empty. "You should get the next round."

"All right."

As I approach the bar, the bartender flicks an ice cube into the air with a metal scoop and tries to catch it in a glass. It ricochets off the rim and onto the floor, but the people on the other side of the bar clap anyway. I guess it looked like he caught it, from their angle.

That's the definition of success. As long as other people are impressed, it doesn't matter if you secretly screw up. The important thing is to look good doing whatever you're doing.

10 minutes later, I still don't have my drinks. It seems like the bartender's serving every new person who approaches the

bar before me. I take out a 20 and lean on the bar, holding the bill in plain view.

The guy standing next to me smirks, and reaches into his pocket. He takes out a 100, which he holds next to my 20. He glances from his bill, to my bill, to me. He raises his eyebrows.

I look back at him and raise mine.

The bartender comes over and asks him what he'd like.

*

"Where does Eric keep the Meat schedule?" I say. I'm recently home from my Saturday shift, which I spent very hungover. Gilbert's here, and he's lying on my bed reading the copy of "The King of Diamonds" I printed out for him. I'm sitting at my computer.

He lowers the sheaf of papers. "Why do you want to know?"

"Curious."

"In a black binder, in the Meat room. I'd be careful, though. Eric doesn't like people snooping around in there."

"Think he might have something to hide?"

"It's possible to care about privacy without having something to hide. For example, I don't conceal that I'm sexually active, but I still don't want any Sheldon Masons watching."

"Did you get with that blonde, last night?"

"A gentleman never pushes the boundaries of the Kama Sutra and tells." He holds up my story. "This is going to cause a lot of trouble for you. It's clearly about what happened with you and Cassandra."

I turn my chair to face the computer.

"What are you doing?"

"Proving you wrong. I'm sending it to Donovan. See if he mentions anything."

"That's definitely a bad idea." He looks down at the manuscript again. "Why does he lock his mother in the dungeon?" He tosses it on the floor. "Freud would have had a field day with this thing."

Chapter Twenty-Nine

In high school, whenever I was rejected by a girl, Mom used to say that whoever it was would look back later in life and regret it. Lately, I've been picturing all the girls who ever turned me down, sitting in a room together and sobbing about letting me get away.

"What have we done?" they'd say. "How could we let failed writer Sheldon Mason slip through our fingers so easily?" Dabbing with handkerchiefs. "He's quite respected, you know, at the local grocery store. Have you heard what an efficient fronter he is? Are you aware how many cases per hour he's known to stock?"

I've taken a few more breaks with Theresa, and they've been fun enough. But I can't discuss anything real with her—not while we're at Spend Easy. I can tell from the way she shifts in her chair that it makes her uncomfortable whenever we stray too close to such topics.

She looks thin.

It's Sunday, and Casey, Donovan, and Gilbert are at my apartment. It's raining outside, and I'm definitely not motivated enough to walk to the shed. We're gonna have to smoke inside.

Gilbert's phone rings.

"Hello? Hi." He listens. "Can't. Busy." He listens some more. "Mom. Your mothering is over. Mother's Day is now purely symbolic. Dad's going with you, isn't he? There you go. Eat a wonton for me." He hangs up, and looks at Donovan. "Wanted me to come to supper."

"You should go," I say. "We're not doing anything important. You should be with your Mom."

"We are doing something important," Gilbert says. He points at Donovan. "Jamaican hot box?"

A Jamaican hot box, Donovan explains, entails turning on the shower as hot as it will go, stuffing a towel under the bathroom door, and smoking a joint.

"Not just one," Gilbert says. "Several joints."

"Or a really big one," Donovan says.

"If you're having a Jamaican hot box, you need to smoke a lot of weed. Otherwise, why bother?"

Donovan rolls one of the biggest joints I've ever encountered, using a quarter ounce of pot and multiple rolling papers. Then we go to the bathroom and turn on the light.

"The fan came on," Donovan says.

"Yeah," I say. "The light and fan are controlled by the same switch."

"That won't do. Do you have a flashlight?"

I search for one. Meanwhile, Donovan turns the hot water on and closes the door. "Hurry," he calls.

I find the flashlight, and rejoin the others inside the bathroom. We're about to close the door when Marcus Brutus starts sniffing around outside and meowing. "Has your cat ever been stoned?" Donovan says.

"Not to my knowledge."

"We should get him in here. It'll be hilarious."

"Could that hurt him?"

"Nah, man. Cats love weed." He picks Marcus Brutus up, rolls of cat fat bunching beneath his fingers, and brings him in with us, shutting the door. He stuffs a wet towel into the crack at the bottom.

We take turns smoking the enormous joint while someone else trains the flashlight on it. Whoever's holding the flashlight periodically jerks the light away, of course, or shines it in someone's eyes, or points it at the cat, who sits as close to the door as he can get, meowing constantly. It gets steamy pretty quick, and soon the flashlight's beam reveals only hazy outlines.

The joint is almost a roach when Marcus Brutus goes silent

Casey points the light at him. "The cat is plotting something."

Gilbert's sitting on the edge of the tub. "So, Donovan. You read Sheldon's story?"

"Yeah, finished it last night. It's based on what happened with you and Cassandra, right, Sheldon?"

"Oh my God. No. It's not."

"It obviously is. She comes off as a huge bitch, too. It's pretty hilarious. I forwarded it to Paul and Claude."

"Why did you do that?"

Donovan shrugs. "Thought they'd enjoy it. Does it matter?"

"No. I just hope it doesn't get back to her."

"I thought it wasn't about Cassandra."

"It's not."

When we open the door, the cat gets down on its stomach and creeps out into the hall. We follow him into the clear, cold air of the apartment. Marcus Brutus paws at empty space. We laugh. He walks slowly down the hall, goes into the living room, and hides under the coffee table. We all sit.

"Now what?" Gilbert says.

"I have more weed in my car," Donovan says. "We could roll it now, to smoke later."

"Who's gonna get it?"

"I will," Casey says. He gets up and opens the door. "It stopped raining."

Marcus Brutus darts from under the coffee table, past Casey, and out the door. "Shit," Casey says. "He's gone, Sheldon."

I reach deep into myself and locate a final reservoir of energy I didn't know was there. I get up and go to the open door. "Here kitty," I call. "Here Marcus Brutus. Here Brute."

Casey and I look at each other.

"He'll come back," I say, and return to the couch.

Chapter Thirty

Her last day in the psych ward, Theresa led me out into the fenced-off garden by the hand.

Seated side-by-side on the concrete bench, she said, "I think you need to talk about the reason you're here, Sheldon. I don't want to pressure you. But to get better, I think you need to start processing why you wanted to kill yourself."

I didn't answer, for a while. I looked out on the busy road beyond the chain-link fence, with cars hurtling past in both directions.

Then I told her about Herman Barry, the man who got drunk one day and drove down Foresail Road.

Even sober, human reflexes aren't fast enough to operate cars. You get distracted for a second, by a text message or a pretty girl or whatever, and something dies. A squirrel, a dog. You. There's a car-related death every 30 seconds. After my mother was hit, 137 other people died before I got the news.

I decided not to attend Barry's trial. The chance to put a face to the name of my mother's killer just didn't appeal. I had no yearning for revenge. There were witnesses, and I was assured he would go to jail. That was enough. I didn't want to think about it anymore.

So when his wife knocked on the door of my new apartment and introduced herself, I was surprised at the anger that welled up, making my heart pound and my vision blur.

She couldn't meet my eyes. Her son could—a boy of around seven, peeking from behind her right hip. She took a piece of folded loose leaf from her pocket and held it out. "Herman asked me to give you this."

I unfolded it. "What is it?" I said.

Eyes lowered, she said nothing.

"Is this an apology letter? Are you fucking kidding me?"

I made a fist. The crumpled note landed on some grass growing through a crack in the concrete step.

"What's your name?" I asked the boy.

He didn't answer.

"What's your name?"

"Herman," his mother said.

"Do you love your mommy, Herman?"

The boy's chin dipped a fraction of an inch. He moved closer to his mother. I was scaring him.

"Your daddy took my mommy," I said. "She's never coming back. She's gone, forever. Because of what your daddy did." My voice cracked. "Do you understand?"

I didn't wait for an answer. I went back inside and closed the door. I took two steps, and then, slowly, I sank to my knees. I let myself fall over onto my side. I hated the tears that started and didn't stop. I hated Herman Barry. And I hated myself.

I stayed there, curled up, crying, for what must have been an hour. Then I stood and opened the door. The letter was still on

the doorstep. It was spread out again, with a stone sitting on top
to keep it in place. I removed the rock and took the paper inside.

In his letter, Barry wrote about a childhood under the yoke of
a chronically drunk father, who took pleasure in knocking him
down, and knocking his mother down, and his sisters, and the
dog. He wrote about having his first drink at 10, and about his
struggles with alcoholism ever since. The AA meetings. The in-
terventions. He wrote about his pride in never touching his wife
or son, except with love. He wrote about divorcing his wife, and
spending long, sober years trying to win her back. And, when he
finally did, getting hammered soon after, and running a woman
down in the street.

He wrote about how, when driving really drunk, you'll steer
toward things you're trying to avoid. You concentrate so hard
on the thing you don't want to hit that you drive straight for it.

It helps, of course, when the thing you're trying to avoid killing is also trying to avoid being killed. This, Barry wrote, was
not the case with my mother. He saw her a few seconds before
striking her, and she saw him. But she didn't move. She didn't
try to get out of the way.

She saw him coming, and she just stood there.

When I finished reading, I found a lighter and burned Barry's letter in the kitchen sink.

(The black marks are still there.) I decided that Barry was a
liar. And I tried my hardest to forget what I'd read.

But over the following months, memories resurfaced that
hadn't seemed important before. Mom sleeping in more, and being reprimanded at work for lateness. Letting her bedroom become disordered. Eating less. Falling out of touch with her

friends. Staring out the living room window, chin in hand—not reacting even when Brute rubbed against her calves, and cried.

The signs were there, but I ignored them. Too caught up in my own shit.

I was sobbing by the time I finished talking, and Theresa held me, and rubbed my back, and told me it wasn't my fault.

I knew she was right. But I didn't believe her.

*

I'm supposed to work the day after Brute ran away, but I call the store and say I'm too sick to come in. I've never called in sick before, and Ralph doesn't ask any questions—he only says he hopes I feel better soon. I thank him, and then I spend the day looking for Marcus Brutus.

It's sunny today, though a little cold. I warm up soon enough, walking in progressively larger loops around the house, expanding my search into side streets and parking lots. "Here, Marcus Brutus!" I call. "Here, Brute! Here, kitty!" Over and over again.

The day wears on, and I begin retracing my footsteps, working my way back to the house. He wouldn't stray too far, would he? Does he hate living with me that much?

My throat's getting sore. If I don't find him today, I'll have to start calling animal shelters, and printing off posters with his photo. A reward might help, but I don't have anything to offer as one.

I knock on Sam's door.

"Have you seen my cat?" I say when he appears.

"No. He's missing?"

"Yeah. He got outside yesterday."

"Sorry to hear. I'll keep an eye out for him. Let you know if I see him."

"Thanks, Sam."

"How are you doing? You don't look that great."

"I'm just tired."

"You wanna come in?"

"Nah. I better keep looking. Thanks, though."

"Okay. Take care, Sheldon."

"You too."

I walk around for another hour, and then decide to head home for a short nap. After, I'll start designing those lost cat posters.

I lie on the couch, but I can't sleep. God damn that cat. As much as he annoys me, I'd give anything to have him here in the apartment right now. To hear his piercing, high-pitched meow. When he gets back, I'll give him two cans of Turkey Giblets in Gravy. Three, if he wants.

Gilbert comes over, and asks if I want to smoke a joint. I tell him no—I'm afraid it'll knock me out for the night, and I want to get these posters done before I go to sleep. He sticks around, though, and we shoot the shit while I work on them.

He leaves just as I'm finishing. I print one off, and it looks pretty good. The clearest photo I could find is one where Mom has him in her arms, their faces pressed together. Mom's smiling, and it sort of looks like Brute is, too.

There's a knock on the door, and I get up to answer it. It's Gilbert, holding Brute, who dangles from his arms, limp.

"Sorry, man," he says. "He must have been lying under the Hummer. I felt the tire go over something, and I got out..."

I take Brute. His body hangs limp in my arms, his head dangling. Red seeps from a gash along his side.

I look at Gilbert. He actually seems kind of upset. I manage to speak: "It's not your fault. You didn't know he was there."

He leaves. I get a Spend Easy bag, and I gently lower Brute into it.

Mom's last remaining culture bomb. For a second, that makes me smile. Then I drop the bag, put my head against the wall, and cry.

Chapter Thirty-One

I call in sick the next day, too.

As an apology, Gilbert brings me a big bag of weed, and the third day I smoke a lot of it and then call in sick again.

I still haven't buried Brute.

"So, what are you sick with?" Ralph asks when I call in for the third day.

"I'm just not feeling well."

"But, what's causing you to not feel well?"

"Not. Feeling. Well."

"I'm going to need you working tomorrow, Sheldon. We're swamped, in here."

"I'll see how I'm feeling."

Going through old photos of Mom, and of Brute, only makes it worse. I put them away and sit on the edge of my bed, staring at the wall. I'm beginning to feel like I did before.

I call Spend Easy again, and ask for Theresa's number. It's a small miracle that she isn't working today, and that she picks up when I call her.

"Hello?"

"Theresa, this is Sheldon. I know it's a lot to ask, but I think I need someone here right now."

"Where do you live?"

She's over within an hour. I tell her what happened, and she gives me a hug, and helps me bury Brute in the backyard. Then we watch *Fight Club*.

Partway through she leans against me, and I put my arm around her.

*

After Therese leaves, I turn on my computer and open the word processor, but nothing comes. I switch it off. I go into the kitchen and sit at the table for a few minutes, staring at the cat, who stares back.

I walk to my room and turn on the computer once more. I look up the number for the penitentiary.

"Hi," I say when someone answers. "I'd like to speak with Herman Barry."

"Is he a prisoner?"

"Yes."

"Inmates can't take calls."

"Oh. Well, can I leave a message? It's important."

"Are you able to tell me his date of birth?"

"No."

"Are you personally acquainted with the inmate?"

"I've never met him. But he killed my mother in a drunk driving accident."

There's a pause. "I see. What's the message?"

"Tell him Sheldon Mason forgives him."

Another silence. "All right. I'll make sure he gets it."

*

I'm back to work the day after Theresa comes over.

"Feeling better?" Ralph says.

"Much!"

But Ralph seems a bit off today, and he's not the only one. A couple of the cashiers, who would normally say hello as I come in, seemed kind of standoffish, too. Does a guy really get this much flak for calling in sick? I mean, sure, it was three days in a row, but I'd never done it before. Doesn't a high case count count for anything around here?

I'm restocking bottles of dish detergent when Cassandra walks up to me. "I read your story," she says.

Uh oh.

"It must be nice, getting to say all those awful things about me."

"I didn't say anything about you, Cassandra."

"Right. Sure. You know, Sheldon, you think you're this fascinating enigma, when actually, you're really boring. Do you know that?" She walks back to the cash registers without waiting for an answer.

Throughout the remainder of the shift, I slowly realize that everyone is like this, now. Co-workers who once greeted me warmly avert their eyes, or avoid me completely. When I go upstairs for a break there are already five employees there, and they all fall silent as I enter. Just like they used to with Randy.

"Told you so," Gilbert says, when I describe the scene to him later.

Paul's working the order tonight, too, and toward the end of my shift I run into him in Aisle Three. He doesn't avert his eyes.

"You read the story?" I say.

"I did."

"And?"

"No big deal."

"So you know I didn't base it on her."

"Oh, it's pretty clear you based it on her, Sheldon. Criticized her, in spite of the shit she's been through. The shit you played a key part in."

"But...no big deal?"

"No, it's not," he says. "Because I'm not worried about Cassandra. She's keeping the baby, you know. Her Dad's going to help her out with it. Plus, she just got promoted to Front End Manager—she plans to work as many hours as she can before maternity leave, and save some money. Cassandra's going to be fine."

"That's awesome," I say.

"I just hope you weren't concerned your writing would have some kind of negative effect on her, Sheldon. Your writing doesn't have that kind of power. So you can put your mind at rest about that."

*

I'm getting sick of this whole 'story scandal', and it's only getting worse. I send it to Theresa, and ask her what she thinks. She says the situation with Cassandra probably did influence it, but that's how inspiration works. To some extent, all authors put their lives in their books.

When I take a break during my next shift, I realize I've forgotten my supper at home, and I don't have any money with me. I go up to the break room, where Gilbert is spraying whipped cream on cookies and eating them.

"Where's your veggie slop?" he says.

"Forgot it."

"Want a cookie?"

"I'm guessing you didn't pay for them."

"You are correct," he says around a creamy mouthful. "No stolen goods for Sheldon, though, right? Wouldn't want people thinking he's unorthodox."

"I'll have one," I say.

He takes two, tops them with whipped cream, and mashes them together. I stuff them into my mouth, whole.

"These are delicious," I say.

"Depravity always is. Wanna smoke a joint?"

Sometimes, on nights he's running late, the guy who brings the order unhinges the truck's cab and leaves the container there for a few hours. Gilbert unlocks the back door, and we go out and crouch under the container, near one of the tires.

I'm pretty buzzed by the time we go back in. Luckily, I keep some eye drops in my jacket for when I'm stoned in public, and I head up to the bathroom to squeeze some in each eye. Then I return to the break room, where Gilbert has resituated himself.

"Can I borrow five bucks?"

"Why? You don't have to pay for stuff, Sheldon. Just take it."

"That's stealing."

"So was eating those cookies."

"Yeah, but I don't wanna take a whole bag of chips."

Gilbert rolls his eyes and fishes a five out of his pocket.

I grab a bag of Cheezies, a can of Pepsi, and a bar. I go to Lesley-Jo's cash register, since she's the only cashier working tonight who doesn't currently hate me. She rings everything through.

"That's $5.37, Sheldon."

I hesitate, and then pass her the five-dollar bill Gilbert gave me.

"This isn't enough," she says.

I take it back. "Screw it, then. I'll put it all back." I gather everything into my arms.

"Why don't you just not buy the bar, or something?"

"I'm putting it all back."

I don't, though. I keep walking, through the warehouse, and up the stairs.

*

I've noticed Eric spends his breaks sitting alone in his car. Last week, on one such occasion, I snuck into the Meat room and found the black binder with the employee schedule inside. After memorizing what nights Eric wasn't working, I snuck back out.

Tonight is one of those nights. It's also a Wednesday: no orders are due to come in, and staff's at a minimum. The perfect night to have a look around the Meat department. Matt's the only one working, and as soon as I see him go up to the break room I duck inside Meat.

I check the desk, rifling through folders and laminates. It all seems like standard Meat stuff, I guess. Information about orders, policies, procedures, and so on.

There's a sound from the next room—the one with the window to the sales floor—and I freeze, holding my breath.

I'm starting to wish I'd stayed sober for this.

Other than the desk, there isn't much of interest in here. Everything's kept pretty tidy. Searching the next room would be too risky, since anyone can see into it.

The last place left to look is the small walk-in freezer that's only accessible from here.

It occurs to me I should have brought a watch—I have no idea how much break Matt has left. I need to be quick, but I'm not eager to enter that freezer.

What if Eric drops in for some reason? There's no camera here.

I go in and start shifting boxes, checking behind them. After every one I glance into the Meat room. But there are too many boxes, and not enough time. Besides, anything hidden behind product would be quickly uncovered by an employee—it's not a good place to hide something.

I don't even know what I'm looking for.

I crouch, and start feeling under the lowest shelves. My hand bumps against some plastic, and I realize it's taped to the metal. I hear footsteps just as I'm ripping it off.

There's no time to escape. The only way to conceal myself would be to pull the freezer door shut, and there's no way I'm doing that.

Matt appears in the doorway. He sees what I'm holding, and his eyes go wide.

I look, too. It's a plastic bag stuffed full of weed.

"You need to get out of here, Sheldon," he says. "Please."

Chapter Thirty-Two

Donovan's fridge is well-stocked. He has grapes. He has Orange Crush. He has the delicious parfaits in a cup we sell at Spend Easy. I grab two of those, and take them into the living room.

"Why don't you help yourself, Sheldon?" Donovan says.

Gilbert takes out a cigar, and lights it.

"Gross," I say. "Don't smoke that in here."

"It's a blunt. It's filled with weed."

"Oh. Awesome."

Gilbert takes a few hits and passes it to Donovan, who does the same, and says, "I'm quitting pot, by the way."

"Sure you are," Gilbert says. "This can be your retirement blunt."

After I found the bag of weed in Meat, I figured Eric must be selling drugs out of his department. Probably packages it up with meat and gives it to customers. And he knocks around his employees who show any signs of exposing him.

Then I showed the bag to Gilbert. "Hey," he said. "That's mine." And he plucked it from my hand.

It turns out Gilbert has stashes hidden in the cameras' blind spots all over the store, for when he's working overnight shifts. He isn't worried about getting caught—there'd be no way to prove they're his.

"Paul tells me he's shopping his book to publishers, now," Donovan says.

"I don't care."

"Maybe you should have sent your book to publishers. Instead of sending it to the entire Spend Easy staff."

"That wasn't me, Donovan. It was you. And thanks to you, working there is now a pain in the ass."

"Actually," Gilbert says, "I've solved that problem for you. Have you checked this week's schedule?"

"No. Why?"

"I lobbied Frank to tell Ralph to schedule us for a bunch of overnights. You won't have to deal with Cassandra. No customers. We can just sit around, get high, and eat."

"Gilbert, I told you not to blackmail Frank on my behalf."

"It's not like I told him to give you a raise."

"Well, I'm not slacking off with you. If we're doing this, work needs to get done."

"Agreed. That's why I told Frank to schedule Tommy to work overnights too."

"Why?"

"He does whatever I tell him. He can do all the work."

"I'll be working, too."

"Suit yourself."

*

Every time I look at the clock now, I see 37. I notice it other places, too. Donovan just bought a 37-inch TV. We drive down Route 37 all the time. I added up the barcode on my favourite flavour of chips, and I got 37.

The first overnight reminds me of the time we snuck in here and ordered 500 boxes of condoms. Most of them are still on a pallet in the warehouse, but they'll probably expire before Frank manages to sell them all. An innovator would give them out for free, to promote safe sex and reap the attendant PR. Then again, I guess that would reduce Spend Easy's future clientele.

We take it easy for the first hour or so, then we get to work. At least, Tommy and I get to work. Gilbert lies on a pallet in the warehouse and goes to sleep, using his coat for a pillow.

We finish checking the Frozen overstock around three, and then we start on the racks. Gilbert emerges half an hour after that, blinking.

"Slow down, cowboy," he says.

"Can't. Too full of energy. I love doing this stuff stoned."

"I can see that. Reminds me of when I first started smoking."

"When was that? Second grade?"

He laughs. "Way before that. Mom swallowed a joint during pregnancy, and I hotboxed the womb."

"Man. We should get Tommy high."

Tommy's restocking canned soup at the other end of the aisle. I call out to him. "Hey, Tommy! Wanna smoke a joint?"

"No."

"Come on. Everyone's doing it."

He looks over. "Stop peer pressuring me."

"I'm not peer pressuring you. You aren't my peer."

He goes back to placing soup cans on the shelf. "Why don't you write a book about it?"

Another overnight, Casey and Lesley-Jo visit us.

Lesley-Jo tells me she read "The King of Diamonds".

"Did you like it?"

"I did. Some of it seemed a bit unrealistic, though."

"Like what?"

"Well, a lot of the characters do horrible things, and the consequences never seem proportional."

I frown. "How is that not like real life?"

Two weeks pass like this. Ralph compliments us on our work—he says he loves walking through neatly fronted shelves to a clean warehouse every morning. "Frank agrees with me," he says. "He wants the overnights to continue."

The truth is, I've been doing less work, and Tommy's been doing more.

Gilbert talks to him a lot about the impending machine take-over. He suggests to him that our mechanical overlords may reward those who work the hardest to sustain the society that will birth the machines.

One night, when we're all in Aisle Three, Gilbert says, "Tommy."

"Yes?" Tommy stops working.

"I'm about to tell you something important."

"What?"

"This is the only time anyone will say this to you. So listen carefully. You're probably going to think I'm joking, or playing a trick. But I'm not."

"What is it?"

"I don't exist, Tommy. And neither does Sheldon."

"You don't?"

"You're the only one who exists in the entire world. Tommy, the machines have already taken over, and they've created this world for you." Gilbert plucks at Tommy's sleeve. "This body— it's not your real body. You're really a brain floating in a nutri-ent-rich fluid, being stimulated electronically, by a computer. This whole reality is simulated. The machines are caring for you right now, Tommy. They're always going to care for you."

Tommy looks up at the fluorescent lights. He clears his throat.

"I don't think I buy it, Gilbert."

"You don't?"

"No. Not really."

"Oh. All right, then."

*

I'm beginning to understand the real reason Gilbert wanted to work overnights. We've started getting frequent visitors, whom Gilbert goes outside to meet. At night, he can sell them weed out of his Hummer with much less risk.

He comes back from one such trip and finds me restocking lima beans in Aisle Two. He stands there for a few seconds.

"Is something wrong with you?" he says.

"I'm fine."

"You've been pissy all night." He pauses. "Wait. Is today your birthday?"

"It was yesterday. It ended at midnight." I'm now 21, but I haven't mentioned it to anyone. "How did you know?"

"Donovan told me it was coming up. Not to mention you've been acting like a little girl this shift. It wasn't hard to piece together."

"Don't make it a big deal, okay?"

"I won't. I wouldn't want to take away your opportunity to wallow in self-pity. But I am buying you a birthday present."

"You don't have to do that."

"I will, though. I know just what to get you."

*

Overnights end at seven in the morning. Gilbert drives me home, and I'm in bed by eight.

At nine, the phone rings. And rings. And rings. Finally, it stops. Then it rings again.

I get out of bed and trudge to the kitchen.

"Yeah?"

"Hi, I'm Bradley. I'm calling you this morning to tell you that you're awesome."

"What?"

"You're an awesome person and you deserve awesome things to happen to you." His words belie his tone, which is flat and bored.

"Who is this?"

"Bradley."

"Yes, you said that, but how do I know you?"

"You don't. For your birthday, an anonymous person has given you the gift of being called every day and told how awesome you are."

"That's a thing?"

"It's a service we provide."

"How long will this go on?"

"30 days."

"Can I cancel?"

"Your anonymous benefactor has already paid in full. So, no."

"Great."

"I'll talk to you tomorrow." He hangs up.

*

Overnights have completely rearranged my sleep schedule. I sleep in the day now, and I'm awake all night, even when I'm not working. To make it worse, I still work the occasional day shift, which really throws things off.

Tonight is Saturday, and me and Gilbert are both off. Neither of us has slept in 24 hours. We're sitting at his kitchen table, high, wide awake. With nothing to do.

"I'll pay you to cancel that daily pep talk thing," I say.

He looks up from his phone. "Sorry?"

"The guy calling me every day, telling me how awesome I am? I need it to stop."

"I'm sure I don't know what you're talking about."

"I know it was you. You said you were getting me a present, and then that started happening."

"Maybe it was Donovan."

"Donovan gave me his pipe."

"All right. It was me. And I'm totally not cancelling."

"Damn." I cross my arms on the table and lean my head on them. Gilbert resumes texting.

"Know of any parties?" I say.

"No. Do you?"

I laugh.

"Wanna go for a drive?" he says.

"Okay."

We grab some fast food and then cruise around town, seeking something interesting. We find it in the form of a party in a three-story townhouse. We don't know who lives there, but the music is loud, and people are dancing in three different windows. The house number is 37.

We park a couple blocks away. As we approach, a guy and a girl leave the house and head down the street together in the opposite direction.

In the porch, four people are standing around smoking weed. "Hey," some guy says when we enter.

"Hey," Gilbert says.

"Who are you?"

"I'm with Sheldon." He jerks his thumb back at me.

"Okay. Well, you guys want a beer?"

"Just one? Between us?"

"One each."

"I'll agree to that."

The guy reaches behind him and extracts two bottles from a case sitting on the floor. Gilbert takes his and inserts himself into the joint circle. "So," he says. "What are we talking about?" He glances back at me, and beckons me forward. "Don't be shy, Sheldon. Join us. Grab your beer." Someone passes Gilbert the joint, and he hits it.

"The Libya intervention," another guy says.

"Why?" I ask. "That was forever ago."

The guy smirks. "Dale's a political science major. He brought it up."

Another guy—Dale, I guess—says, "We're talking about whether protecting civilians from Gaddafi was a good enough reason for all those countries to send in armed forces. I think it was."

"That's not why they went," Gilbert says.

"Yeah it is."

"No, it's not. They went because all the uprisings had them spooked about the oil supply. The U.S. has defended their energy interests in the Middle East for decades. Now the rest of the West is waking up to the fact that oil's running out. This is only the beginning. The resource wars haven't even started yet."

"The what?"

"Are you a poli-sci major?" Dale asks.

"I just read between the lines. Can we have more beers?"

The guy who gave us the first two shakes his head. "I only bought a dozen."

We finish the joint, and our former beer supplier takes a second one from behind his ear. He holds it up. "This joint is a descendent of the first one I ever smoked. When we're finished, I want the roach back. I'll rip it up and put it into my next joint. The cycle will continue."

"That's legendary, dude," the guy to his right says.

When we're done, Gilbert ends up with the roach. The guy takes out a Ziploc bag and opens it. "Okay," he says. "Drop it in."

"What's it worth to you?"

"Didn't you hear what I said? It's a lineage." He steps closer.

Gilbert holds the roach near his mouth. "I'll eat it. I will put this roach in my mouth and I'll swallow it."

"Okay, man. Okay. I'll give you a beer."

"One for my friend, too."

"Two beer. No problem."

"Give them to Sheldon."

He does. Gilbert deposits the roach in the baggie. "Come on, Sheldon." He starts up the nearby staircase. "Let's check this shit out."

I follow.

The staircase reverses direction halfway up, and Gilbert disappears around the bend. When I reach the top, he's already talking to a girl leaning against the wall, drinking a cooler. He turns to me. "Look, Sheldon. I found you one!"

I sigh. Gilbert knows I'm dating Theresa.

"What's your name?" Gilbert asks the girl.

"Shianne."

"This is Sheldon," Gilbert says. "He's an honest man in a world without truth."

"Yeah?" she says. "What do you do?"

"I'm a writer," I say.

Gilbert puts a hand to the side of his mouth and shouts at Shianne over the music. "He works in a grocery store." He walks down the hall, leaving Shianne and I looking at each other.

"Oh my God," she says. "I lost my phone and I haven't been on Facebook all weekend."

"Everyone must be wondering what you're doing."

"I know!"

I bid Shianne adieu and go down the hall. I turn into a room with just one guy in it, sitting on a couch, playing a guitar, and singing. I approach him, and stand nearby. This close, I can hear him over the music.

He sings, "Discouraged by our limitations, we pursue ine-briation to make them grow—it's fun, you know." He stops, and looks up at me. "I just made that up."

"It was pretty good."

"Thanks. I don't think I know you. Who invited you?"

"I'm with Gilbert."

He nods. "Right on."

Gilbert comes in. He's holding a new beer. He points at the guitarist. "Play *My Fair Lady*!"

"Um, that's a play," the guitarist says.

"Play *The Starry Night*!"

The guitarist frowns. Gilbert leaves.

"Who was that?" he says.

"I have no idea."

I go into another room, where a tall guy wearing a fedora is standing behind a bar, pouring shots for a bunch of people. I guess he's the host. I walk up to the bar and lean on the end.

"Hey," the fedora-wearing guy says, pointing at me. "I don't know you."

"I'm with Gilbert."

"Yeah? Well, who's he here with?"

"Um, he's with Sheldon."

"Whatever. We're doing shots. You want one?"

"Sure."

He pours me one. "What's your name?"

"Sheldon."

"You have the same name as the guy your friend came with?"

"Yeah."

We all down our shots, and the host pours another round. He repeats this several times.

I find Gilbert talking to a pretty brunette in the kitchen. "Is this Sheldon?" she asks.

"Yeah," Gilbert says. "Sheldon, meet Stacy."

"Hi."

Stacy wraps her arms around one of Gilbert's. "Me and a few friends are talking about going DT," she says. "Would you guys be up for that?"

"Going what?" I say.

"DT," she says.

"What's that?"

"It stands for downtown."

"Why didn't you just say downtown?"

"It's what they say on the internet," Gilbert says.

"That's fucking stupid," I say.

The girl glares. "Asshole." She stalks away.

"Whoops," I say. "Didn't mean to salt your game."

He raises his eyebrows, takes a sip, and says nothing. There's an open bottle of rum on the counter with a third left. I pick it up and take a swig. Some of it dribbles down my chin and neck. I take another.

Some time later—I'm not sure how long, exactly—I'm standing on a coffee table, shouting at a group of people gathered below me. "Never trust alliteration," I say. "Never! If someone feels it's necessary to convey a message using words that all begin with the same sound, you should be suspicious!" I drink from my beer. I sway. Someone steadies me. I hold the bottle up in the air. "When you use alliteration, you're not using the most appropriate words. You're just using words that sound similar.

Meaning gets sacrificed on the altar of alliteration! So does heart! And soul!"

Everyone laughs.

Gilbert appears. "We have to go."

"Why?" I say. I shout: "I'm only getting started!"

More laughter. I hold up my beer.

"I just played a central role in breaking something very valuable," Gilbert says. "I'm leaving right away. If you choose to stay, you will probably be required to produce a large quantity of money."

I step down from the coffee table. "Let's go DT."

We walk swiftly through the party, weaving through the packed hallway toward the staircase. "Excuse me," I say. "Excuse me. Excuse me."

When we're halfway down the staircase, someone shouts from above. "There he is! That's him!"

I look up. Fedora guy is standing at the top of the stairs, next to the guy who gave us the beers when we first arrived. The beer guy is pointing at Gilbert.

Fedora guy runs down the stairs toward us. Gilbert grabs me by the shirt and drags me around the corner and down the second flight. Fedora guy catches up with us at the front door, and grabs one of my arms. For a few protracted seconds, they play tug-of-war with me. Finally, Gilbert grasps my shirt with both hands and yanks me outside. Fedora guy is quick, though. He leaps after us and grabs my arm again.

Gilbert plucks the fedora off his head and throws it into the street. Fedora guy looks at his fedora lying there on the asphalt, and looks back at us. He looks at the fedora. A car is coming.

He lets go. We dash toward the Hummer.

Gilbert jumps in the driver's seat, and I open the passenger side door. "Wait," I say. "You've been drinking."

"Yes. I have. And if you don't get in right now, you'll be arrested."

I get in. Gilbert backs up to get clear of the car parked in front of us, whips around to face the other way, and drives into the night.

After a minute I say, "We're far enough. Find somewhere to park."

"Why?"

"You're drunk. You're driving drunk."

"So?"

"It's illegal."

"So is driving stoned."

"This is way different. I saw you drink a lot at that party."

"Not as much as you."

"Let me out. Pull over."

Gilbert rolls his eyes. "This isn't my first time driving after having a few."

"Pull over, Gilbert."

He stops the car in the middle of the road. I glare at him, open the door, and get out. I don't bother closing it.

Neither does he. It closes by itself as he speeds away.

Chapter Thirty-Three

I haven't spoken to Gilbert much since the party. I did ask him to make Frank take me off overnights. I no longer trust myself to work hard without supervision.

I've been experiencing strange things during overnights. I've seen stuff fall off the shelves without being touched. And, as I front, I keep seeing movement in my peripheral vision—like someone walking briskly past the aisles. Twice, I ran to check if anyone was there.

One time, with my earphones in, I thought I heard a woman call my name. I turned off my MP3 player and listened, but it didn't happen again. The voice sounded just like my mother.

I don't believe in ghosts, but at night, this place is freaking me out. I'm still seeing 37 a lot, too. More than before.

*

Why is everyone looking at me?

"Sheldon? You okay?"

"Yeah. Fine. Why?"

"You've barely said anything since we left the apartment."

Theresa and I are at the mall. We biked here with plans to see another movie. There are a lot of people here. More than I expected, I guess. And they all seem to be staring at me. Do people normally stare this much?

A cashier from Spend Easy passes in front of us. She sees Theresa, and seems about to say something to her, but then she sees me. She breaks eye contact and keeps walking.

I'd like to call out to her. I want to stare her in the face and ask her how her day is going. Make her uncomfortable. Make her pay for not talking to me.

Except, I can't remember her name.

"I need to use the washroom," I say.

"Sure."

I go into the Men's room and splash water on my face. I smoked with Gilbert after work, and I still feel stoned. I look stoned, too. My lids are heavy, and the skin under my eyes is dark. I wonder if Theresa knows.

She said I seem depressed, lately.

I rejoin her outside the restroom, and we walk to the theatre. The movie begins in 15 minutes, so we rush to buy our tickets and food. I get a large popcorn. It comes with one free refill. I want to kill this high as quickly as possible.

When we enter the theatre, the previews have already started. We find two seats together near the front. During the opening credits, I think about how vulnerable I am to the person sitting behind me. If that person had a knife, or a gun, he or she could easily take me out.

As discreetly as possible, I twist around and glance at the person sitting behind me. It's a little girl—probably five or six. I face forward.

"I need to use the washroom," I whisper to Theresa.

"You just went."

"Yes." I get up and start edging past people.

I call Gilbert from the restroom stall. He answers on the sixth ring.

"Gilbert, I feel like I'm going nuts. I keep thinking everyone's out to get me. A security guard looked at me, and I was sure he was about to throw me out. I'm tripping, here. I think the pot was laced with something."

"We used a vaporizer, Sheldon."

"So?"

"It only vaporizes the THC—nothing else. It wouldn't matter if it was laced."

"Why am I tripping balls, then?"

"Because you tend to trip balls."

"What? What do you mean?"

"You trip out. Over nothing."

"No I don't."

"Right."

"Thanks for your help, Gilbert." I hang up.

I go back into the theatre and resume cramming popcorn into my mouth. Theresa isn't saying anything. Is she upset with me? She probably thinks I'm a loser. I can't even stay sober long enough for one date. She doesn't smoke pot at all. She probably thinks I'm a huge stoner. This will likely be the last date we ever have.

After the movie, when she asks me what I thought of it, I have very little to say. I barely watched the movie. My thoughts kept repeating in my head, on loop, loud.

Scott Bartlett

On the bike ride home, it feels like the ground is rushing past underneath me. I keep asking Theresa to slow down. "We're not going that fast, Sheldon," she says once, but she slows down each time I ask.

I ride with her to her apartment. She gives me a kiss before going in. "Call me, okay?"

"Okay," I say. I get on my bike, and ride away.

*

I quit smoking pot. Theresa didn't ask me to, but I'm afraid it will start causing problems with us, if I continue. I got really scared, during our date—it made me realize how much it would hurt me to lose her.

That isn't the only reason I quit. When Gilbert asks why, I say, "I don't know. You'll probably think it's stupid."

"Probably. Why?"

"I started feeling like the only time I'm happy anymore is when I'm high."

"Were you happy before you started smoking?"

"Not really. Sometimes."

"Well, synthetic happiness is better than no happiness."

I visit my mother's grave, for the first time in months. Someone's planted something on it. I get down on my hands and knees and study it up close. It looks like a bunch of little ferns.

I stand up. I clasp my hands together and I bow my head. I say, "God, if you exist, please make my Mom happy, if she still exists somewhere."

I look up at the sky. There are a few clouds. I don't think they're trying to tell me anything. I don't feel any better, or any worse. Nothing has changed.

"I'm going to be okay, Mom," I say. "I'll come back."

Chapter Thirty-Four

Since I quit smoking weed, Theresa and I have gotten a lot closer—joking around a lot more, trusting each other more. We've been together almost every day, and a couple times we've stayed awake till the morning, lying in each other's arms, talking.

That's how I know this is a bad idea.

"How long has it been since you smoked?" Donovan says.

"Almost two weeks."

"Oh, man. This is gonna mess you up, then." He passes me the joint.

"Thanks." I take a hit and pass it back. "Do you have any eye drops?"

"Nope."

"Damn. I left mine home. Didn't think I'd be doing this tonight."

We're on break, standing behind the strip mall across the road from Spend Easy. The sun is setting. Someone drives past, and Donovan hides the joint behind his back till they're gone.

"Hey, man," Donovan says. "Are you okay?"

"Huh?"

"You don't look good. You wanna sit down?"

But then it's like the sun plummets below the horizon, and it all goes dark.

*

Shaking. Someone's shaking me.

"Sheldon? You all right? We have to get back to the store, man. We've been gone too long."

I open my eyes. Donovan's face hovers over me, concerned.

"Wasn't expecting that," I say.

He chuckles. "Yeah. I have a cousin who faints sometimes, smoking."

"Was I saying anything?"

"No. You cracked your head off the side of the building, though. You all right?"

"I feel warm." I look down at myself.

"I think you pissed yourself, dude."

"Fuck."

We walk back across the road to the Spend Easy parking lot, and Donovan grabs me some napkins from his car's glove box. I mop up as much of the urine as I can. I ask if he thinks it's noticeable, and he says yeah, it sort of is.

"I suggest you walk to Aisle One as quick as you can, pocket some eye drops, and go to the customer washroom."

"Yeah. Sorry, man. You probably weren't counting on this being so stressful."

"I'm not stressed."

I follow his advice. I walk through Aisle One, grabbing some eye drops off the shelf without stopping. The bottle comes encased in a cardboard box, which I stuff into my pocket and then walk to the customer restroom, making my strides as long as possible while attempting to appear casual. When I get there, I try the knob, but it won't turn. It's locked.

"Hey," someone says behind me.

I turn around. Eric is leaning against the wall, his massive arms crossed.

"Looks like you didn't make it in time," he says. He nods at my crotch.

"I spilled something," I say.

He uncrosses his arms, steps forward, and seizes the rectangular bulge in my pocket. "That feels like an awkward thing to be carrying around in your pants. What is it?"

"None of your business."

He reaches inside and takes it out. "Eye drops. Your eyes bothering you?"

I don't say anything.

He bends closer, and squints at me. "Looks a bit like pink eye. In both eyes. Do you have a receipt for this?"

"No."

"And if we ran it through the system, would it come up as purchased? Or stolen?"

Again, I say nothing.

"Let's head to Frank's office, shall we?" He makes a sweeping gesture that ends with his left hand pointing toward Aisle One. "After you."

I start walking slowly toward the store office. I can feel my heart beat. I struggle to put my thoughts together into some sort of plan. All I can think about is how difficult it would be to get a job anywhere else. This is my only work experience.

When we get to the office, Eric holds up the box of eye drops and tells Frank he found it on me, and that I was unable to produce a receipt. Also, that my eyes are red, and I smell of marijuana.

My pants are damp against my thighs.

Frank's eyes are locked on the box of eye drops. "I'm afraid we'll have to let you go. Employee theft results in immediate termination. We won't press charges. You will receive your final paycheck in the mail."

Eric smiles. Frank's eyes dart to his computer monitor. Sweat gleams on his forehead, and he's slowly clenching and unclenching his hands.

"Toodles, vegan," Eric says.

I take a breath. And another. I turn toward the door. Eric moves out of my way, still smiling.

I don't leave.

"I'm sure Randy has a Facebook account," I say.

"What does Randy have to do with this?" Frank says.

"I'm just saying that I can easily get in touch with him. And I have some compromising information about you, Frank. I think I'll go home and write it on his profile, for everyone to see."

"What's he talking about?" Eric says.

"Bye," I say. I take another step.

"Wait," Frank says. "You're not fired. You can stay."

The box of eye drops crumples in Eric's hand. "What the fuck?"

Frank's face is red. "Everyone in this room has a secret now, Eric. All three of us. Either all the secrets stay in this room, or they all get out. This isn't how I want it. But it's how it is."

"What's your secret?" Eric says.

"What's yours?" I say.

Eric glares at me, his hands clenched so tight they're shaking. "Get out, vegan. Get out before I throw you out."

"Sure thing, asshole."

*

The shift after our confrontation, I take a TV dinner and walk past the Meat department with it. Eric's restocking hamburger, and I hold up the dinner.

"Have you tried the Chicken Parmagiana, Eric?" I say. "It's fucking delicious."

His eyes narrow.

Another day, Theresa catches me stealing a bag of chips on her way back from the washroom to the front end. She sees me take them off the shelf and walk toward the warehouse.

"Are you going to pay for those?" she says.

"No."

"I didn't think you'd steal, Sheldon."

"It's just chips."

"What would your Mom say?"

Gilbert's sitting on his cart halfway down the aisle, tossing a box of popcorn into the air and catching it. He watches as I place the chips back on the shelf, and chuckles.

Theresa goes back to the front end. "What would your Mom say?" Gilbert says, mimicking her.

"Shut up."

"Life is a prison," he says. "Girlfriends are the jailors."

*

I asked Gilbert to arrange for me to work overnights again. We're a couple hours into one, smoking a joint in front of the store, when Matt rides up on a bicycle.

"Hey, Matt," I say.

"You need to stop giving Eric trouble," he says.

"What are you talking about?"

"He's worried about you exposing him. And he's taking it out on us."

"By hitting you? Why don't you call the cops, Matt? Why do you let him do that?"

"He threatens to hurt my family." Matt's voice is growing ragged. "He knows I have a sister from searching my Facebook profile, and he specifically mentions her. He's crazy, Sheldon. And he's military trained. He says if I tell, and they arrest him, he'll just pay bail and go after my sister."

"If you tell what?"

Matt sobs, and doesn't speak.

"What does he do to you, Matt?"

"He rapes them," Gilbert says, in the croak peculiar to people holding smoke in their lungs. He exhales, and I can see it disperse in the light shining out from Spend Easy.

I look at Matt. But Matt won't look at me, and he doesn't speak.

"Matt," I say. "You need to do something about this."

He shakes his head. "It's my fault. He says I sent him signals. Sometimes I think I could be gay. I probably did give Eric the wrong impression."

I put my hand to my forehead. "Even if that was true, he has no right," I say.

Tears roll down Matt's face. He stays silent.

"Go home, Matt," Gilbert says. "Go on, you poor bastard."

Matt gets on his bike and pedals away.

Gilbert holds the joint out to me. I take it and throw it on the ground, crushing it against the sidewalk with my foot.

"Eric rapes his employees?" I say. "Grown men? He just rapes the entire department, and no one does anything?"

"Not all of them," Gilbert says. "One or two, at any given time. The ones with the lowest confidence. Makes them think it's their fault. You heard him." He opens the door and heads into Spend Easy. I follow. "He screens all his new hires. A lot of his workers are poor. It's not that surprising no one exposes him. Statistically, men raped by other men are the least likely to report it."

"How long have you known about this?"

"A while."

"Why haven't you done anything about it?"

"Eric knows I'm blackmailing Frank." Gilbert leads me down Aisle Five, grabbing a bottle filled with caramel corn on the way to the warehouse. "If I screw him, he'll screw me. Pardon the pun."

"That's disgusting. You're fucking disgusting."

He whirls around, and jabs me in the chest with the caramel corn. "Back the fuck up, Sheldon. Quit being self-righteous long enough to use your brain. Eric's an insane motherfucker. If I recall correctly, he's suspect number one for locking you in the freezer. How do I know he won't really go after his employees' families, if he's exposed? How do you know? Are you going to take that risk?"

I say nothing. I'm grinding my teeth.

"What do we do in this society, when we see atrocity? Huh? What do we do, when we learn our favourite clothes were made by kids in sweatshops? What do we do, when it comes out that first-world governments are torturing people? We look the other way, and we say thank God it's not me. Then we go see a movie. Read a book, maybe."

He turns again and walks toward the warehouse. I stay where I am.

"If Eric goes down," Gilbert says as he leaves, "he's taking all of us with him. Me, Frank, and even you, Sheldon. You're part of this, now, too."

*

I sleep past my alarm, and get up late—too late to make it on time for my shift. I trudge to the washroom and start brushing my teeth.

The bristles hurt my gums. That's weird. I look down at the toothbrush, and there's a tiny bead of blood.

I brush more carefully, and when I'm finished I rip off some floss and insert it between two molars. The floss gets stuck, though, and I wiggle it back and forth, trying to work it out. Four of my teeth fall out, and a large section of my gums comes with them, tearing away like play-dough. It all falls into the sink with a *splat*, and lies there, glistening.

I wake up, drenched in sweat, to the phone ringing.

Just a dream.

"Hey, Sheldon? This is Ralph. Just calling to make sure everything's all right."

"I slept in."

"No problem. Try to make it in as soon as you can."

"Actually, Ralph, I'm not feeling well. I don't think I can come in, today."

"Very good." He hangs up.

I walk into the living room. For a long time, I sit on the couch with my head in my hands.

Chapter Thirty-Five

I'm working another overnight, and I just want to be baked. So baked I can't think.

But Gilbert has no weed. He says the biggest local dealer got busted, and the town's all but dry.

If he has none, the town must truly be dry. According to Donovan, Gilbert's phone is full of drug dealers' numbers. He doesn't have a regular supplier—he buys it from whoever's selling it cheapest, to increase his profit when he resells. Which is pretty ironic, considering I've heard plenty of people say Gilbert sells the best dope.

We're sitting in the break room. Tommy's not on tonight, and I don't think either of us is likely to do any work. I'm not sure what we're going to tell Ralph tomorrow.

Gilbert looks up from his phone. "We should have a party."

I nod. "By all means. You should throw a party. There are so many reasons to celebrate."

"I said we should have a party. Tonight. Inside Spend Easy."

"That's pretty funny."

"I know. It would be hilarious."

I sigh. "Are you being serious?"

"It'd be easy. All I'd have to do is go outside, put on a mask, come back in, and disable the cameras from Frank's office. We'll make sure everyone's gone by morning. Then we could tell Frank a bunch of guys broke in and prevented us from leaving while they trashed the place."

"How would they prevent us from leaving?"

He shrugs. "Tie us up."

"This is a profoundly bad idea."

"I'm texting people now. I'll get Donovan to bring a mask."

Donovan shows up in 15 minutes, and I follow Gilbert as he walks through the store to meet him. "Can't Frank access the cameras from home?" I say. "What if he notices the feed's stopped?"

"It's past midnight, Sheldon. Frank's not that motivated."

"What if someone driving by notices a party? Think they won't report it?"

"I'm sure everyone realizes this is party-at-your-own-risk. I don't think we need a disclaimer."

"I'm not worried about them."

"Go back to the warehouse and get some overstock or something. You can't come with me while I do this."

Within an hour, there are at least 40 people in the store. When he texted them, Gilbert told them each to park in a different place—some at the strip mall across the road, a couple at the nearby gas station, a few more behind Spend Easy.

Gilbert made one rule: stay away from the windows near the front. Otherwise, he told them to do whatever they want. It'll only make the 'takeover' seem more realistic.

So the guests/intruders are helping themselves to everything in the store. That's not limited to eating—one guy tears a little hole in two bags of macaroni and takes to flicking them about, twin streams of pasta flailing around Aisle Two. In Aisle Five, someone sets up a bowling lane, complete with pineapple pins and the roundest watermelon to be found. And in Produce, a girl starts puncturing and draining coconuts for people to use as flasks.

As for Gilbert's rule, no one follows it. People are standing around the cash registers, talking, drinking, and smoking. There are at least 10 cars parked right out front. This is the sketchiest thing I've ever participated in.

I can't see Gilbert anywhere.

I'm halfway down Aisle Three when something whizzes past my right ear and hits a bottle of canola oil, leaving a neon orange splatter.

I turn around. There's a guy standing at the end of the aisle with a paintball gun pointed at me. He waves.

"Sorry, bro! Thought you were someone else." He disappears from view.

Wonderful.

As I enter the warehouse, Tool starts blaring from the ceiling speakers. I find Donovan and a few others gathered around the cardboard compactor. There's an open box of beer sitting on a pallet. I take one and open it.

"Have you seen Gilbert?" I say.

"He's in the break room," Donovan says.

"What's he doing?"

"Well, he has two girls in there with him, and they have the door barred. So your guess is as good as mine."

"What are you doing?"

"Playing a game."

"What game?"

"We're calling it Put It in the Compactor and Press the Green Button."

A girl places a carton of whole milk on top of the cardboard and hits the button. The machine descends, crushing it.

"That was kind of disappointing," she says. "You could barely even see the milk come out."

What was she expecting?

"I did so much coke tonight," Donovan says to me. "I'm blitzed."

"Do you know about Eric?" I say.

"What about him?"

"How he's...abusing his employees."

"What are you talking about?"

"He's sexually abusing his employees. Matt's one of them. I'm thinking about going to the police."

"You think they'd believe you? How would you prove anything, even if it's true? Holy shit," he says, looking at a guy wearing a yellow hoodie, who has taken out a blunt and started passing it around. "Where'd you get weed in this town?"

The guy chuckles. "Pretty sure I'm the last one within a 30-mile radius with any. If you see someone smoking dope tonight, they got it from me."

Donovan hits it, and passes it to me. I hit it too. I pass it to whole milk girl.

"Can you believe Gilbert invited people here?" I say to Donovan.

"Gilbert doesn't give a fuck, man."

"It's getting out of control. I'm gonna start kicking people out."

"That would piss him off. I wouldn't piss Gilbert off."

"What's he going to do me? We're friends. He'll get over it."

Donovan laughs. "Really? You really think Gilbert's your friend?"

I hesitate. "Yeah, I do."

He puts a hand on my shoulder, still laughing. "Sheldon. Buddy. Gilbert's the one who locked you in the freezer."

Someone passes me the blunt. "What did you just say?"

"Gilbert locked you in the freezer."

"He wasn't working that night."

"I know. See, Brent never used to write down his schedule— he just called every night to find out if he was working the next day. I was here the night before you got trapped, and Gilbert told me to tell Brent he wasn't scheduled. The next night, Gilbert snuck in, hid till you went into the freezer, and then closed the door behind you."

"Why?"

"He figured you'd assume it was Jack, and he wanted everyone in Grocery to think Produce was out to get them. And he wanted everyone working harder—to pacify Frank long enough to get more dirt on him."

"Hey," says the only guy in town with weed. "Are you gonna smoke that, or are you afraid you'll piss yourself?"

"What?" I say.

"Donovan told us how dope makes you tinkle."

I look at Donovan. "Thanks a lot." I throw the blunt at him, and he bounces it between his hands a couple times before catching it.

"Hey, man. I consider us friends."

I turn around and walk toward the stairs.

328   Scott Bartlett

"Don't bother Gilbert, Sheldon," Donovan says.

"Shut up."

I knock on the break room door twice. No answer. I try to push it open. Something's blocking it. I throw my shoulder against the door. It opens an inch before swinging closed. I slam my body against it, and it opens farther.

I'm backing up for a third time when the door opens a crack, and Gilbert peers out at me.

"What?"

"You lied to me."

"What are you talking about?"

I kick the door. Gilbert steps back. I kick it again and squeeze through. The table was blocking it. Two girls are huddled together in the far corner, attempting to cover themselves, with partial success. I ignore them. Gilbert's leaning against the counter wearing only underwear.

"You locked me in the freezer," I say. "I could have frozen to death."

"No I didn't."

"Donovan told me, you asshole."

He doesn't say anything for a couple seconds. "Now, why would he go and do that?"

"I could have died in there."

"Someone found you, didn't they? I would have let you out, if no one else had."

"That's not the point."

"It addresses the point you just made."

"I thought we were friends."

"We weren't really friends, then. We weren't even hanging out."

"I'm done with you, Gilbert. Done."

"You're breaking up with me?"

I swing my fist at him, but he grabs it, twisting my arm and slamming me face-down onto the table.

"How far are we going with this, Sheldon? How much do you want me to embarrass you?"

"Fuck you, Gilbert."

He lets me up. I glare at him a moment longer, and I start to leave.

"Sheldon."

I look back.

"I didn't lie to you nearly as much as you lie to yourself."

I leave the break room, walk down the hall, and descend the staircase. On my way through the warehouse, I pass Donovan, who's holding a CD in one hand and a marijuana bud in the other.

"Where are you going?" he says.

"Home."

"But you're working."

I keep walking. Donovan chases after me.

"Hey," he says. "I think you should know. That weed we just smoked? It has silica dust in it. Look." He rubs the bud on the CD, and it leaves a scratch. "That means it's grit weed. Dealers do that sometimes, to increase the weight, and rip people off. We now have silica particles in our lungs."

I walk faster. Donovan does too, holding the pot and the CD, gaping like an idiot. A paintball zooms by and splatters on the floor in front of Aisle Five. Donovan stops.

"Whatever, Sheldon." He goes back into the warehouse.

In the front of the store, some of our guests are lining up shots on the Service counter. I grab one as I walk by, toss it back, and throw the shot glass in the trash.

"Hey!" someone shouts.

There's a case of beer sitting on the floor underneath the window. I grab a bottle and twist off the top, tossing it over my shoulder. I leave Spend Easy.

I'm halfway across the parking lot when I hear sirens. Two patrol cars are speeding closer, to my left. I walk toward the Cart Corral, trying to be casual. If they're headed here, hopefully they won't notice me.

Both cars pull into the parking lot. Before they can reach me, I place the bottle inside the Corral.

One of the cruisers stops nearby. An officer gets out, glances at me, and opens the back door.

Frank emerges. He looks me in the eye.

"Have you been drinking?" the cop says.

"No."

"I saw him hide a bottle," Frank says.

"Are you sure about that, Frank?" I say. "We all have secrets. Remember?"

"Right," he says. "I forgot to mention, Officer. I'm gay."

The cop gives a slight nod. "Noted." He walks toward the Cart Corral, and finds the beer bottle. He holds it up. "I saw you put this here, too. Looks like you're coming with us."

Chapter Thirty-Six

I quit weed again.

I watched a video recently in which a bald Chuck Palahniuk explains how he shaves his head every time he finishes a novel, in order to discard his old self, start fresh, and begin writing the next book. I decide to apply the same idea to my marijuana habit. I buy electric clippers, and stand in front of the mirror. The hair falls from my head in clumps. I remove the uneven stubble that remains with a safety razor.

I hate the way it looks.

Good.

"If I smoke again, I have to shave it again," I say to my reflection.

The police could have charged me with being intoxicated in public. But given my lack of a criminal record, they decided against it. Frank had already told them he intended to fire me. "Hopefully termination will be lesson enough," one police officer said.

I assume Gilbert lost his job too, and Donovan. I haven't spoken with them.

I can't stop thinking about what Eric is doing to his employees. Someone has to say something. But Eric threatened to go
after their families—would he really do that?

And who's going to believe the guy who just got fired for
throwing a party in a grocery store?

I decide to tell Theresa. She'll know what to do.

She knocks on my door the morning after I shave my head.
She doesn't say anything about my lack of hair.

"I have something I need to talk to you about," I say.

She looks down. "I can't do this anymore, Sheldon."

"What?"

"I'm sorry. I can't."

She's breaking up with me.

"But—I quit smoking pot," I say, without much hope.

"It's not about that. When I first saw you again, at Spend
Easy, you seemed so collected. You seemed like you were better.
You made me happy." She sighs. "You're a mess, now, Sheldon.
I'm afraid that if I stay with you, I may not stay better. It breaks
my heart, because I care about you a lot. But I've worked too
hard to risk my health like this."

I wipe my eyes. "I care about you too, Theresa. So much." I
try to keep my voice from cracking. I fail.

She's crying, now, too. "Can you try to understand, Sheldon?
Can you at least try?"

"I understand," I whisper.

She takes my hand, and for a moment, I think she's going to
kiss me. But she lets go, and then she leaves.

I forgot to tell her about Eric.

The phone rings. I walk to the kitchen.

"Hello?"

"Hey, this is Brad. I'm calling this morning to tell you that you're awesome."

I hang up. Then I pick up the phone again, and dial Gilbert's number.

*

Donovan's having a party tonight, and Gilbert says he'll pick me up, and bring a joint for us to smoke on the way. I pace around my apartment all day. Nothing interests me—not even the internet. And the apartment is so silent. It was never this quiet, with Marcus Brutus around. I could turn on some music, but I don't.

When the Hummer pulls into the driveway, I already have my sneakers on. "Nice haircut," Gilbert says when I get in.

"Thanks."

"The town's still dry. I only have a couple joints. I don't wanna waste them on anyone at the party. All right?"

"All right."

"By the way—just so you don't try to tell me this weed's laced, I got it from a guy who buys from Sam. If you start tripping out, that's all you."

He lights a joint and pulls out of the driveway.

"So," I say. "Are you looking for another job?"

He shakes his head. "I'm working with a guy now to end this dry spell. Who knows—maybe after this, I'll be the town's main dealer." He chuckles. "I can't go back to a normal job, where I actually have to do work. Not after Spend Easy."

"Nice haircut," Donovan says when we walk in.

The party isn't really a party. It's only Donovan, Casey, Lesley-Jo, and a girl I don't know, sitting around and drinking.

"Hey, Sheldon," the girl says.

"Hey," I say. "What's your name?"

"We, uh, went to high school together."

"Oh. Sorry. I have a terrible memory."

"It's Rita."

"Right. Sorry."

She raises her eyebrows, and says nothing.

Gilbert brought a bottle of liquor with him, which he's pouring down his throat at a rapid pace. He keeps offering me shots, but after the first I don't take any more. Everyone else is drinking beer. I brought a half-case, but I haven't opened it yet. I don't feel like drinking.

They're talking about hockey when I interrupt. "How much silica dust entered my lungs at the Spend Easy party last week, do you think?"

Everyone looks at me.

"There was silica in that weed?" the girl from my high school says.

What's her name, again?

"Were you there?" I say.

"Yeah."

"I heard it'll kill you, after a while," Donovan says. "After you smoke grit weed, it's only a matter of time."

"Oh my God," I say. "Holy shit." My chest feels tight. I take a deep breath. I can feel my heart beating.

Gilbert rolls his eyes. "You'd have to smoke pounds of it. You're not going to die from smoking it once. Jesus."

"That's not what I read," Donovan says.

"On the internet?"

Donovan doesn't answer, and Gilbert laughs.

The conversation returns to hockey. Donovan isn't saying much, though, and I notice him glance at me a couple times. I think he suspects I'm high.

Actually, he definitely knows. Gilbert's better at hiding it than me, but it's easy to tell when I'm baked. Donovan will probably ask me soon. I can't lie for shit. He'll be pissed off when he realizes we held out on him.

The girl who went to my high school looks at me. "Are you gonna drink any of those?" She glances at my beer.

"Sorry, what's your name again?" I say.

"You forgot it already?"

"I'm bad with names. I'm really sorry."

"Rita. My name's Rita."

"Okay. Sorry. I'm really stoned."

For a moment, the conversation goes silent.

"You're stoned?" Casey says.

"How are you stoned?" Lesley-Jo says.

"Just kidding!" I try to laugh. "Sorry. That was a dumb joke."

Donovan stands up and bends closer. "You are, aren't you? I can smell it. I thought I smelled it earlier, but I assumed I was going nuts. Where'd you get dope?"

"I—" I can't think of a single thing to say. I make sure not to look at Gilbert. Hopefully they won't suspect him.

"I had some," Gilbert says. "We smoked it on the way over here so we didn't have to share with you yahoos."

"Jerk," Donovan says. He sits down again. And their conversation resumes.

I text Gilbert to ask if I can speak with him in private.

Across the room, Gilbert's phone buzzes, and he picks it up. "Sure, Sheldon," he says in a robotic monotone. "We can speak in private."

He's making fun of me.

We put on our shoes and go outside.

"Hey, man, sorry for giving you away, in there," I say. "I'm so baked, I don't know what I'm saying."

"It's not a big deal. Besides. They don't know I have more." He takes the other joint out of his pocket and wiggles it between his fingers.

We get in his Hummer and light it. He turns on some music and we smoke it in silence. After a couple passes, Gilbert's phone vibrates.

"That's Rita," he says. "She's asking if we're smoking more weed." He starts tapping on the screen.

"Are you telling her?"

"Hell no."

The front door opens, and Donovan sticks his head out. He spots us, and comes outside. He's not wearing any shoes. Rita and Casey emerge behind him.

"Gilbert!" I say. "Look!"

He glances up, and then fishes his keys out of his pocket. He starts the engine.

Donovan begins running toward us. Gilbert slams the gear shift into reverse, and pulls out of the driveway. He speeds away, beeping his horn at them. We're both laughing.

He passes me the joint.

"Wait," I say. "You're drunk."

"I'm fine."

"You should pull over, though. You—"

"Shut up, Sheldon."

"Okay. I'm sorry."

"Right."

"I trust you, you know."

"Okay. Give me the joint."

I pass it. "I shouldn't question you, all the time. You've done a lot for me. I know that."

"Okay."

"You're the best friend I've ever had."

He glances at me. "Yeah?"

"Whoa, watch out for that guy, Gilbert. You're going off the—"

"Where?"

"Right there!"

Chapter Thirty-Seven

I'm walking along Foresail Road. It's still dark.

Donovan's party is over, I guess.

I left with Gilbert. Right? We smoked the joint, and we drove—

Where?

Maybe I should call him.

My phone isn't in my pocket.

I don't have my phone. Did I leave it at Donovan's?

I guess I'll have to walk home.

My apartment is in the opposite direction. Where am I going? Is there somewhere I need to be?

It must be pretty late.

It's cold.

And I'm scared.

I come to a 24-hour gas station. I go in, and ask the attendant what time it is. He tells me it's 3:37 AM.

I return to the road and continue walking.

I touch my head. Tiny little bristles. I need to shave it again, don't I? I smoked pot again.

I think I have a drug problem. Maybe a drinking problem. I think I need some help.

I keep walking.

By the time I arrive at her grave, it's no longer dark.

I lie down. Six feet above Mom.

I fall asleep.

*

In my nightmare, it turns out Tommy was right, after all. He was just off by a few months.

*

When I wake up, I'm lying on top of those ferns somebody planted. I'd forgotten about them.

How deep do fern roots go? Could they reach down one day, and get tangled in her bones?

I start digging, with my fingers.

I still feel high. There was definitely something extra in that weed.

This plant is not ferns.

This plant is a carrot.

It only takes me a few seconds to dig it up. The earth is loose.

It's a small carrot. It's July, so it hasn't had long to grow.

I'm still high, and I'm tripping out.

I take a bite of the carrot. I chew. I take another bite.

That helps.

*

On the way home, I stop into the same gas station and ask to use their phone. I try to call Gilbert, but there's no answer.

Where is he? What happened last night?

I'm still high. Something very strange is going on. I have a lot of questions.

But I know, now, where to find the answers.

At my apartment, I go straight to the closet where I keep everything Mom owned. I've barely looked in there since I moved into this place. It was too painful to go through her stuff, deciding what to toss and what to keep. I just shoved it all in here, and tried not to think about it.

I close my eyes and open the door. I reach inside. My hand closes on a book, and I take it out. I open my eyes. It's Mom's Bible.

I never knew Mom to believe in God. She bought this shortly before she died, and I have a hunch she did start believing, then. I think she was right to believe. When she died, I think she found herself in heaven.

Recently, Mom's been sending me signals. In the form of 37.

I don't know how I didn't see this before.

I open to page 37, and start reading. I'm surprised to find that the stories are all about me.

How have I missed this? I've read Bibles. But I never noticed that every single sentence is about me. About how, all these millennia, history has been leading to my birth.

I start flipping to random pages, amazed at how blind I've been. Every passage bears a coded message, meant for me. The hairs on the back of my neck are tingling.

I learn that I had a life before this, which spanned eons upon eons.

I lived in Hell.

I am the antichrist.

Mom knew this—the Bible tells me that, too. She tried to teach me to be good, but the guilt of having birthed the antichrist became too much. When Herman Barry ran her down, she welcomed it.

As the antichrist, I am fated to end the world.

"No," I whisper. I'm crying.

I am good. I won't participate.

Destiny can be averted. All I have to do is die.

I go to the kitchen and open the cutlery drawer. I select the longest, sharpest knife I can find.

I go into the washroom and plug the tub. I turn on the hot water and wait for it to fill up, kneeling on the floor. I roll up my sleeves and lean with my forearms against the lip of the tub. The knife dangles from my fingers.

When the tub is full, I place the blade against my wrist. I breathe deep. I don't want to do this. I'm afraid. I'm afraid it will hurt, and I'm afraid to die. I want to live.

But if I don't go, everyone else will. I think about Theresa. After I lost Mom, I convinced myself I didn't need anyone.

I need Theresa.

But I won't let her die. I'll kill myself before I let that happen.

My hand shaking, I pierce the skin.

This isn't right.

I think I'm supposed to do this in the shed, instead.

I stand up and walk back through the apartment.

Sam is standing in the living room.

I bring the knife behind my back. "I didn't hear you knock," I say.

"What are you doing with the knife?"

I give up trying to hide it.

Sam takes a step backward.

"Please put that down," he says.

"Get out of my way, Sam."

"Are you threatening me?"

"No."

"Then please put down the knife."

I drop it. It sticks in the carpet and doesn't fall over.

Slowly, Sam moves forward. I watch as he grasps the handle and pulls out the knife. He brings it back to the kitchen, and then returns to the living room.

"Sit down." He points to the couch. I sit.

"Why don't you tell me what's going on?" He sits beside me.

"I—" I can't say anything, because I'm going to cry again.

"What's the matter?"

Tears run down my cheek. I manage to speak: "I don't feel like I'm real."

"What do you mean?"

"I feel like I'm dead, or something. Am I dead, Sam?"

He shakes his head. His eyes are wide. "No. You're not dead, Sheldon."

"Can you hold my hand? Please."

His eyes narrow, and his own hand twitches. "Why?"

"Please. I feel like I'm going to disappear."

I'm the most frightened I've ever been.

Sam takes my right hand in his left. I look at his face. My vision blurs, and his face becomes distorted. It twists around. He becomes ugly.

"Sam?"

"Yes?"

"You look like a demon."

"Thanks."

"No offense, I mean. I didn't mean—"

"None taken. What's going on?"

"I think I have a drug problem. I can't quit. And last night, I smoked a joint with Gilbert, and I'm still high. I haven't come down yet. It's been hours and hours. I don't understand why it won't end."

He stands up. "Come with me. We need to get you out of here."

I follow him outside. There's a brown car parked in our driveway. He sits behind the wheel, and I sit in the passenger seat.

"Who owns this car?"

"My cousin. He's visiting, and he let me use it to go search for you."

"Why were you searching for me?"

"Never mind that."

We drive. I look at the clock. It's 7:37. I watch until it changes. It takes a very, very long time.

"The clock just took like 15 minutes to change, Sam."

He glances down at it. "I don't think so."

"Did you mess with it? Are you playing a joke?"

"I'm not."

"Where are you taking me?"

He clears his throat and doesn't say anything. He turns on the radio.

It's a talk show. "He throws all his junk in the backyard and leaves it there," a lady is saying. "It's an eyesore, and he doesn't care one bit. I've put in several complaints to the Town, but no one listens. That trash heap he calls a yard is reducing my property value. It's not at all fair. If he moved to Australia tomorrow, I wouldn't miss him. Not one bit."

"Sam?" I say. "Are you taking me to the airport? Are you sending me away?"

"No, Sheldon."

I think he's lying.

A commercial comes on: "His name is Bubbles Z. Clown, and he's the funniest clown around town! He does kids parties of all ages, and he's even been known to keep a roomful of adults entertained. Juggling, balloon animals, jokes, dancing, and laughter—these—"

"Sam?"

"Yes?"

"Do you think I'm a clown?"

"Let's turn that off, okay?" He hits a button, and the man's voice cuts out.

"Where are you taking me?"

"The hospital, Sheldon. I'm taking you to the hospital."

*

While we wait, Sam lets me use his phone as much as I want. I try about 20 times to reach Gilbert. He's still not answering.

I told a nurse everything that's happened. Sam and I have been sitting around for hours since then. I get the sense there's something he isn't telling me, and I spend most of the time wondering what it could be.

"Sam?"

"Yeah?"

"Is Capriana pregnant?"

"Who's Capriana?"

"Never mind."

*

Throughout the day, Sam grows more and more agitated. His answers to my questions become terser.

He keeps checking his watch.

Finally, nine hours after our arrival, a nurse tells me the doctor is ready to see me. She leads us through a series of corridors. Sam holds me back until we're out of her earshot.

"If they give you a choice," he says, "between staying in the psych ward and going home, tell them you want to stay."

"But I don't want to. I hate it here."

"Trust me."

"You just want to get rid of me."

"No. Wrong. I'm giving you very good advice."

After hearing what's happened over the last 12 hours, the doctor says it seems likely I'm experiencing acute psychosis brought on by marijuana use. She says that for a small percentage of users, high doses can trigger this. She gives me the option of either staying in the hospital's psychiatric ward and

awaiting treatment or booking an appointment and being treated as an outpatient.

"What do you think I should do?"

"I'm afraid I can't make that decision for you."

I hesitate. "What time is it?"

"10 after five."

I clear my throat.

"I'll stay, I guess."

*

No one ever smiles, in here. If you smile at someone, they'll
only look back at you, blank-faced. I haven't personally tried
smiling, but I've seen it happen.

Sam brought me my essentials—toothbrush, MP3 player,
Velcro shoes.

"What am I missing, Sam? What's going on?"

But he remains silent, and stares into space, his jaw set.
Eventually, I stop asking.

I guess sometimes the mind just skips, like a CD. You can try
taking it out and putting it back in. If that doesn't work, you
can try cleaning it off with your sleeve. And, as a last resort, you
can buy one of those scratch repair kits.

If all else fails, you throw it on the trash heap.

I see another doctor the day after I'm admitted. She pre-
scribes a half milligram of an antipsychotic—another drug
that's supposed to correct the chemical imbalances that plague
my brain.

I refuse it.

They call Sam, and within a half hour he's standing with me in front of the Nurses Station. We both stare down at the little half-pill sitting in the tiny plastic cup.

"I don't want it," I say.

"Taking it is part of staying here, Sheldon. They're trying to get you back to where you were."

"I don't like where I was."

"Then aim for a better place."

"It's another drug, Sam. The doctor said it was marijuana that caused all this."

"This pill isn't pot. This pill is designed to rebalance your neurotransmitters. Pot did the opposite."

"You smoke pot. It doesn't do that to you."

"Your brain is different from mine."

I take a deep breath and flick the half-pill into my throat, washing it down with water from a paper cup. Sam and I look at each other, and he gives a small smile. "It feels like it's stuck in my throat," I say.

I spend most of my time in here feeling guilty. My doctor seems to pick up on it, and now she questions me about it every session. But I have no answers for her. All I know is that there must be a reason I keep ending up here.

At first, I was convinced that everyone I've ever known secretly hates me, and is working to make sure I'm stuck in this psych ward forever. A lot of the people I see look very familiar— patients, nurses, doctors, visitors. One woman resembles one of my seventh-grade teachers, and I wonder if it really is her, in disguise. Another woman resembles my deceased grandmother. Did she really die, or did she just pretend, so she wouldn't have to see me anymore?

I include Sam in this—he drove me here, after all. He's probably done with me. Just wants to make sure I stay put. Once and for all.

And where's Gilbert? I try to call him every day. I feel like it's important that I reach him.

For a few days, I believed I was the star of a reality TV show. The most popular one in history. Incredible ratings. Viewers on the edge of their couches—amused and enthralled by my suffering.

But now, I've concluded that I'm really in Hell. Not the fire-and-brimstone Hell you've heard about. Hell is nothing like that, it turns out.

Hell is a place where you hurt the people you love, without meaning to.

I realized yesterday that I've been in Hell for a long time, without knowing. As for how long, exactly, I believe there are two possibilities.

One is that I got here a year ago, when I tried to commit suicide. Except, I really did succeed in killing myself. My memory was simply altered, so I believed that I was still alive.

The second is that I've been in Hell all my life. I lived a life before this in which I sinned a lot, and now I'm paying for it, by spending a second lifetime in Hell.

If the first possibility is true, then I assume Sam is Satan. He's the one who escorted me into Hell, after all—by 'saving' me from hanging. Plus, the names are sort of similar.

If the second possibility is true, then a patient named Lou must be Satan. It's pretty conspicuous, actually—Lou could be short for Lucifer. Also, he keeps challenging me to play chess. I think he wants to play for my soul.

As for how I feel about all this, I guess I'm taking it in stride. Or rather, I've grown accustomed to the fear that's been with me since I found myself walking alone on the side of the road. Becoming accustomed to fear is a lot like being calm. Other than the jitters, and the jumping at every sound, and the wide eyes I see every time I look in a mirror.

At any rate, I'm certain I deserve everything that's happening to me.

On my fourth day, I'm visited by Paul and Cassandra. They're a couple, now.

"Your belly's big," I say.

"Your hair is all gone," she says.

Cassandra knew I was here, because I sent her an email and told her. Patients are allowed access to the internet between 1 and 2 PM, in the Occupational Therapy room.

They do most of the talking. Sam says I've barely said anything since I was admitted. Cassandra tells me a publisher accepted Paul's novel, and they're even paying him a small advance. (Now that's the kind of irony you'd expect in Hell.) Apparently his editor thinks Paul really captured the 'zeitgeist', and predicts the book will sell well.

"Why did you ask Cassandra to come here, Sheldon?" Paul says.

I hesitate. "I just wanted—I want to—"

'Apologize' is the word that's sitting in my brain, waiting to be said. But what am I supposed to be apologizing for? I know there's something.

"I think I figured something out," I say to them instead. "I think that marijuana was my personal forbidden fruit." Their faces are blank. "I wasn't supposed to smoke it. See? Smoking it put me here, and in here, I have knowledge of good and evil."

I take a breath, and go on: "I now know that in order to live, you have to kill. You know what I mean? You have to kill, or someone has to do your killing for you. Life consumes life. The symbol for eternity is a snake eating its own tail. And a snake told Eve to eat the apple. But the Bible doesn't even mention an apple. I googled it this morning, and in certain texts that apple is referred to as fruit from a 'forbidden tree.' So why not a forbidden plant—that is to say, pot?"

Paul seems angry, now. "Pot isn't why you're here, Sheldon. It's not what caused your brain to break."

"Paul," Cassandra says.

"What do you mean?" I say, slowly.

"What do you remember from Friday night?" Paul says. "What's the last thing you remember?"

"Stop it, Paul," Cassandra says. "The doctors told us—"

"What are you talking about?" I say.

But Paul is silent. He glares at the wall, and Cassandra avoids my gaze, too.

"How is Matt?" I say.

They look at each other.

"Matt was arrested," Cassandra says.

"What?" I say. "Why?"

"He attacked Eric with a knife from the Meat room. Eric managed to get it away from him, and then called the police."

"I always thought he was a little off," Paul says.

"Didn't Matt say why he did it?"

Cassandra shakes her head.

"Eric sexually abuses Matt. That's why he attacked him. Eric threatens to hurt his family if he tells."

Paul stands up. "Come on, Cassandra. I've had enough."

I stand, too. "You have to believe me. Please."

Paul puts his hand up. "Back off, Sheldon. Don't contact us again."

They walk toward the door.

"Wait," I say. "Have you been talking to Gilbert?"

"No one has," Paul says. And they leave.

*

Later, a nurse finds me in the common area and says there's someone here to see me. She leads me through a couple doors that she has to open with a key. She holds them for me and watches as I pass. I've noticed that the nurses never turn their backs to me.

She brings me to a room with a long table, and closes the door once I'm inside. I hear her lock it.

There's a police officer standing with his hand on the back of one of the chairs. A doctor is sitting at the head of the table—she's the one who admitted me.

"Hi Sheldon. I'm Officer Benson. Have a seat."

I sit. He sits across from me.

"I have a few questions for you."

I look at him in silence.

He clears his throat. "Are you acquainted with Gilbert Ryan?"

"Yes."

"Do you know his whereabouts?"

"No. Do you? I've been trying—"

"I don't. That's why I'm asking you."

"Okay."

"Are you acquainted with a young man—younger than you and Mr. Ryan—named Leonard Reynolds?"

"No. Who is that?"

"Where were you on July 13th, at 2:32 in the morning?"

I consider this. "I can't remember exact times," I say. "I was either at a party or in Gilbert's car."

"Were you intoxicated?"

"Yes."

"Was Mr. Ryan?"

I don't say anything.

"It's a crime to lie to a law officer, Sheldon. Was Mr. Ryan intoxicated?"

"You don't have to answer if you don't want," the doctor says.

I hesitate. "He was drunk," I say.

"What happened during your car ride?" Officer Benson asks.

"I don't know."

"You don't remember?"

"I was in the car, and then I was walking on the side of the road. I don't remember what happened in between."

"So, you claim to have localized amnesia."

For a few seconds, Officer Benson looks at me, and I look at Officer Benson. Then he stands up. "Thank you for your time. Another officer may come by another day, for another chat."

"Do you know what happened?" I say.

The doctor clears her throat, and they exchange glances.

"I'm afraid I can't talk to you about that," Officer Benson says.

He leaves.

*

I ask Sam who Leonard Reynolds is, and he looks at me without speaking for a while.

Then he asks where I heard that name. I tell him about the visit from the police officer, and his lips get tight, and he marches down the hall toward the Nurses Station. I watch him make sweeping gestures with his hands, and I can hear him shouting. I can't make out the words, though.

I go into the TV room, and Lou is there, watching some cooking show. The chef is processing lean cuts in a blender.

"Have a seat," Lou says.

I remain standing.

The chef pours the meat mush onto a countertop and uses cookie cutters to make little shapes. He places these on a cookie tray, and slides them into an oven. 40 minutes pass in a matter of seconds, and he takes out the meat shapes.

"Delicious meat cookies!" the chef says. He puts on some sprinkles. They look just like regular cookies.

Lou glances at me, and grins. "Look good, don't they?"

He changes the channel. A TV preacher appears, staring me right in the eyes.

He's saying, "The Christian person's job is to spread God's message as effectively as we can. But we have our work cut out for us. It's almost impossible to transfer an idea perfectly from one mind to another. Language is not sufficient."

Lou turns off the TV. "You know," he says, "I'm all religions. Christian, Muslim, Buddhist. Atheist, even. I'm whatever I need to be."

I don't say anything.

The preacher is right. Words don't mean what I thought they meant. They're like simple tools I've forgotten how to use.

Sam is returning from the Nurses Station as I leave the TV room. He's red in the face.

"Sam?" I say. "What are my shoes made of?"

"Leather."

"I know, but—leather from what animal?"

"Cows."

"Are you sure?"

"Yes."

"How do you know for sure?"

"What else would they be made from? Come with me, Sheldon. I brought you something."

We go to my room, and he takes out the framed photo that I keep on my bedside table at home. It's a picture of Mom and me. He places it on the desk near my bed.

I bend closer and study it. Mom is smiling, but the smile doesn't touch her eyes. I never noticed that before.

*

The next time Sam visits, Theresa is with him. I'm sitting in the common area, and I see them come in and stand at the threshold, looking around the room for me. Theresa has her hands in her back pockets, and when she sees me, she smiles. It's strange to see her in here again. She looks healthy and beautiful. This time, I'm the only one who's a mess.

They walk over. "Hi, Sheldon," she says.

I stand up. "Hi." I want to touch her—make sure she's real. But I don't have the courage.

She hugs me.

I look at the floor. "You shouldn't have come here," I say. "You shouldn't risk—"

"I'm not risking anything."

Looking at her, all I want is to narrow my realities down to one. I want the old reality back—the one in which I take it for granted I'm not in Hell. In which it's easy to believe everything is as it seems, because what else would it be?

Looking at her, I want to get a job, and start writing again, and not be such a mess all the time.

For most of her visit, she holds my hand. I don't say much, and neither does she. When it's time for her to go, she gives me another hug.

"Theresa, I—I love you."

She pulls back and looks at me, her hands on my shoulders.

"Let's not talk about that right now, okay?"

I lower my eyes. She puts a hand on my cheek.

"I'm not going anywhere. I'll come back and visit you soon. I want to help you get through this, Sheldon. I want to help you get better. After that, we'll talk about everything else. Okay?"

"Okay."

She kisses me on the cheek, and leaves. Then it's just me and Sam.

"See, Sheldon?" he says. "You have people who care about you. I'm not going anywhere either, you know."

I answer by hugging him, too.

"Thank you, Sam."

The metal trolley arrives, bearing supper, and Sam stays while I eat.

"Are you and Frank together, now?" I say.

He nods. "He left his wife. He still talks to his family, but he lives with me, now."

"I'm happy for him," I say. "That seems better."

"It's been hard," Sam says. "But I think he feels more comfortable with himself." He chuckles. "I learned something weird about him, the other day—his first name isn't actually Frank. That's his middle name, which he goes by. His first name is Sam. Crazy, hey?"

*

I have the old dream, about the day my mother died. This time it's different, though. This time, I'm driving the car that hits her.

I wake up panicking. I get up, and the horrible feelings left over from the dream follow me into the hall.

I ask to speak with a nurse. She lets me into a private room and follows me in, closing the door behind her.

"What's wrong, Sheldon?"

I close my eyes. Through my eyelids, the fluorescent light looks red.

I say, "I had a dream. I think—I think something terrible happened. Before I was admitted."

"And what's that?"

"I don't know. I—"

"Yes?"

In my mind's eye, I see streaks of blood on a windshield.

"Sheldon?"

My eyes are wide. My breath catches. I draw my knees close to my chest, and I stare into space.

I remember.

I remember saying "Holy fuck," and Gilbert remaining completely silent.

I remember sitting in the Hummer for what seemed like forever, and finally, Gilbert opening his door and getting out. Stumbling as he did.

"Sheldon?" the nurse says. "Would you like to go to your room?"

I remember opening the passenger side door, my heart pounding with terror, my mind screaming *don't look run away pretend it didn't happen.*

I remember seeing the torn, motionless heap that, moments ago, was a boy, surely no older than 16. I remember earphones trailing from his ears, connected to nothing—his phone lying on the asphalt several meters away.

"Would you like me to call Sam?" the nurse says.

I remember hearing the car door close, and looking back, making eye contact with Gilbert through the blood-spattered windshield.

Him backing up, driving past the corpse, and disappearing around the next turn.

*

Sam is here. He says the police will have more questions for me once I'm released from the psych ward, and I'll have to appear in court. I give a slight nod. I'm staring at the desk that's next to the bed across from mine. My eyes feel dry.

A nurse comes in. "How's he doing?" she asks Sam.

"Still pretty upset."

She nods. "Would you like some Ativan, Sheldon?"

I look at her hands, clasped at her midsection.

"It'll help with your anxiety," she says. "We'll only give you a small dose."

One of her thumbs is rubbing the back of the other hand.

"Will I get you some?" she says.

I look at her chin.

"No," I say. I want to say: I need to feel this—I deserve to. But I don't, because nothing is worth saying.

"What's that?" she says. "I didn't hear you, dear."

"He said no, thanks," Sam says.

"All right. Let me know if you need anything."

She leaves.

Gilbert is gone. The police officer said they don't know where he is.

I'm the only one left who knows about Eric, and no one will believe me, now.

"Would you like to go out into the garden, Sheldon?" Sam says.

I look out the window. It's raining lightly.

"Okay," I say.

We walk down the hall. Sam tries to push open the door, but it's locked. He goes, and returns with a nurse. She sticks her key in the lock.

We go out and sit on the wet bench. We gaze through the chain-link fence at the busy road beyond.

I look up. A crow is perched on top of the fence. I think it stares back at me, but I can't be sure.

Its head twitches. It caws, and flies away.

Acknowledgments

My Mom read this book three times at various points during the revision process and provided valuable feedback on its development. So thank you to her, for that and for the endless support she's given me since the day I decided to be a novelist, eleven years ago.

Thank you also to my Dad, who gave me feedback on an early draft and who has also been extremely supportive.

Thank you to my friend and fellow writer Matthew Daniels, who gave extensive feedback on an early draft as well as the second-to-last one. Matthew and I have been swapping feedback on each other's work for years, an arrangement for which I am very grateful.

Thank you to the Newfoundland and Labrador Arts Council, who gave me a grant to write *Taking Stock* and who awarded it the Lawrence Jackson Writers' Award. The NLAC's logo can be found at the bottom of these acknowledgments.

Thank you to Samuel Thomas Martin, who provided very encouraging and helpful feedback as adjudicator for the Percy Janes First Novel Award.

Thank you to the Writers' Alliance of Newfoundland and Labrador, for accepting me into their excellent Mentorship Program. Successful applicants are assigned a professional writer with years of experience, who then offers extensive comments on a manuscript over a five-month period. Thank you to Sara

Tilley, who was my mentor. Her comments helped me view the manuscript from angles I hadn't considered, and *Taking Stock* benefited tremendously from her careful scrutiny.

Thank you to Michael Winter, who provided feedback on the first chapter as Writer in Residence at Memorial University of Newfoundland.

Thank you to Lezlee Coombs, Danielle Tucker, and Raven Warren, who made editorial contributions on the first draft.

Thank you to my beta readers for helping me develop the final draft. They are Sandra Bos, Melanie Jensen, Agnes Mason, Andrew Mercer, Nicole Parsons, Kyle Rees, Eben Viljoen, Kimberly Walsh, and Sam Westcott.

Thank you to my cover artist Susan Jarvis, who once again produced art I couldn't be more proud to have representing my writing.

Thank you to the many people I've connected with through my website, Twitter, and Facebook, who read my stories, write reviews, and help spread the word. I couldn't do this without you.

Newfoundland and Labrador Arts Council

About the Author

Scott Bartlett was born 1987, in Newfoundland Canada, where he currently lives. He has been writing for over a decade.

His fiction has won several awards, including the H. R. (Bill) Percy Prize for his medieval comedy novel *Royal Flush*, as well as the Percy Janes First Novel Award and the Lawrence Jackson Writers' Award for *Taking Stock*.

Scott blogs about his writing and other subjects at ScottPlots.com, and he loves connecting with readers.

CPSIA information can be obtained at www.ICGtesting.com
Printed in the USA
LVOW07s2348051015

456960LV00002B/2/P